Hood's Bow

By

John Mowbray

Hood's Bow

Cover art by Laura Preston

First Printing: January 2019

This book is dedicated to Helen, Matt and my mam. Without all your help and input, Hood's Bow would not have been possible.

Prologue

"Wealth is a small thing, Hood, it's tiny like a grain of sand. It seems large only to those who do not possess it," said Lord Smyth, his eyes wide, attempting to remain calm.

Hood watched in excitement from the landing atop Smyth's grand staircase. His hazel eyes filled with glee as he counted the lords and ladies his band of men had held up. It wasn't hard, the robbing business, not for Hood anyway. The wily young man maintained that all he needed was a group of loyal men with all the morals of a hungry pig. The thing about pigs, though, is that they're nasty bastards when they're hungry.

"Calm yourself, Gilbert, you wait your turn now!" scolded Hood. Gilbert was the biggest of the lot of them, the dumbest too. He held tightly onto a young woman in a sky-blue dress, her hair was auburn and her skin was soft and young, his grip almost snapping her neck. Gilbert often got carried away with the women they robbed. Hood didn't much like it, but didn't hate it enough to stop him.

Hood strolled slowly down the winding staircase; his features were handsome and strong, his dark hair tied neatly back. The young man tossed his beloved bow from one hand to the other playfully; it was a fine bow, crafted with love from one cut of strong yew. "I'll tell you what, Lord Smyth, we'll have a little wager." Hood waved his hand at Stutley, the oldest man in his group, to move the dagger away from Smyth's neck. Hood moved swiftly through the hall of the previously dignified lords and ladies to stand before Smyth. He was taller than Hood, fatter too. The blue satin around his collar was stained with the trickle of blood from Stutley's blade.

"I don't gamble against thieves," muttered Smyth, holding onto his courage.

Scattered laughs from his band of men sounded around the hall. Hood smiled, his teeth always showed when he smiled, he liked it that way, something carnal about it. "Oh Lord, you will wish to place this bet." Hood shoved his bow into Smyth's hands and gifted him a single arrow from his quiver. He walked back to the far wall, near the spiral staircase, then leapt onto a table of polished oak. Gilbert loosened his grip on the girl and began clapping happily, a simple smile upon his ugly face.

Lord Smyth looked down at the bow in his hand; his chins wobbled as he spoke with confusion. "And what am I supposed to do with this?!"

Hood stood upon the table in his green garbs, his arms stretched out wide. "You get one chance, Smyth, one chance to hit me with that bow. If you do, you have my word, my men will leave you all unharmed."

"And if I don't?" Smyth already knew the answer.

"None of you leave here unharmed; actually, I'll be honest, probably not even alive. Your corpses will be stripped of their belongings and the proceeds spent on whores and ale. Your manor will be emptied of its trinkets and burnt to the ground."

Crying had started in the crowd now. Hood didn't like crying, it grated on him.

Smyth gulped, spit moving down his throat in a fat ball. His hand was shaking as he notched the arrow into the bow. All eyes were watching, all except Hood's, his were on some silverware he'd noticed on one of the mantels.

The string was pulled back lamely by a weak arm and the arrow was shot. Hood wouldn't have said it was shot, it barely reached him and bounced off the wall to his right. The cries were louder now and cheers went up from Hood's men.

The young man hopped down from the table and snatched his bow back. "You see, Smyth, I was always going to win, for this bow would not dare put an arrow in me."

Chapter 1

The smoke from the Lord Smyth's manor still clung to Hood's lungs; a painful cough heaved from his chest and turned into laughter as the men recalled the fat lord's shot at Hood.

"Lord lard arse couldn't even pull the bow back," chuckled Gilbert, as he laid down his chest of loot. Gilbert neared seven foot, his shoulders were wide and his face was ugly. He dropped the bound lady from his shoulders and onto the camp floor, loosening the rope he called his belt.

"Gilbert!" said Hood, his voice sharp.

The giant's head swung, his hands paused and the lady's eyes looked up to the young outlaw leader in hope.

"Not bloody here, at least take her where we can't hear your grunts."

Gilbert smiled and revelled in the new found fear from the lady's screams.

The rest of the group moved into the camp slowly; Scarlett sat down across from Hood, searching through his sack of loot and Stutley came in slowly, pushing Lord Smyth into the camp.

"I tell you, Hood," said old Stutley, "John would not be happy about this."

Hood laughed suddenly, his face softening. "I won't kill him. He's to serve as collateral."

Smyth was tired, his fine clothes were black from smoke and a deep gash was on his cheek from where Stutley's knife had slipped. "You outlaws are beasts," he muttered.

Hood stood, brushing down his black leggings. "Finding some courage, are we?"

"You low-born men are all the same. You all get caught and hanged eventually."

"Hood ain't low born," said Scarlett. "He's a nobleman."

He wasn't.

Smyth started to snigger, the type of snigger that got a man's throat cut.

Hood felt anger rise in him, bubbling like a poison. His young face remained composed and he knelt down in front of the fat man, a dagger in his clutches.

"What're you going to do? You said yourself, I'm worth more alive than dead," said Smyth.

"Hold his head and his neck," ordered Hood. "Scarlett, open his mouth."

Stutley rolled his eyes. "I should have bloody took that bet up with you, Scarlett, I thought he'd of been able to resist it this time."

Hood smiled. "Never try and predict the actions of an unpredictable man, you two, it won't work in your favour."

Smyth wanted to struggle, but he couldn't. He was a weak, soft man with little or no fight in him. All he could do was let out a high-pitched squeal as Hood's jagged knife cut the tongue from his mouth.

It always surprised Hood how much a tongue would bleed. He'd seen fingers cut off before and they never bled as much, but the tongue could fill the mouth with blood in moments. The beauty of the trick is that if they survive, then they can never speak again, not without great difficulty anyway. And if they died, well, it wasn't overly pleasant for the victim. Lord Smyth had choked for several minutes before he suffocated, his face blue and his eyes wide.

"There goes the collateral," sighed Stutley, his old eyes staring down at the dead man.

"Fun to watch though, eh?" smiled Hood. "The Sheriff probably wanted him dead anyway, we would have got nothing for him."

The men looked at Hood blankly. Smyth's bowels had loosened only moments ago, the sound, at first, comical. However, the stench was now overwhelming.

Hood looked down at him and then to his men. "You think the Sheriff would have traded John for this man? You think even four of this worthless sack would get John back?" He kicked Smyth in the stomach, more air releasing from his bowels. The sound only amplified Hood's point.

Gilbert burst from the trees then, his huge form slouching with disappointment at the sight of the dead lord. "Aw, I missed it, you could have told me!"

"There will be others," said Hood, brightly. "Where's the girl?"

"Broke her."

"Of course you bloody did," said Scarlett. "You never leave them for the rest of us, selfish prick."

Gilbert was about to charge the man, but the sound of a distant shout stopped them. "Grab the loot, time to go," said Hood, setting off through the forest.

Guy of Gisborne sat on his horse watching the plumes of black smoke rise from Lord Smyth's manor; there was no way anybody was alive inside. Even outside the dead were scattered, their throats slit, or their stomachs opened up.

The priest turned to him, his pale face filled with worry. "We should pray, bury the dead and pray. Hood will be punished."

"God helps those who help themselves," said Guy, spitting to the ground. His grey eyes looked back at his men; they were lightly armed and barely seasoned. "The Sheriff wants me to catch Hood and he gives me ten fools along with a priest to patrol."

Guy was the Sheriff's man, he had been for years. The partnership started out simple, the Sheriff paid and Guy killed. Soon he was hired and brought into the Sheriff's service full-time. It used to be important men he had to dispatch, but in time the Sheriff used him for any old peasant. However, now he had Hood as a target, a formidable man. A dangerous man.

Guy dismounted his horse and addressed his men. "Check the bodies, see if any can still breathe a word, and if they can, get them to tell us any details, their direction, their numbers. Once you've done that, finish them and put them out of their misery."

The men nodded and gave a wry smile to each other. He knew what they were thinking; rich men and dead women, their rings and purses up for the taking. But Guy knew a man like Hood wouldn't leave a stone unturned.

His narrow eyes looked up at the sun. It would be set in no more than two hours, that's when Hood would have the advantage. Guy's hand came up and stroked his bearded face and then pulled his dark hair away from his eyes. He saw boot prints, big ones, going off into the west. Only one man he knew had boots that big – Gilbert.

The men were disappointed with their lack of findings

when Guy had called them to follow him into the edge of Sherwood Forest. "I'll tell you what," Guy had said to the sunken men. "When we kill Hood and his men, you boys can have whatever they've got on them."

"Sheriff wouldn't be too happy about that," said the rat-like priest.

Guy turned to him, his young, sharp face darkening. "Who's going to tell him?"

The priest swallowed hard and shook his head. "Not me, Guy."

He smiled. Giving the men something to work towards was key to potential victory, a man who is driven is like a hungry wolf amongst fat sheep.

They pushed through the trees and walked for a while, Guy following what tracks he could. The canopy of greenery blocked what little sunlight there was left, so he had the men spread out wide, searching for whatever signs they could find.

"Guy, fire!" one of the men shouted, pointing towards a small glow through the trees in the distance.

Guy cursed under his breath and strode over to the man, grabbing him by the collar. "I'd kill you now if we weren't about to face the enemy." He threw him down and gestured silently for the men to follow.

As they neared, it was clear the camp was deserted, so Guy lowered his sword and moved in slowly, sitting himself on a log by the fire.

"Good heavens!" gasped the priest, almost falling from his feet.

"Yes, there's our Lord Smyth," said Guy, looking down at the fat man. All dignity was void, his face blue and his open eyes were blood red. "I always forget how bad the dead smell."

The men came in around Guy, ready to move on.

He looked into the darkening trees, there was still half an hour of sunlight and they couldn't be far. But as soon as the light was gone, this was Hood's game. There were indents on the floor, chest indents, at least four. That would slow them down.

One of the men came from the trees then, a look of horror on his face. "Lady Ryla is there, her body's mangled, looks as though her back's been snapped."

Guy sighed and stood. He knew he had to follow now.

The priest turned to him, his green eyes wide. "You think they knew she was the Sheriff's sister?"

"I don't think it would have mattered."

Unease was creeping into Guy's bones like a sharp chill. His men could feel it and he could sense it in their movements. The forest was too quiet, all that could be heard were footsteps crunching on dry leaves. The darkness had almost fully settled in, a tiny glow of sunlight was the only comfort, and it was dying, fast.

Guy heard a whooshing, the type that only lasted seconds until it hit its target. There it was, the first of many arrows embedded itself into the forehead of one of his men. Guy held his composure and his sword high, his men, however, did not.

A deep roar came from near the priest. That was Gilbert; his long sword swung with power and cut the head clean from the priest's neck, his head bouncing onto the forest floor. It seemed to Guy that arrows came from every direction, taking all of his men before any of them could swing their sword. Of course, Gilbert clove his way through a couple too.

Before he knew it, he was all alone and Hood stood just feet away from him, his bow in his hand and an arrogant smile on his face. Guy knew he could reach him with his sword, it would mean certain death, but he was probably going to die either way. He tried to lurch forward but felt the cold steel of a dagger resting on his throat, an old man breathing down his neck.

"Stutley, if I didn't know any better, I'd have said you were a dancer in your past life," said Hood cheerfully.

The old man behind Guy gurgled a laugh.

Guy sighed with frustration. "At least do the honourable thing and face me yourself with a sword."

Hood laughed. "Honourable? A man whose job it is to hunt down and kill people attempts to preach about honour to a man who is known for his abilities to rob and murder. Quite a reach, don't you think?"

Scarlett stepped forward. "Could ransom him, Hood, a trade to get John?"

This time Guy laughed, the sound sickly. "The Sheriff won't make a deal, not now that you've killed his sister."

Silence followed the comment and Hood's hazel eyes fell on Gilbert.

Guy's face was one of shock and pleasure. "Oh you didn't know, did you? That young lady back there all broken up was one of his sisters. His favourite too."

"Shut him up," said Hood simply, his head turned away.

Stutley turned his dagger backwards and smashed the pommel onto the back of Guy's head. He fell, blackness engulfing him as he tipped towards the forest floor.

Chapter 2

Hood watched as Guy of Gisborne crumpled to the ground and hit the leaves. "Why not make him bleed?" asked Stutley, the old man itching for death.

Hood shrugged his shoulders. "Someone needs to tell the Sheriff of our deeds."

Hood made a point to show he had no interest in the consequences of what had happened. With the illusion of consequence gone, there is nothing that can stop a man like Hood. They began the walk to their loot-cave, deep in the forest. It was a long, quiet walk in the dark. Each man with their own thoughts, but all circling the same thing – the Sheriff's sister. Before this, Hood knew, he was wanted and a sharp thorn in the Sheriff's side. But this incident brought it to a new level; they knew now there'd be a constant hunt for them. Hood smiled at the thought. "You reckon the King's men will be after us now?" asked Hood, turning back to his silhouetted men.

Stutley was the only one close enough to hear. "I reckon there'll be a few royal guards, aye. I've seen more for less than this."

"Think there will be posters?"

"Oh aye, a reward even," agreed Stutley.

"Better be a handsome one, whatever bastard catches us lot deserves it." He could tell Stutley smiled at that.

"Would you have left the Sheriff's sister if you had known it was her?"

"I don't think you need me to answer that one,

Stutley." Their conversation was interrupted by a clatter and Scarlett's deep, roaring laughter. The black outline of Gilbert had disappeared and moonlight shone on the loot that had fallen from the chests he carried. The seven-foot shadow reappeared and brushed himself off.

"I'm tired, lads, can we not just stop here for the night?" asked Gilbert, his voice drained.

"Almost there," reassured the bowman.

The cave was large and deep, naturally built into a small rise of earth in the forest. Scarlett started making the fire before the cold of the night latched onto them. Gilbert threw the chests of loot down dramatically and went for his stash of moth-eaten blankets. Stutley lowered himself slowly, massaging the old joints in his knees. Finally, Hood made his way to the back of the cave, checking over their hoard of trinkets and coins.

Over the last few months, the group had made a good living; they'd robbed rich people and got nothing, they'd robbed poor people and hit the jackpot with rings and such. They veered from priests for a while, but then they met Gilbert. Gilbert had a thing about priests, he didn't like them one bit, said they were like vultures, the type to latch on to something good and devour it, rip it to shreds until it's nothing. Hood tended not to agree, that was until they hit their first church, that was the biggest take they'd ever had.

Hood sat, his eyes watching the dance of the flames, he was drawn to the gold of the fire, always the gold. Since Hood was a young man, he'd been obsessed with the idea of wealth. He'd been in London with his father, following him for work. Hood had learned two things on that trip; the first was that London was a real shit hole, filled with cheats and rats. The second was when he saw the royal guard push them aside, leading a magnificent carriage, gilded with gold and led by giant stallions. He had seen the face of King Richard that day; the king was happy and proud. Despite the peasants around him living in squalor, they worshipped him, revered him, respected him like a god. It had made Hood wonder; the only difference between this man and the dirty, kneeling people around him was his gold. The young boy that was Hood had felt a fire ignite inside his chest, a cosmic urge that led him down his bloody, glorious path.

Hood had offered to keep watch while the other men slept that night. The fire was warm, the smell of wood smoke comforting. He jolted as he saw Scarlett sit down opposite him, the man's green eyes looked up and he smiled with a set of broken teeth. "I snatched this from fat Smyth's." Scarlett pulled a dark bottle from the blanket next to him and pulled the cork; his crooked nose touched the top of the bottle and his face grimaced. "Hope it tastes better than it smells." He threw the bottle back and glugged the dark liquid inside.

Hood held out his hand and Scarlett passed him the bottle. "Good find, Scarlett, my friend. It's been a while since I tasted anything other than cheap ale." Hood drank deeply, his face twisted as he lowered the bottle. "I think I prefer pissy ale."

"It grows on you," said Scarlett, gesturing for it back, a warm grin on his face. The two sat in companionable silence for a while. It was comfortable, it always was with Scarlett. John had often said it was a rare talent to be able to put a person at ease as naturally as he could.

Hood looked up, he could see the round, silver moon peeking through the trees above them. "All these riches and here we are, in the middle of the forest, four men living in a cave," he began to laugh. "A cruel joke sent down from the heavens."

Scarlett shook his head. "We've got what riches can't buy, Hood."

"And what's that?"

"We'll be legends, that's what. Carved into history; the outlaws of Nottingham, the men who foiled them all."

Hood's young face brightened in the fire-light, he'd never thought of it that way before. Perhaps those were the riches he was looking for after all; the type that stay with you till your bones are dust. Thoughts of John captured had initially depressed him, potentially sealing the group's fate if they attempted a rescue. But now he felt driven, now he wanted to topple the odds and carve his legend. "You're not as dim as you look, Scarlett."

"And you're a cheeky bastard, Hood," he said with a dry chuckle. Swallowing the last of the wine, Scarlett threw the bottle and stretched out, snoring instantly.

Hood turned his eyes back to the fire, picturing a different kind of wealth, a wealth that could not be bought.

Hood had awoken that morning feeling bright. He'd risen before dawn, grabbed his bow and gone on the hunt for breakfast; deer were a rarity in this part of Sherwood, but rabbits were not. The hunt was a proxy, his mind twisting around Nottingham Castle, attempting to figure a way past the guards and into the keep. He rubbed at the bow with his thumb as he gripped it, his mind working, clearing as he moved.

His arrow found its target over and over, but still he could not think. John was a thinker, he would have had a plan brewing from the moment the obstacle arose. John was a man that was two steps and a leap in front of everyone else.

The young bowman made his way back to the cave, four rabbits swung over his black tunic; his hair tied back. He could see through the trees from a distance that the men were up. Scarlett had caught his eyes through the many trunks. "Where the bloody hell have you been?" he shouted, birds scattering from their branches.

Hood walked slowly into the camp and dropped his catches in front of the fire. "Been for breakfast, what's wrong with you?" He gazed around the camp, Stutley wasted no time on beginning to skin the rabbits.

"You've been gone hours! Gilbert's been out looking for you, like a hound without its master that man is. He went bloody frantic."

Hood threw his arms in the air dramatically. "Well, where the hell's the big bastard now?"

"There he is," said old Stutley, his bony finger pointing beyond the two men.

Scarlett and Hood turned, their mouths dropping open. Gilbert stood crimson from head to toe, his face blank and his long sword gripped tightly.

Hood took a step slowly towards him and placed his bow carefully onto the forest floor. "You alright, Gil? Whose is this blood?" He stepped closer and raised his hand to the giant's cheek, slapping it hard. The sound made Scarlett and Stutley wince, they half expected him to snap the bowman in two.

Gilbert's dark eyes twitched from that and focused on the small man stood before him. His face began to soften and manic laughter started to bellow from his lungs. Hood looked back and smiled at the two stunned companions behind him. "Come, Gilbert, we have breakfast."

Eustace the Monk was a holy man of sorts; his talents lay in realms of dark magic and other things the priests of England abhorred. His mind tried to focus beyond the hunger and the chill of the morning air. His garments had been stripped of him when the priests of the north decided to begin the transfer to Nottingham. He found shame to be a big thing with these holy men.

His pale eyes looked outside of his wooden cell on wheels, he was being pulled behind a horse-led wagon, four priests atop it and two fat ones either side on horses. Trailing behind were two guards, clad in wolf skins.

All this for a man accused of being in league with the devil. You think I'd be in this wooden box if I were in bed with Satan? he thought, bitterly.

A wind blew, a strong wind, sifting through the dense trees and onto the narrow road surrounding it. Eustace felt a cold that he knew. It was the same cold that death came tiptoeing after.

The carriage stopped and his cage jolted to a halt. His eyes could see just between the men sitting at the front of the wagon, they were staring at something. One of the priests rose from his seat and dropped down to the road. Now Eustace could see clearly; it was a giant, surrounded by the howls of death.

"Clear the path, man, men of the cloth are passing," the priest's voice lacked confidence. When the giant didn't move, the two guards dismounted. They walked up to him, their swords drawn. Eustace could see the man clearly now, something was missing from him, the look on his face was empty, void of anything. The giant reminded him of a bull he'd seen as a young man in España. The torero would coax and tease the bull until its temper got the better of it. But just before it would snap, it had a blank look in its eyes, as though all rational thinking had fallen from its skull and out its ears. After that, it would charge.

And charge the bull did. Within mere moments and with speed unprecedented from a man that size, he'd smashed the two guards' heads together, an explosion of blood and skull followed. After that followed a rage that Eustace had never witnessed before. The giant went from priest to priest, killing them with his bare hands, smashing skulls and breaking necks. He struck one so hard in the chest Eustace saw the cavity collapse, the dying man attempting to suck in his last breath. By the end, the big man was dripping in blood, he hadn't even cast an eye at Eustace. Despite being confined to his cell, the monk did not feel safe. The giant wandered between the bodies, making sure each one was dead, like a hound assuring itself. Before long, he'd wandered off and the monk was left shivering in his cell.

Hours had gone by and flies were gathering around the corpses. Before long, more travellers would come and no doubt Eustace, already having a questionable background, would be somehow held to blame.

A voice came from behind the caged man. "If you're going to fight, then you must fight. Strike hard before your enemy's words cut into your chances."

The monk tried to twist his head, but his restraints held him back.

A black-garbed man walked around to look at him, his face handsome, a quiver on his back and a bow in his hands. "That's what Gilbert said to me a couple of years back when I first met him." The bowman's eyebrow rose as he looked around the carnage. "I met him in similar circumstances to this actually. More guts though."

"Are you going to let me out or not, bandit?" said the grey-haired monk.

The bowman smiled. "Bandit? I prefer aggressive activist. Now, what're you in here for?"

"I was fighting against your kingdom, a mercenary of sorts. I'm an important man, or was. Until I was captured. The problem with being a mercenary is that when you're gone, you're gone. Your employer no longer pays you and there's no loyalty."

"So you were on your way to meet your end until my friend kindly saved you?"

"I don't think his intent was to save me, in fact, I don't believe he noticed me at all."

"He probably didn't," said the young bowman, turning and signalling into the trees. Three men appeared, one was old, far older than Eustace but had a vicious look to him. The next was a burly man, with bushy brown hair and thick stubble. The last was unmistakably Gilbert, the beast who had torn into the priests. The giant looked different now; he was smiling as he searched the bodies of the priests, a boyish excitement about him.

The older man chucked the bowman a set of keys from one of the bodies. "I believe these are the keys to your freedom," he said, jingling them lightly. "Now I've got a trail of thoughts in my head that I'd like to put to you." He began to put the key in the first lock. "You must be a useful man with a weapon, or with your mind at least, if you're an important mercenary. Unless, of course, that was a lie to coax me into ransoming you.

But I'm sure you've realised by now, that I'm more of a take and kill sort of man rather than one who might sit around and wait for a ransom." The lock unclicked, and he began on the second at his feet. "You're loyal to gold, and as a man who has acquired a lot of that in my days of taking and killing, I can supply it." He moved behind the cage and began about the chain on his wrists. "And I imagine you're currently unemployed, since you're in the middle of chilly old England in chains." Eustace could stand now and he hobbled down onto the forest floor, face on with the young bowman. "And I'm currently down a man. How would you like employment?"

Eustace stretched, his body was tall and strong, his appearance much younger than first assumed. He opened out his hand and shook the bowman's own. "I'm expensive."

The bowman smiled, his teeth baring. "I don't doubt it, but I'll make you earn every penny, don't you worry about that."

Chapter 3

Guy of Gisborne had woken slowly. The confusion came first, then came the pain. Around him it was pitch black and as he raised his head, he saw the white moon through splayed branches. He vomited as dizziness overcame him. For a moment there was relief and clarity flooded his thoughts. Guy touched the back of his head and winced at the pain; he wanted to lie down and sleep, but he knew the cold might kill him if he did.

He grabbed hold of the gleaming hilt of his sword and stabbed the blade into the ground, helping him rise. No notice was taken of the bodies around him, they were utterly useless and deserved their places strewn across the forest floor. He felt a pang of anger as he too could have been amongst the rotting.

Finally, he'd stumbled his way to the edge of the forest and recognised the area. It was at least four hours' walk back to the castle, four painful hours. His ego was bruised and his need for Hood enhanced. The bowman made him curious. Why had he let him live? Did he think the Sheriff's reprimand is worse than death? No, it wasn't that. Hood enjoyed the chase, he enjoyed the challenge. "Cocky little sod," he said to himself, a smile almost creeping onto his face.

Dawn had come and in the distance he saw the castle. Carts had started to make their way through the gates from the surrounding villages, attempting to sell their wares at the market. The sight of the structure should have brought happiness, his home was there, better yet, his wife. But the burden of informing the Sheriff about his corpse of a sister lay heavily on him.

Guy looked down at his belt where his throwing knives would usually hang. He would have them there when he told the Sheriff, for the Sheriff can be a rash man, unpredictable even.

Guy made his way down the stone path and towards the gates, the men on guard knew him and nodded their acknowledgement as he moved by. His clothes were stained and trickling blood had dried to his hair and neck. No one would question him though, they knew who he was after and they knew who he was reporting to.

The young man eventually came to a crossroads, looking up at the castle and then turning his eyes down a street of houses to his right. He wanted to go there first, he needed to, for love commanded it. Guy saw his doorway, green with black metal strips. His legs were about to move for it until he caught his reflection in a pane of glass beside him. He looked like death. Guy moved to an inn nearby and threw the keeper a copper as he made his way up the stairs and to the washrooms.

The water was cold as he bathed himself in the tin tub, but the dirt was sliding off him nicely. He brushed his thick hair back as he looked in the mirror. His skin fresh and his eyes dark. He could have been dead, as he thought back to the incident with Hood. Guy shook the ridiculous thoughts from his head. Life and death are one, nothing in life is promised, except for death. His father would say that, he told him it the first time as he stood above his mother's corpse. He told him it the last time as he lay on his own deathbed. People will say anything if they find comfort in it.

Guy held a borrowed daffodil lightly in his clean hand as he knocked on his green door with the other. Jule opened it and her shining eyes lit up, her small frame wrapped around the bigger man with excitement. Guy kissed her lightly and ran his hand through her hair, bringing it to his nose. He exhaled. "The scent of you is something I'll never tire of. Where's the little one?"

Clara ran around the corner at the sound of his voice, screaming with joy. Guy lifted his daughter from the ground and handed her the flower. "A pretty flower for a prettier girl," he said. Clara smiled at that and pulled her father in, showing him the sweet pastries her mother had made.

As Guy looked around his home, at his beautiful family, he felt fear. Stupid man, he thought, love makes you vulnerable. But he was too happy to really care.

The Sheriff stood tall watching the priest give his sermon. There was a row at the front reserved just for him and his two sisters. The row behind them was empty, for the Sheriff would not have peasants that close to his back.

The priest was round and old, his eyes small but his voice powerful. "We wish to climb the steep path that leads to bliss, but Jesus asked, 'For what is a man profited, if he shall gain the whole world, and lose his own soul?'."

The Sheriff grimaced at this, but, these things must be said to keep the sheep content within their hovels. For if they ever come to realise their true worthlessness, the peasants will strike first at the wealthy with their pitchforks. Despite this, the comment had made the Sheriff uncomfortable and the priest would pay in due course.

The Sheriff and his sisters were led out of the church with their guard and back to the castle. A fire was lit promptly as the large room had a particularly bitter draft. A serving maid brought the Sheriff a glass of wine and his sisters Mary and Athella joined him. The Sheriff was an unsightly man, his body long and slender, his forehead was bulbous and his chin was too long. The hair on his temples had started to grey over the past few years, but he didn't mind, he thought he was becoming with age.

"Are we still going to Lord Smyth's banquet this evening?" asked Mary sweetly.

The Sheriff smiled at his younger sister, she had always been his favourite, she knew her place and was always polite when speaking. One day she would make a man a fine wife. "You are, Mary."

The young lady clapped with delight.

The Sheriff's dead eyes turned on Athella. "You—" A dog cut him off, barking from outside the manor. He shivered, irritation coursing through him. "You will not."

"Surprise," said the brown-haired sister, sarcastically.

"You need to learn when to—" The dog was barking again, cutting through his words.

Athella chuckled, attempting to retrieve the laugh as quickly as she'd let it out. He rose and his bony hand swiped backwards with power, striking her on the side of the head. The Sheriff turned sharply and began to storm outside with speed, moving down the corridor and out into the courtyard. He didn't slow down as he strode towards the barking dog and the guard holding onto its collar, attempting to calm it. The Sheriff knelt down and gripped the dog's head, twisting it sharply. The neck snapped and the barking ceased. The guard instinctively reached for his dagger until he saw it was the Sheriff.

The guard's eyes widened as the realisation struck him, his dead dog was the least of his worries now. "Go on!" shouted the Sheriff. "Take it out."

The guard hesitated and looked around him. Other guards had turned to watch and his sisters had their heads pressed against the manor windows. "Now!"

The guard pulled his dagger and held it loosely.

"Stab yourself," commanded the Sheriff.

"What…?" said the guard, baffled.

"If I need to repeat myself or wait another ten seconds, then believe me, you won't have a choice where you're stabbed."

The guard looked around anxiously, panic beginning to rise. He swept the blade down and into his thigh. The guard screamed in agony, pulling it back out. Dark blood began to pump.

The Sheriff started to laugh wildly, his dead eyes finding their gleam. "You damned fool, you've struck an artery. You'll be dead in minutes."

He turned sharply and began to walk away, chuckling lightly to himself. The guard wanted to use his last ounce of strength to leap at the evil man. However, his body would not let him. Instead, he dropped. His comrades rushed to his side, attempting to give him one last comfort before he died beside the dog.

The Sheriff's mood was sombre, he sat in his chair once again and the moon was high in the sky, piercing in through a window and onto the floor. He swirled his glass of thick red wine, picturing it as blood, Hood's blood, the priest's blood, the dog's blood. Uncontrollable thoughts like these used to trouble him as a child, but then he learned to embrace it. He thought once an evil was embraced, one could control it. But that wasn't so, he soon found it sought control of him.

The wine was glugged down in one and he held his bony hand out with the glass in it, a serving maid filled it up briskly. The room was silent, all that could be heard was the crackling of the fire and the occasional gulping of the Sheriff. "Did you not want to go to Lord Smyth's tonight?" asked his servant.

The Sheriff sighed. "You can't help yourself, can you, Katheryn?"

The plump, older woman smiled. She'd been in the service of the Sheriff for years, since he was a very young man. She knew when she could say something and when she could not. She knew when he had softened and when he was on the brink of lashing out. "I just don't like silences, that's all, Sheriff."

"Silence is the only pure thing I have in life, Katheryn, it's my salvation. Let me have it," he said, still staring into the fire. She was quiet then, for she knew to be. One more word from her could turn the peaceful man into a wild beast.

There was a draft in the room, something suddenly sucking the warm air from around him. His head slowly turned and he saw the serving maid trying to turn his sister Athella away and out of the room. "Let her come in, Katheryn, I don't mind."

Athella sat herself on a padded leather chair at the other side of the fire. The Sheriff's dark, drunken eyes looked at her with disgust. She was the image of his mother, something in him despised that. Every time he looked at her his blood boiled and his mood soured.

The shadows from the fire danced on her face, the resemblance was uncanny. "Why do you hate me?" she asked plainly.

The Sheriff drank again. "She was a cruel bitch our mother," said the Sheriff, averting his eyes and moving them back to the flames. "You'd be too young to remember this, you were just a babe. Me though, it's clear as day. She bloody hated me, anything I loved, she took away. She drove father to the grave with her damned complaining." He looked back at Athella. "She chained me up for saying that, below the old house in the basement for two days." He laughed once more. "The rats were better company than her. Hope she's rotting in hell." His glass was held out and Katheryn came to fill it.

Athella had no words for him, their mother was a subject she did not dare to venture.

"Before you ask, Athella, the reason why you didn't go to that fat bastard Smyth's is because you're too plain. Your nose is too long and you've got a chin like your older brother's," he said, smiling, tapping the glass against his own. The Sheriff knew she was far from plain. Many doted on Athella and her features were far softer than his own, the man felt elevated when he trod on others.

Athella stood suddenly, anger exploding from her. "I hope that bandit Hood gets you, they say he's after you, you know? All the guards are whispering it."

"Stupid girl," he said, half rising. "I've got Guy out for him! And as soon as Guy of Gisborne has a name, they're already dead."

Athella stormed out of the room and slammed the door. The Sheriff, too drunk to care now, slumped down, downing his glass of wine before falling asleep.

The Sheriff woke, his mouth dry and his neck cold.

There was a blanket around his body and a smouldering fire in the hearth. He looked to his right and downed a cup of water that he knew Katheryn would place beside him. His stomach churned and his head bleated as he rose. The tall man sniffed his way to the kitchen and ate the cooking meat on offer, easing his stomach.

The cruel man readied himself, donning his cape and shaving away the bristles. He strolled stiffly through the courtyard with his guard closely behind him. Blood stained the floor from the previous day, he smiled at the memory and regretted not watching the scene for longer. His dark eyes looked to the sky and saw it was almost noon, he would be on time for his meeting, he always was. The Sheriff had the leaders of his patrols meet him daily, this was to give direct orders and receive updates on local activities.

As the tall man walked through the streets, soldiers stood to attention and peasants moved away swiftly. The Sheriff's reputation preceded him and he felt respected for that. He took a shortcut along one of the high walls and looked down at the city for a moment. Not far from him was the eastern gate, leading out onto the main road. Many men, women and children were travelling through there, mainly hunters and farmers, selling their stock. His eyes narrowed as he focused them on a wagon being pulled by horses with something trailing behind it. The Sheriff turned to the younger guard behind him. "What's being pulled by that wagon?"

"A prisoner, sir, the dark monk captured from the north."

"Ah yes," smiled the Sheriff. "I shall have some fun with him later." The Sheriff, with his mood brightened, moved off towards his destination.

When he arrived at the meeting hall, six of his officers were waiting outside, talking amongst themselves. "Why are you all standing out here?" demanded the Sheriff.

A heavily bearded man came forward from the silenced troop. "Guy of Gisborne has requested he sees you alone, Sheriff, he's inside waiting."

The Sheriff reddened and entered the hall without another word, his guard waiting outside. The hall was long and had cold, stone walls. Tapestries and shields sporting the emblems of the surrounding houses hung on half-rotten fixings. A long table was in the centre with many seats around it, Guy sat at the end and stood as he saw the Sheriff.

"Do you command my men now?" asked the Sheriff.

"My apologies," said Guy. "But I thought you would like to know what I have to say privately."

The two men remained standing despite the empty seats. "Well," said the Sheriff, "I assume you completed my task, or you would not have taken the time to bath and get a change of clothes." He looked down at the knives hanging at his belt. "Or clean your weapons."

"Hood is not dead. He and his men ambushed us, killed everyone except me—"

The Sheriff interrupted him. "So you're telling me, you don't do what I ask, get my men killed and—"

"There's more," said Guy, his young face stern.

The Sheriff's fist clenched. "Don't you interrupt me, worm, you—"

"They robbed Smyth's and butchered everyone there."

The Sheriff stopped. Silence, that beautiful silence, allowing his mind to contemplate. "Mary?"

"Dead." Guy braced himself. His hand ready to unsheathe his knife.

The Sheriff smiled, a cruel line forming on his face. "An opponent, a worthy opponent comes to the table. Finally!" Laughter began, no humour within it, just madness.

Guy was on edge, confusion running through him as he watched the unpredictable man.

The Sheriff stopped and threw his hands down on Guy's shoulders, his dark eyes staring. "We will make this man rise, rise to the King's attention. Then we will capture him. Once we have him, we will reap riches unimagined and I'll bask in pleasure as I peel the skin from his screaming face."

Guy wondered if the man stood in front of him was insane or instead, deeply struck with grief. Either way, he had no choice. It's much safer to work with the Sheriff than against him.

Chapter 4

Hood liked Eustace, the monk was a different kind of man than he was used to, not the bandit scum he'd usually meet on the road. He'd told him some more about where he was from, which kings he had fought for and why he was here. Hood didn't care about that though, the past was the past and it was there for a reason. People say you can learn an invaluable amount from a man's past; Hood disagreed. People are constantly changing, something they did a day ago they might decide never to do again. That's how humans are, they adapt and change. A person who claims they do not, well, they're liars or blind.

Hood watched Eustace move to the back of the wagon, sifting through the items. He grabbed a long handled axe with a single, razor-sharp blade at the top and swung it with skill. "I'm afraid that will be going back, monk."

Eustace looked at Hood, his pale eyes filled with confusion, his grip tightening on the axe.

Hood laughed and patted him on the shoulder. "Don't you worry, you'll get it back soon enough. But I need a way into that castle and this is my ticket."

Eustace looked around at the men, they were stripping the priests, picking bits of clothing from one or the other that weren't covered in blood. Hood leant into the wagon and pulled out a hand full of heavy brown robes. The bowman handed the robes out to his men and then passed Eustace a roll of bread and a skin of water.

"Apologies, monk, but if we're to make it there

without questions being asked about our delay, then we need to move now," said Hood, gesturing him to move back into the cage.

Eustace sighed and stepped back in.

"Don't you worry, plenty of gold to be made and Englishmen to slay."

Eustace watched as Hood closed the cage door and loosely closed the padlock on it. He moved around the scene of dead priests, clapping his own men on the back and fixing their garments where they could not see. When the young man moved towards Gilbert, he saw the giant light up. Gilbert admired Hood above all and felt great pride when any attention was thrown his way. Hood tried to straighten out the big man's outfit, he was literally bursting from the seams. The bowman took the largest of the brown gowns he had given him and draped it around Gilbert's shoulders, hiding the ruined priestly clothes.

The wagon slowly teetered down the crest of the hill that overlooked Nottingham Castle. The sun was bright, shining down onto the settlement and Hood smiled. "Good old Nottingham," he said to Eustace, walking alongside his cage. "Looking at it from here you'd think it wasn't such a shithole."

The group of outlaws looked almost passable as priests to the eye that wasn't casting suspicion. Stutley probably suited it the most, his grey hair flailing at the side of his bald head and his old face mimicking frailty. Gilbert sat in the wagon, attempting to shrink himself as much as possible and Scarlett sat at the front, his brown hood draped over his head, holding the reins of the two horses leading them.

As they neared the gate, other folks were giving

them attention. People were asking who the prisoner was or asking for blessings; they'd tend to veer towards Stutley for this. "Bless ye, child of God," he'd say softly. He covered his desire to throttle them well.

They finally reached the gates, two guards were on watch and stopped the wagon. "Who's this then?" asked one of the guards, prodding at Eustace through the bars.

Hood moved in close to the guard. "I would not touch him. This, my friend, is a dark monk, captured from the eastern isles."

The guard stepped back, as if in disgust. "What's a dark monk do?"

"What don't I do," hissed Eustace, opening his mouth, waving a tongue that was split in two.

Hood nodded solemnly. "A demonic man. We're taking him to the castle, the Sheriff's going to have his way with him."

The second guard moved in and shoved the first out the way. "Bloody let them through. They're expected, you idiot."

Hood nodded kindly to him and signalled Scarlett to move the wagon through the gates. The wheels rolled through slowly and Hood turned to Eustace. "Do me a favour and never show me that mess in your mouth again. I could have cut it off myself."

Hood's eyes were constantly on the move as soon as they were past the gates. His gaze drank in every alley, every solid rooftop or misleading route. It'd been a while since he was inside these walls and even then he wasn't too familiar. Old man Stutley was acquainted enough, he walked at the front of the wagon, guiding them on their route. Stutley used to be a guard in his younger days, long before the Sheriff. After that, he'd even spent some time in the dungeons as a prisoner. Stutley's iron rule about never paying a woman for sex bit him on the arse when he found himself drunk in a whorehouse. He spent two months in a damp cell for that.

They could see the tower now where John would be kept and it began to dawn on them that they had no plan in place. "There will be guards up there, Hood, what should we do?" asked Stutley.

Hood was trying to muster a plan up in his head, counting the different scenarios. To fight their way in would drastically increase the odds of being caught. To do it covertly would mean no weapons could be carried and getting caught would be deadly.

"You there!" came a voice. "Halt that wagon."

The wagon stopped and four guards with their swords drawn walked over.

Hood's heart was beating rapidly in the quiet moments that followed, he felt the rush he craved so dearly. He looked around, armed men approaching, their own weapons tucked away in the wagon with Gilbert. One of the men was nearing Stutley and another the wagon.

"I recognise you," said the guard, pointing his finger at Stutley's chest.

The guard closer to the wagon had one eye on Gilbert as he slowly stepped nearer. Gilbert's glare focused, his face blank, as the guard reached over the wagon and began riffling old cloths and blankets. The weapons lay underneath and Gilbert licked his lips.

The guard talking to Stutley pulled back his brown robe to reveal the bloodstained priest's clothes. Hood smiled at this and for him, time moved slowly. He then watched with glee as the guard near the wagon spotted their weapons under the dirty cloths. Those dirty cloths would be the last thing he saw, due to Gilbert's shovel hands wrapping around his head, squeezing until blood poured from the eyes.

In the same breath Stutley wasted no time. Move first, that's what the outlaws did, they didn't wait for reaction. Stutley had pulled the dagger from the guard's belt and impaled it into his neck. Hood swept up the sword from Gilbert's fallen man and took on the remaining two. The clash of steel rang out, bouncing from building to building. Stutley edged behind one of them and used his stolen dagger once more, severing a pressure point in the neck. Hood watched with joy as blood spurted towards him and past his final assailant, distracting him for just enough time for a blade to enter his chest.

The outlaws stood, a bloody scene around them. "So much for going in quietly," said Scarlett, fishing out the weapons and handing them around.

Eustace was let out from his cage once more and threw on one of the brown robes. The grey-haired monk hafted his axe and swung it through the air. "That was not quiet," said the dark monk. "More men will be coming, we must be quick."

Eustace saw Hood pull back his bowstring and fire it towards him, an arrow whooshing by his head. The monk heard a thud and turned, a guard with his sword half raised was falling, an arrow in his chest.

"This way, lads," said Stutley, jingling the keys he'd found on one of the bodies. The dungeon tower holding John was on the crest of the road and the guards must have been switching shifts. When they reached the tower they all stood silently, looking over their shoulders and waiting for Stutley to find the right key. He worked through them, trying different ones. The dungeon gate was metal, ornate bars twisting and entwining creating strength. Through it, they could see stone stairs leading downwards and upwards. Stutley insisted John would be kept down in the dungeon as the tower hadn't been used for years.

The lock clicked and they were in. Hood went first, his bow on his back and a short sword in hand. Scarlett stayed on watch, ready to shout or die if there was any trouble. The stone stairs curled downwards and were lit by flickering torches. The air was growing colder and damper the further they went down. Hood couldn't help but feel uneasy trapped beneath ground with nowhere to run. The patter of feet on stone stopped as they finally reached the dungeon. A long hall preceded them with cells set in the walls either side, torches glowing outside of each.

The outlaws looked around, thinking about where to start. "John!" said Hood, in a loud whisper. The sound echoed off the walls.

"Hood? That you?" came a voice from the second cell.

Hood ran to the bars to see his friend, happiness overcoming him. He stuck his hand through and gripped John's. "Didn't think I'd abandon you, did you, John?"

"Not for a moment, brother. Now, get me out of here."

Stutley started to search through the set of keys once more. "It's that one, Stutley," pointed John. "I've watched it turn many times."

The cell clicked open and John was free, he stepped from the small cell with a great smile on his face. His hair was dark and curly and his eyes wide and blue. He stood tall and his shoulders broad. John had a chivalrous look about him and could have passed as a king in the right clothes. "Gilbert, it's good to see you." He looked him up and down, seeing the bloody priest's outfit latched onto him. "Odd choice of attire." He looked at the rest of them. "Started a church have we?"

Hood chuckled. "A ploy you would have been proud of. Now, let's be off, Scarlett's up there waiting."

"Who's this?" asked John, facing Eustace, his eyebrow raised.

Eustace stepped forward, the two were almost exactly the same height and width, but Eustace looked meaner; could have been the axe in his hand.

Hood moved between them. "He's a friend, he can be trusted."

"How do you know?" asked John.

"You know I've always been a good judge of character."

Then came a voice, a familiar one. "Hood!"

The group turned their heads to the far end of the corridor, it was Guy of Gisborne, standing, a door open to his side and sword in his hand. His eyes were locked on the bowman.

Hood sighed. "Enough of this," he said, notching an arrow in his bow. Then he felt a hand push his bow to one side. It was Eustace, his large figure moving in front of the group, his axe in hand.

"You," said Eustace, staring at Guy. "You are the man who captured me. You are why I'm here."

"Fate has brought us together once more, dark monk," said Guy.

"It's choice, not chance, that determines our fate. Now, we can have a fair fight without your men."

Eustace turned to the outlaws and signalled them to leave. "I'll see you again, Hood, I need my gold."

Hood smiled. "I hope so. You know where to find me."

With that, the outlaws ran from the dungeon clattering back up the winding staircase. Guy took a step forward towards the monk, gritting his teeth and freeing the muscles in his sword arm. Eustace removed his brown robe, letting it drop to the floor, revealing his huge bare chest. They moved closer, raising their weapons. And then they clashed, and a brutal fight to the death was underway.

Chapter 5

Three months earlier

"Hunger is the enemy, Hood, not because it starves, but because it clouds the mind. It distracts a man and blinds him to what is important," said John, staring over the half frozen lake, watching two men in their boat wafting slowly out.

Hood looked at him, his gaunt face confused. "John, none of us have eaten in days. We know the rest of their camp have food and supplies, let's catch up with the lads and sack the place."

John shook his head slowly, not taking his eyes off the men on the lake. "Think about it, Hood. Why are these men coming out here? There's no fish in there, it's not a nice day for a relaxing paddle. They're up to something, I can smell it."

"Perhaps they are. Let me know when you find out. In the meantime, I'll be filling my belly with whatever food their friends have." Hood disappeared through the snow-covered forest, a wolf pelt wrapped around his shoulders and his bow in hand.

John stayed watching, his eyes never leaving the two men on the lake. After a while, they reached the middle and John held back the nibble of a doubt in his stomach. Then he saw it, a long pole with a hook on the end was pulled from the belly of the boat. They dipped the pole deep and kept raising it back up with nothing on the end. John's gaze brightened as they finally hooked what they were looking for. They pulled it up slowly, struggling with the weight. A huge chest was heaved from the water and onto the boat. Even from that distance, John heard the thud as it hit against the timbers.

The men began to sail back to the bank from where they'd come. John was careful now, silently moving, focused like a madman. Every step was naturally calculated, his heart slow and his movements sleek. The prospect of riches did this to John, he became unnatural, possessed even, until his thirst was quenched.

John was a devious fox waiting within the trees, watching as the chickens neared, their fate coming closer to being sealed with every second that passed. The two men carried the chest from the boat and dropped it onto the land within the trees.

John heard jingles, definitely coins, he thought, no trinkets in there.

"About time we collected this, Rob," said one of the men. "We've stashed this loot for too long."

"Aye, you're right, Wendell, the heat's off now though. We'll be able to buy a bloody castle with this stash."

Wendell looked up at his friend. "You saying what I think you're saying?"

"Let's leave the other bastards. If we take it back, they'll just waste it, better split between two than eight."

"Rob," said the young man, seriously, "I've never agreed with you more." The two began to laugh and collect their things, but as Rob turned back to the boat, Wendell drew his dagger and thrust it in his neck.

Rob began to choke, falling forward into the shallows of the lake. His companion kicked him down, holding his head under the shallow water with his boot.

The thrashing stopped and Wendell exhaled with

relief. When the young man turned back to the chest, he saw John and stumbled with fright. Now John wasn't terribly intimidating under normal circumstances, but these circumstances were far from normal. A sword was gripped tightly in either hand, his chest was heaving like a bull's and he stood taller than a bear. Mud was smeared on John's face and clothes, a wild look in his eyes.

Wendell had met many different types of men in his life; agreeable men, violent men, cowardly even. But never had he seen a man quite like this. He began to scramble away, his knees and hands attempting to climb over the body of Rob back into the water.

John stabbed his blades down into the ground and took one large stride towards Wendell, grabbing his ankles and dragging him back to the chest of coins. He kept the man on his belly, one foot on the top of his back and one of his right arm. John bent down and lifted the chest with effort. "This is a good find, Wendell."

"You can have it," pleaded the man. "Please, just let me go and you can have it."

"And what if I don't let you go? Does that mean I can't have it?"

"What?!" said the man, panicked.

"You know," said John, feeling the weight of the chest, then looking down at the back of Wendell's head. "I once saw a chest of three hundred silvers fall on a man's head, his eye was pushed from its socket, his jaw was snapped and all his teeth were ruined. He died about three days after that. If this chest has more than that, then you'll certainly die. If it's got less, then you'll probably live; for a little while."

Wendell was sobbing now, his words just noises.

The chest dropped. A great crack and squelch was heard and the sobbing ceased. John stepped off and lifted the chest, smiling.

"At least five hundred there, cheers, Wendell."

John followed the prints of Hood and emerged at a camp; six dead bodies were piled in the snow next to packs of supplies. Hood, Gilbert, Stutley and Scarlett sat on logs around a roaring fire, stuffing their faces with meats and bread.

Hunger struck his belly like sharp lightning and he rested the chest of coins easily onto the floor. None of the men except Hood looked up at him. The young bowman put his food to one side and rose, trying to conceal his lust for the chest as best he could. "John, you truly do have a talent for this occupation."

"You don't need to tell me that, Hood. You, on the other hand, need more training. If I hadn't kept on the trail, this would have been long gone. The two in the boat were planning a runner."

"Have you managed to open it?" asked Hood, kneeling down, inspecting the lock.

"Nope, waited for you."

Hood smiled, his teeth in view. "Ever the gent, aren't you, my friend?" The bowman saw blood on the edges of the chest, staining the snow it leant on. "I see you've measured the contents already."

John smiled. "Told you I would do that one day, completely crushed his skull."

The other men perked up at that. "Must be a big one to do that. That lad in Grimsby had his head crushed by two-fifty."

"It was three hundred," said John.

Stutley ambled over and began to pick at the lock,

no one could pick a lock like that man. The skill came to him as if God had made him just for that reason alone.

The lock clicked and Hood gestured for John to lift the lid. It was a beautiful sight, none of them had seen that much gold in their lives. Gilbert was the first to turn away back to the food, that man was ruled by desires more base than wealth. The rest of them laughed merrily, planned what they'd buy and constantly ran their fingers through the heavy coins.

That night John was the last to sleep, the rest of the men snored lightly, covered by their thick blankets next to the glowing fire. He sat staring at the open chest, the coins glittering in the fire-light. He felt restless, unsatisfied, hungry for more.

The group of outlaws overlooked a large wagon rolling towards Nottingham castle. They were on the crest of a snowy hill, no more than a quarter of a mile away from it, the wagon was less than two miles away from the castle.

"John, we can't do it, we've got to just let it go!" said Hood with urgency.

"It's there for the taking, Hood, we can't let it go. There are less than four men with it and it's being pulled by two geldings. Have you seen the size of them? Can you imagine the weight of the loot they're pulling?"

"Aye, that's what worries me. It's clearly a government wagon, the quality of the build and coverage indicates that. But what concerns me the most is the men with it," said the bowman.

"What about them?" said John, snow falling on his dark curls, his blue eyes filled with frustration.

Hood turned to the rest of the men; they were stood

a little while away, occupying themselves while John and Hood talked tactics. "Gilbert, come here."

The giant strode towards them, happy to hear his name. "What do you need, Hood? We attacking?"

"Look at the wagon, should we go for it?"

"Of course we should!"

"Why should we?" asked Hood, standing between the two big men.

"Easy, ain't it?"

"What's easy about it though, Gilbert?"

The giant squinted his eyes. "The men, they'll be easy targets, they've got no armour, no weapons. We'll take them down in less than a minute."

"Exactly!" said the bowman with passion. "It's too easy. It's all too easy. Where have they come from? Why haven't we seen them sooner than this? We would have picked them up far earlier in normal circumstances. They don't even have thick clothes on for Christ's sake!"

"You're thinking too much into it!" argued John.

"And you're not thinking enough. We haven't even scouted the perimeter around them, there are a dozen places men could be hiding."

John shook his head with frustration. "There's no time to scout, it'll reach the castle if we do. Lads!" he called. Scarlett and Stutley came over. "You think we should go for the wagon?" he said, pointing down at the target.

Hood stepped in swiftly. "You need to hear the facts, boys."

"We've heard 'em," said Stutley.

"The whole of Nottingham has damned heard them," chimed in Scarlett.

"And?" asked Hood. "Hand up if you think we

should loot."

Gilbert and John raised their hands, Scarlett slowly raised his. "Sorry, Hood," said Scarlett. "Too good an opportunity to miss."

"That's settled then," said John, hastily. "Arm yourselves. Gilbert, you're with me, we'll come in from the south. Stutley and Scarlett, you flank them from the east. Hood, well, you just grab your bow and do what you do best."

Hood nodded reluctantly, his jaw clenched.

The group lumbered down the land, splitting off to form an assault on the wagon. The method was executed many times in the past, their dynamic like a pack of wolves. John and Gilbert the powerful ones, using brute force as they went. Stutley and Scarlett stealthy and efficient, making their way to the enemy while they're blinded by the force of the first two. Then lastly Hood, the leader of the pack, cunning and calculated, formulating the best method of execution whilst picking off the biggest threats from a distance. They ran like clockwork, most of the time.

This occasion was different though. Hood was uncomfortable with the circumstances. A bad taste lay waste to his mouth and the scenario sat curdled in his stomach.

Hood saw it all unfold from the treeline as he was notching his first arrow. Gilbert and John ran at them, the two colossal beasts about to swing their swords at the escorting men. That's when Hood heard the order from a distance. He could see galloping horses cresting the hill below them and men streaming from the treeline closest to John.

The bowman could see Scarlett and Stutley further

down the curving trees, fighting off a handful of men. Hood moved in closer and went down on one knee, picking off two men while the others were downed. He turned his attention back to John and Gilbert at the wagon; they were doing a marvellous job, their blades cutting the enemy down two at a time. But that wouldn't last for long, not when the horses reached them.

"Run!" shouted Hood at the top of his voice.

Gilbert and John seemed to break out of their battle trance after that, in the same moment the last of the footmen were slain. They had a chance to run, to reach the safety of the forest before the horses got to them. Hood watched as Gilbert ran for it, his big frame moving as fast as it could.

John, on the other hand, seemed stuck. His head was twisting between the unguarded wagon and the trees. "Run, you greedy prick," muttered Hood under his breath. Scarlett was pulling at Hood, trying to get him deeper into the forest.

John made the decision and Hood bowed his head in disappointment as John bolted towards the wagon. The horses reached him just as he'd pulled the cover off, discovering nothing but empty crates.

At least thirty armoured horsemen formed a semicircle around him and Hood felt sick as he prepared himself to see the end of John. The leader of them dismounted, he was the only one without armour and Hood recognised the man. It was Guy of Gisborne. He was a length shorter than John, but his stature was just as powerful. He pulled his sword from its sheath and stepped towards John, gesturing his men to stay back.

The sound of steel clashing rang out through the

snowy valley and the two fought like heroes; parries and ripostes, one after the other. But in moments like these, skill and endurance always triumphed. John was good, but Guy was better. The weapon was battered from John's hand like a toy from a child and the exhausted outlaw was pinned in moments.

That's how they captured John, the infamous outlaw that was doomed by his own greed.

Chapter 6

Hood was leading his outlaws back up the steps of the dungeon, their feet clattering against the stone once more. This time faster, with more urgency. His mind reeled as he thought of Eustace facing Guy. The move was an honourable one; Hood saved the monk's life, so he was doing the same. Not only that, but he had no doubt in his mind Eustace would be butchered facing Guy. Despite having a powerful physique, the monk was much older, well beyond his prime. Hood had seen Guy use his blade many times, in his duel with John his skill was dizzying.

Scarlett's head popped into the dungeon doorway, looking down the stairs onto them. "We've got company, lads." The group wasted no time, they poured out of the dungeon door and onto the street beyond to face a group of soldiers that had emerged. One of the best methods of attack was to take the enemy by surprise. The soldiers thought the outlaws would stop at the sight of them, but no, the group didn't hesitate. Hood and his men understood a moment's hesitation could cost the fight. If they'd stopped for even a moment to contemplate, or take in that they were outnumbered two to one, then the soldiers might have formed order. Not now they didn't.

Hood's bow loosed an arrow upon exiting the dungeon that took a man in the throat, another was instantly embedded into the guard beside him. Gilbert took on three of them at once, the sheer size the man sprinting at them, wielding a longsword made their bowels loosen. Stutley and Scarlett made a fine team too; Stutley guarding Scarlett's flanks expertly while Scarlett swung his sword like a madman, and as they fell, Stutley would finish the job. John was weakened from his time in the dungeon, but that didn't stop him knocking an armed guard from his feet and caving in his skull.

Near silence was upon them as the last man fell, the death rattles were the only thing that broke it. Rumbling could be heard coming from the main road. It was more soldiers, at least forty of them running with speed, a horseman at the front leading the charge.

Hood looked around, the slim man's hazel eyes assessing his surroundings, marking the exits. "You two," he said to Stutley and Scarlett. "Make your way down there, and split off where you can." He turned to Gilbert and John. "You two do the same but down that way. We'll all meet back at the cave in two days. Now go!"

"What about you, Hood?" asked Gilbert, worrying for his leader.

Hood smiled. "You don't worry about me, lads. Now off you go, quick!"

The men nodded and reluctantly left the bowman. The group of soldiers were nearing and he knew he needed to be the distraction so his men could make ground. He notched an arrow in his bow and steadied his breathing. His shot was loosed and an arrow struck the horseman that was galloping ahead of the foot soldiers. The horseman toppled off, an arrow piercing his chest. The horse found more speed when free of the weight and galloped towards Hood. The bowman was ready, watching the hoofs and counting the seconds before he made his move. The horse closed in and

Hood leapt, grabbing the pommel of the saddle and stepping into the stirrup, levering himself up onto the galloping steed.

The horse manoeuvred round towards the soldiers and Hood started loosing arrows into the thick of them. They began to part, self-preservation overruling their initial task. This was the key to a surprise, they can't bet on it, so the chances are that they'll revert back to their instincts.

Hood laughed loudly, his heart pounding as he sped down the main road of Nottingham. He peered back at the soldiers, they were looking around aimlessly, staring at Hood, then towards the avenues in which the others took. It was easier than herding pigs to slaughter, thought Hood.

As the bowman came to a quieter part of the town, he dismounted the horse and made himself disappear into an alley. Hood had thought of exiting through the town gates promptly, but thoughts of leaving his brothers behind galled him. Strangely, he felt guilty for dragging them into this. The plan didn't move as smoothly as he thought it would and now his outlaws were spread across the large town, where capture meant certain death.

He wandered for a while through the various alleyways and at times heard soldiers run by, their swords drawn, the men shouting at the top of their lungs. He'd soon ditched his oversized priestly clothes and dumped them on the ground. Hood looked down at himself; he didn't look like an outlaw, aside from his bow and quiver. His black tunic was clean and well made, his leggings were of dark green wool and his leather boots brown with spots of mud. The bowman heard the bustle of the market coming from the town square. He laid his bow down in a hidden place within an alley, moving away with one eye on it. Hood composed himself and walked to one of the stalls, purchasing a pack to roll his weapons into. Once done, and his bow safe again, he decided to walk amongst the crowd at the market, keeping his eyes up and attempting to blend in. "You there!" said one of the stallmen.

"Yes?" said Hood, his eyes searching for someone else he may have been calling.

"You would look fine in one of these," said the jolly stallman, handing him a dark green hat, it had a wide brim that was turned up at the back and pointed at the front like a bird's beak, a brown feather stitched neatly into it.

Hood looked at it and smiled widely, placing it on his head. "It'll keep the sun out my eye when I shoot," he said closing one eye and blocking out the sun with the beak.

"It's a bycocket, all the rage with the nobility these days." He went to grab it from Hood's head and the bowman moved back. "It's expensive mind," said the stallman, his eyes narrowing.

Hood reached into his pocket and threw him a gold coin. "That'll cover it."

The stallman was struck with disbelief as he looked between the heavy gold coin in front of him and Hood, who had turned his back on him, disappearing into the crowd.

Gilbert had stood, listening to Hood's plan intently. "What about you, Hood?" He couldn't help the words pouring from his mouth.

"Don't you worry about me, lads. Now off you go,

quick!" said the young bowman confidently.

Gilbert looked between Hood and the mass of soldiers coming towards him. Hood wasn't worried and Gilbert knew if there was one man who could get out that situation alive, it would be the bowman. The giant turned and began to run down the alley with John. His longsword was sheathed and his long legs were moving him as fast as possible.

Eventually, John slowed and came to a stop, his chest heaving, sucking in air. "You go down there," he said, pointing to a quiet alley. He brought his hands up to Gilbert's face. "Remember, the cave in two days. Don't get killed!"

Gilbert simply nodded and watched John walk briskly in the opposite direction. The giant stood, no one was around and the sun was shining brightly. He enjoyed the heat on his skin and went to roll up his sleeves then stopped. There was blood on them, splattered all over his old brown tunic. The thing was filthy anyway, it would only blend with all the other dried blood eventually.

His mind circled and the ugly man began to wander down the alley John had instructed him to. Gilbert didn't like being alone, all his life he'd had someone to guide him, to tell him what to do. He'd grown up on a farm up north. His older brother was a soldier and often came home, practising swordplay with him. He was as big as Gilbert, but had brains, he was the thinker of the family, everyone said it. One winter he didn't come home and they were issued with a statement from the military saying he'd been killed in some civil skirmish. Gilbert was beside himself, his brother was a man he admired. But worse was his mother, her death came soon after and his father's even sooner after that.

Gilbert found himself alone on a farm where he had little understanding of how to run. He'd just been a worker, doing what people told him as best he could.

As expected, the farm turned to shit within weeks and Gilbert didn't have the mind to do anything about it. He was frustrated and felt lost. He was a sheep without a shepherd.

Gilbert had packed his things and grabbed his brother's old sword, setting out for the road. Days had gone by and Gilbert soon found himself lost, hatred filling his head. He was angry, angry at God. Why had his family been taken from him? Why was he not blessed with a mind like everyone else, so he could figure out how to survive?

He had sat on the side of the travellers' road, rain pouring heavy, his cloak saturated and his stomach weak off berries he'd picked from a bush to graze on. He saw in the distance through the rain, a covered wagon rolling slowly towards him. His spirits lifted as he saw it was a holy convoy, priests and their horses.

He rose as they began to move by. "I'm glad to see you lot here, I'm in great need, Father. I've lost everyone," he'd said to the priest leading them, a heavy hood over his old face.

"Back, peasant!" he scorned, brandishing a small knife. "Holy men are to be revered, not begged. Where is your dignity?"

Gilbert stepped back in shock. The rain seemed to fall heavier and more priests walked past. One pushed him in the chest, making the giant fall back and out the way of the wagon. Gilbert's sadness left him and in its place was raw fury. His vision misted and he drew his long sword furiously, running at the man who had pushed him. The priest didn't know he was a dead man until the longsword pierced his back and was jutting through his stomach. Gilbert began to roar at the top of his lungs and lift the sword while the priest's body was still embedded onto it. The man was wailing in agony. Gone was his bitter attitude towards Gilbert, words veiled by blood dribbled from his mouth.

The other priests had run at him with their short knives and clubs. Gilbert threw the body from his sword and began cleaving into his enemies. But even for a man such as Gilbert, fifteen priests attempting to stab at him was almost too much. He held them back with wild cuts and maiming wounds. The priests started to lose their courage as the giant, blood covered demon felled them one by one. They broke and ran. Gilbert watched and was about to take heed after them, but his legs halted as he saw their path was blocked by a slim man garbed in black, a short bow in his hand.

Gilbert slowly walked towards them, his bloody sword held loosely in his hand. The six remaining priests turned in fear, the lead priest who had initially spurned Gilbert spoke quickly, desperation in his voice. "You must help us, bowman."

The bowman laughed, his handsome face baring its teeth. "Where is your dignity?" he said, mimicking the old priest's voice.

The priest was taken aback, words caught in his dry throat.

Hood smiled. "Oh relax, I overheard you when my companions and I were lying in wait to ransack your convoy." The horrified priests looked around then, searching for the bowman's men. The bowman pointed past Gilbert and at the wagon beyond. Two men were upon it, once more looting the dead. "There they are," said the bowman proudly. "They are really the best at what they do, you know?" One of the priests dipped his hands into his pockets pulling out an expensive gold necklace with a jewelled pendant on the end. "Oh we'll get that too, don't you worry about that, old boy."

The bowman walked through them now putting his arm on the leader priest's shoulder, angling him away from the others and back towards the wagon. The young man turned back to the blood-covered giant. "Finish them off, my good man, then come and join us for some food." Gilbert smiled, it was the first time he'd smiled in weeks. His grip tightened on his sword and they were torn to parts within moments, none escaping.

That night they had sat a little way from the roadside with the stolen wagon and horse. It was when he'd first seen Hood's trick, where he'd hand the enemy his bow and offer a deal – strike him with his own bow and he was free, miss and he was dead. Of course, the lead priest missed, they always did. Gilbert was in awe of the bowman from then. They went on to sit around a warm fire and ate fine meat stolen from the priests. Gilbert was welcomed into the group that night. Hood had opened his arms and let all know he was now one of them, a brother of the forest, an outlaw.

Gilbert could already feel his inner control being lost as he walked through the alleys of Nottingham, his anxiety rising and his heart beating rapidly. Every time he was alone he seemed to lose control. Hood had saved him, the man had welcomed him into a new family, where he was controlled and instructed. "Some men just need a gentle push in the right direction to fulfil their potential," Hood had said to him once. Gilbert agreed and knew that he was one of those men.

He heard the sound of several sets of heavy boots making their way down the road outside of the alley, the jingle of armour following. Gilbert's instinct was about to take hold of him, an urge to grab his sword from its sheath and step out in front of them, taking down the enemy swiftly. But he quelled the urge and tried to think, what would Hood do? Seeing a door beside him, he grabbed for the handle and pulled it down. The door was unlocked and Gilbert's huge frame slid in. The giant was proud of himself, giggling as he heard the group of soldiers pass through the alley, missing him completely. He turned around and inspected the house around him. Looking down he saw a small girl, her eyes wide with fear at the bloody intruder before her. Gilbert bent down. "Come here little 'un, aren't you a canny little girl."

The little girl walked towards him and did as she was told. Gilbert stroked her hair and felt it between his fingers.

"Clara, come here!" came a sharp voice.

Gilbert looked up suddenly, his hand grabbing on to the little girl's arm, clutching it tightly. The girl began to cry at the pain and Gilbert gripped tighter. "Shush!" he said, putting his huge hand over her mouth, covering her face completely.

The slim woman ran over immediately, screaming at Gilbert, punching him and kicking.

Gilbert held on, bracing himself until it stopped. He looked up and saw the woman, she'd fallen back, tears streaming from her eyes. "Pretty aren't you?" he said, a wide grin on his grisly face. He stood, releasing his grip on whatever he was holding and moved towards the sobbing woman. Gilbert grabbed her, turning her over and lifting her dress. His giant form dwarfed her own, his hands cupping around her ribs squeezing tighter and tighter. Gilbert compressed his grip as much as he could as he finished with her, a large crack sounding from her spine, causing the feral wailing to cease.

There was silence after, an eerie silence, the kind that followed something awful. Gilbert's mind focused once more as he looked around the room, realising what he'd done. He reminded himself of a hound he had when he was a boy. The beast was loving and loyal to those around it, guarding on the nights and playing in the days. But when there was food, meat in particular, the hound's eyes would glaze and it'd do anything in its power to get hold of it. Gilbert's father had broken its neck prying it away from a boy it'd seen on the road near the farm, the boy had dried meat, chewing away at it in front of the dog. In that moment of error, the split second instinct had taken over the mind, that dog was dead and the boy maimed.

"Perhaps I'm more beast than man," thought Gilbert. The insight was more than he cared to probe. Then he remembered Hood and the cave. His head began to hurt as he tried to figure out a plan of action.

"Fuck it," he said aloud, unsheathing his sword. "I'll cut my way out of here."

The giant walked from the house and into the street beyond, looking for the southern gate.

Chapter 7

Stutley and Scarlett ran from the scene as Hood had told them to. They both had no concern over the bowman, he knew what he was doing, he always did. Hood had never failed the group and he gave the impression he never would.

The two men ran for a little while and Stutley began to slow as they passed more people. Stutley removed his blooded brown robe and threw it through an open window. "Get rid of yours too and put this on," the old man said, pulling out two oversized, moth-eaten tunics from his deep pockets.

Scarlett pulled off his priestly garments and threw them, replacing them with the dull, clean pauper's tunic. "What're we doing?" asked Scarlett, his green eyes upon him. "Hood told us to run and split."

"And that's the correct thing to do when speaking to two giants such as John and Gilbert, those two stick out like a weeping wound. If he had more time he would have told us two to stick together, he wouldn't have wanted to confuse Gil, that's all."

Scarlett looked at the older man in wonder. "You think?"

"Aye, we look like normal folk, it'd be more out of place for us to be walking alone than together."

"Shouldn't we at least run a little further? Guards will be coming very soon."

Stutley smiled, the older man's yellow teeth gleaming. He looked around and gestured to the milling throngs of men and women around them, going about their day to day lives. "And when they do come and they ask the public if they've seen any killers, they'll be pointed to the people they saw running."

Scarlett laughed. "Sometimes I think you're as bright as Hood."

"Perhaps I am. But he's a born leader and enjoys it. I, however, can't lead, I'm not likeable enough."

"I like you," said Scarlett. "You're like a sweet old grandmother."

The two men laughed. "Watch it," said Stutley. "This grandmother will gut you when you sleep."

They heard the heavy boots of soldiers running down the wide alley from the direction of where they'd come, the traffic of people split for them and the swordsmen stopped. One of them, a helmed man addressed the small crowd. "Have you lot seen any men run down here? They're outlaws, they were dressed in holy robes." No one was saying anything and the guards started to get impatient.

Stutley, appearing even older in his torn and used tunic stepped forward, his hand grabbing Scarlett's, holding it to his shoulder as if to mimic a need. "I saw a couple of men, they headed that way, pushed right by me and my son here, 'orrid men," he said in his most feeble voice he could muster. Scarlett was taken aback at how frail the sharp old man had made himself appear.

The soldier nodded gratefully and pressed his men onwards, stamping further down the alley.

The crowds realigned and went on with their day once more. "You're a bloody fiend," said Scarlett, his lips curving into a smile.

Stutley stood himself back up straight and moved through the throng heading for a large, oak door. "That wouldn't even begin to describe what I am. Now, let's get ourselves in here for a drink, see if we can buy some more robes."

The two friends sat at a table in the corner of the inn, tankards of dark ale sitting in front of them. Stutley purchased two robes from the innkeeper. They were thick, woollen and used. The garments probably had lice, but they kept the bite of the wind off them. "Nice of that bloke Eustace, wasn't it? Staying back and fighting Guy," said Scarlett, foam coating his brown stubble.

"Aye, it was, a fine man. You can tell he's got noble blood in him somewhere along the line, such acts of chivalry aren't often found in men around here."

"We could have stayed, helped him kill Guy."

Stutley scoffed. "You saw how fast those soldiers arrived. They would have had us trapped down there and by now we would have had our heads hacked off ready to be spiked on the walls."

"Bahh," said Scarlett, sipping his ale. "Hood would have got us out of there somehow, he always does."

"I have great faith in the bowman too, Scarlett, but we mustn't forget he's just a man, he's no god."

"A demi-god perhaps then," smiled Scarlett. "Like those Greek legends."

"I think you've had too much ale, lad. Although, the day we met him I wouldn't have doubted it if you'd told me."

Stutley thought back to the day, it was just over four years ago when they'd first met the revered bowman. Scarlett and Stutley had been in the far north and decided to head south to avoid the bitter winter of Northumberland. The two had travelled for days, food scarce and warmth even more so. In those days Scarlett carried a bow, Stutley's hands would not hold a straight aim if he wanted them to. One clear, cold morning they'd seen a stag, a hell of a beast on the edge of thick forest staring right at them. Before Stutley could tell him to hold his fire, Scarlett had loosed the shaft, stamping itself into the lower abdomen of the animal.

They'd heard a yelp and it'd run off into the trees. "You dolt!" scorned Stutley. "These are royal forests, permitted for only noblemen and the King to hunt in."

Scarlett shrugged. "Then we leave it and carry on, it's that simple."

"It's bloody not that simple. That stag will be making a hell of a noise, royal foresters will catch it in no time and then they'll be looking for the ones responsible."

"We deny it, Stutley, there'll be more men than us here."

"Believe me, Scarlett, I did some foresting when I was young, a bit of summer work when this type of place is teeming with people and they needed an extra hand. They don't go easy on lawbreakers, especially on the King's land. We'll have our fingers off or worse." Stutley's old head looked around at the emptiness of the landscape. "There's no one here this time of year except foresters, making sure the stock can breed."

The two men decided, against their better judgment, to go after the stag, hoping to catch it before anyone else could. It didn't take them more than an hour to find it, it'd slowed down, its senses dulling due to the injury. Scarlett pulled back his bow and shot, the arrow finishing the magnificent beast off. "Now what?" Scarlett had asked, as they stood over the dead animal.

The old man looked down at the carcass. "Be a

shame to waste it with our bellies this empty, come on, help me heft it and we'll carry it out of here."

They heaved it up with difficulty. A stag's an awkward thing to carry, they're all antlers and legs. An arrow whooshed by, slashing against Stutley's arm and hammering into Scarlett's leg. The stag dropped and as if out of nowhere twelve men in forester's clothes, stitched with the King's emblem appeared from the thick.

The captain of them neared as his men held their bows and swords upwards. Not that they needed them against two starving men, but it was all for show, it always was with the royal soldiers. The leader was bald-faced and young, his expression had an air of pompousness and his thin, blonde hair was already receding. "My, my, what do we have here?" It was a question that demanded no answer. Stutley stared with malevolence, he could almost feel his daggers warming around his waist, itching to be embedded into the man before him. Scarlett suffered silently with the shaft in his leg, more concerned with the threat of death.

The young captain inched closer to Stutley, pulling one of the many daggers at the old man's belt and pushing it against his throat. "This is your final day, old man." He nodded towards Scarlett. "His too. This will be the last face you see before your soul flies free."

Stutley pulled a dagger of his own with the quickness of a much younger man, holding it at the captain's throat. The captain tensed and blood began to trickle from Stutley's neck.

"What's all this?" came a voice. It was oddly free of hostility, yet commanding, instantly cutting through the tension.

Everyone turned their heads and the captain eased

his eyes over. "These men, they've shot one of the King's deer."

"God's man, lower your weapons, the lot of you. This is my deer and my arrows, these two men are with me."

Stutley began lowering his dagger now. His pale eyes turned to see a young man holding a fine bow loosely at his side. The bowman's tunic was black and his leggings were dark green, his young face handsome and strong. Beside him was a tall man with giant shoulders, his look was one of nobility and his blue eyes shone with something akin to madness, though it wasn't. More likely bloodlust, he thought on reflection.

The captain moved away from Stutley and brushed himself down, attempting to dignify himself once more. "Well, even so, I'll need to see your permit."

The young bowman pulled out a piece of parchment and handed it to the captain. The dazzled soldier looked up from it and stared at the bowman. "Apologies, Lord Loxley, I wasn't informed you'd bought a permit for this time of year."

The bowman's eyes narrowed. "Your name, boy, you've shot my man and threatened another."

The captain's face dropped. "It… it was an accident," his voice lost all command and he suddenly looked like a child dressed in a fancy outfit.

"All men must pay for their actions, be it sooner or later, the day comes for everyone."

The captain had given the parchment back to him and wandered away through the forest with his tail between his legs. The other soldiers following him, smiling to themselves at their leader's misfortune.

Stutley and Scarlett had been beckoned to follow the two strangers, the big one carrying the huge stag over his shoulders. They'd settled in a cave mouth and lit a fire, devouring the stag.

"The shot should always punch through the chest, puncturing both of the lungs and giving a swift death. That's why the meat's so stringy, the stag was too scared, it could feel death looming," said the bowman, eating the meat from a plate cut from bark.

"Where's your castle, Lord… what was it? Loxley?" asked Scarlett.

The big man beside the bowman grinned with humour and they both began to laugh. "I am Hood, and these trees around us, this forest, this whole bloody island is my castle. Men like those back there are my jesters and everything that belongs to anyone is mine."

Stutley smiled at the memory, it was a golden time when they first came together. It still was, he'd never had so much fun in his life since he met the madman named Hood. "If I was forty years younger, Scarlett," he said, sipping his ale. "We'd have been a bloody unstoppable force us lot."

"I think you'll find we already are, we're in the belly of the dragon and it still can't consume us," said Scarlett, tapping his fingers off the wooden table, as he always did when he didn't want to tempt fate.

"Come on, finish up, we should get out of this town and back to the cave. Better sooner rather than later."

Chapter 8

John had raised his hands to Gilbert's unpleasant, wide face as they came to a fork in the alley. "Remember, the cave in two days. Don't get killed!" he'd said to him. Gilbert had stood aimlessly for a moment and John turned his back, sprinting down the alternative route. Usually, John would stay with Gilbert a little longer, explaining the situation in detail and guiding him through the steps. But there was no time in this instance, men were going to be upon them and John had just gotten his first taste of freedom in months.

John didn't know the town of Nottingham well, he'd been on few occasions and they weren't friendly visits. The big man was dressed in tatters from the dungeon, his leggings covered with holes and dirt. Dried blood was splattered on his face and hands. He looked worse than the beggars that lined the poorer streets and John knew that the guards would be able to pick him out of a crowd.

The avenues John walked weren't busy, in fact, the properties there spoke of riches. His mind wandered and he thought of the potential loot they could acquire in such an area. John admonished himself and brought his thoughts back to the issue at hand – leaving the town alive.

The area was too open, if any man or woman spotted him they'd probably alert the guards themselves. His blue eyes narrowed as he spotted a target edging around the corner. John ducked behind a fixture and moved into the porch of a building. He watched as the guard walked slowly, almost with no care. That's when he knew he wouldn't have been alerted to the commotion he and his outlaws had caused yet, if he had then he would not have been dawdling.

John moved out of cover and sat down on the steps of the porch, lowering his head.

The guard strolled up to him, he could see by the armour he was a royal one, hired to patrol the higher class areas. "You there, peasant, you can't be here. Move on."

John didn't budge until the guard went to kick him in the side. The giant's grip lashed out, grabbing his leg and hauling him to the ground.

The guard fell and John attempted to smash his chin on the ground, but the guard was bigger than John had first thought, his strength outdoing the weakened outlaw's. He'd pinned John and was about to rain his huge fists down onto him.

The two men heard a creak at that moment, an old woman had opened the door of the property and the guard's head turned to her, pausing in his movements. John took the opportunity and slammed his fist as hard as he could into the guard's throat – struggled gasps sounded and the guard fell back. John was atop him in moments and twisted his head viciously, snapping his neck. The giant outlaw pulled the guard's dagger and strode towards the old woman standing in her doorway, shock upon her face. "Sorry, love," he said. "You opened that door at the wrong time." His hand grabbed her wispy, white hair and he dragged the blade across her throat. A quiet sob sounded and then her old body hit the deck. His head turned as he entered the house and he saw an old man sitting, his eyes wide at the scene. John swore with annoyance and ended the old man's life where he sat. The old man went quietly with no fight, as if it were welcome after what he had just witnessed.

It was all so easy, too easy, thought John as he dragged the soldier into the home, shutting the door behind him. He stripped the guard of his armour and cloaks, donning it himself. It was as if the outfit was tailored to fit and John chuckled as he looked at his image in a long mirror. "I could have been a damned knight," he said, pulling his sword with a new found ferocity.

Before John left the property he'd piled the bodies, pulling the rings from the old woman's bony, stiff fingers and searching through her jewellery up the stairs. Of course, then came the second priority – filling his stomach. John never was a man who really enjoyed food. He ate for the convenience, for the energy. His gaze wandered beyond the sweet pastry and he grabbed cuts of fatty ham, stuffing it into his mouth with dry bread and washing it down with a jug of cool water.

Excitement entered him as he left the front door of the defiled property. He straightened the helmet on his head. It was a nasal helmet, where a single strip of metal stretched down over the face, guarding the nose. His chainmail breast was older on closer inspection; some of the rings had begun to rust, but the patterned surcoat that fell over the top of him hid this superbly.

John strutted down the wide path, passing men and women stared momentarily before quickly moving by. Children watched in awe as the giant moved beyond them, many asking him to unsheathe the sword on his hip. John would swear at the children with threats of death to scatter them.

The outlaw found himself being drawn to the least busy avenues, attempting to move through the town as best he could with the least attention being acquired. He felt almost invincible in the armour and yearned to test it against another man, but he kept hold of his senses and moved on searching for an opportunity of exit.

His heart quickened as he moved around a corner, seeing a similarly dressed soldier standing guard by a long gate. The guard's head was turned towards him, his body language one of aggression, yet, he hadn't pulled his weapon. "Where've you been, you simpleton? I should have been off duty fifteen minutes ago," said the soldier as he came closer.

John didn't say anything as he watched the furious guard shake his head at him and walk away down the wide street. The giant looked around in wonder, almost disappointed that his sword had not been unleashed. He was about to walk from the scene until he heard a deep voice. "Open the gates."

It came from the other side of the gate John was supposedly guarding, he turned and saw a long courtyard leading to a great manor. Soldiers on horses were coming towards him slowly, they surrounded a figure, guiding them out towards the gate.

John shrugged and grabbed the handle, heaving the gates open. Four great stallions came first and then behind them came a man John recognised as the Sheriff. His face was shaded under a wide-brimmed hat and his dead, dark eyes stared right through him. They moved beyond the outlaw followed by another four horsemen. John thought about trying his luck against them, but he'd be a fool to risk it after coming this far. The aim was not to kill, but to become rich and invisible to fiends such as the Sheriff. "Ugly bastard," muttered John as they disappeared out of sight. Then he smiled to himself as he looked around the empty courtyard and at the doors of the Sheriff's fine manor. What self-respecting thief would miss an opportunity such as this?

John wandered through the gates and towards the manor, he did all he could to stop himself from running. The door was huge and studded with metal, he tried the handle and it was loose, opening without effort. As he stepped in, his eyes widened at the sheer size of the place. He'd robbed many properties in his lifetime, but none had he seen as fine as this. The ceilings were high and the crystal chandeliers hung low. Masterpieces were mounted on the walls and finely made rugs lined the polished wood floors. "Rob smart," he thought to himself as he grabbed a satchel he found by the door. A man can only carry so much treasure before it becomes a burden; therefore he must steal the smallest and most valuable things he can find. John made his way up the grand staircase before any of the lower rooms, from experience he knew this would be where the finer-made things were, the things people kept closest to their hearts.

The giant outlaw moved with cat-like grace from room to room, taking rings, necklaces, fine jewels and any gold coins he could see. His blue eyes were drawn to a beautiful short-sword hanging on the wall next to a finely made sheath. The silver handle was inlaid with blue jewels and the sword edge was razor sharp. Some blades were made for decoration, they would bend easily and be given as trinkets or prizes. Some swords were forged for battle, made plain but brutal, rarely blunting. But this piece of art was both beautiful and battleworthy. John picked it up feeling the perfect balance of weight in his hand, revelling in it. He grabbed the sheath and tied it around his waist so it hung on the other side of his belt, then slid the pretty blade silently in.

His satchel of loot was full and he made his way through the empty manor to the back, searching for the stable. In no time at all he saw the large structure out back at the end of an extending yard, sheltering great horses. John made his way towards it without worry and found the biggest horse there was, taking his time to saddle it and hang his satchel carefully.

"Are you stealing from my brother, guard?" came a voice.

Startled, John turned around, half pulling his sword. Upon realising it was a lone woman, the big man turned back uncaring, continuing to ready his mount. "Is it really stealing, if it's probably all stolen anyway?" he said, his back to her.

She laughed and edged herself around to face him. "I hope you don't get caught, soldier, the Sheriff isn't a forgiving man."

John continued to fasten what he needed to. "I don't much care what he is, if he's rich, then I'm stealing from him," he said. The giant looked up. The woman was young and dark-haired, she had large eyes and a slim body. Her face was delicate, yet, some features a little too prominent. "His sister, eh? I don't see it. You're not ugly enough."

She laughed then. "You're the man they're all looking for aren't you?"

"Aye," he said plainly. "How'd you guess?"

"I'm confined to this place most of my days and know the guards on rotation from sight."

Shouting could be heard from the manor and John turned, seeing seven guards running towards him. He looked up at the woman and shook his head. "Did you do this?"

"I'm afraid so," she smiled. "You're an outlaw, worse would be done to me for letting this happen."

"What's your name?" he asked with wonder, the guards still approaching.

"Athella," she replied.

"Well, Athella," he said, grabbing her by the shoulders and swinging her in front of him. "I can do worse than the Sheriff, and some of the lads you're going to meet will make him look like a suckling babe." His sword was pulled and rested lightly on her slender neck.

The soldiers running for him came to a sudden stop, maintaining their distance from John and Athella. "You lads let me get upon this horse and the lady will not die," he said calmly.

"Let's let him kill her," one of the guards said. "We'll be able to take him once she's downed."

"You could," said John. "But there are not many men that can best me with a blade, I'd bet I'd be able to kill four of you before you killed me. And you wouldn't just walk away from this. I imagine the Sheriff wouldn't be too happy at being left with only one sister."

"My other sister is dead, Hood and your friends killed her," Athella said coolly.

John laughed heartily. "Those boys are always helping me."

The guards looked between each other sheepishly and began to back off a little, giving John some space. The outlaw stepped into the saddle, pulling Athella up and sitting her in front of him.

The horse was kicked into action and John grinned with pleasure as he moved past the furious guards, heading around the front and out the gate.

Chapter 9

Every so often time slows around you, sticking you between two beats of the earth. That's what happened to Guy of Gisborne as he watched John and the outlaws run from the dungeon behind the towering Eustace. Guy did not fear the monk stood before him, he'd seen him fight when they first met, he'd watched as the monk took down five of his men before being thrown to the floor. Guy had stood idly that day, seeing what the man had in him, what he was made of. In the end, he found he was made of blood and guts like everybody else. No dark god watched over him, protecting him from normal men.

"You are afraid, Guy?" asked the monk, his accent strange and deep.

Guy scoffed at the question. "I don't fear death, I fear dying though, so try to make it quick if you will." With that Guy's blade rang out against the tall, grey-haired monk.

The monk blocked the swing of his sword with the haft of his long-handled axe. The wood of the haft had been strengthened and no blade would be able to mark it. Eustace moved his axe in ways unknown to Guy, he'd never fought a man with such a weapon. He'd battled men with short, large winged axes, but never this. Guy was a man who understood duelling; he knew it was not a single art that could not bend, the duellist had to morph to suit the different variables thrown at him. So the swordsman let Eustace come, he learned the axe's movements and watched the reach of the monk. Within a few minutes, Guy decided to make an attack, arching his body back as the axe swung high, Guy's sword slicing into Eustace's side.

The monk grunted and blood pattered onto the floor. It was a light cut, nothing a few stitches wouldn't fix, but the intent was to leach his confidence. And that it did. Eustace began to step back, on the defence with his axe until he reached the dungeon stairs.

Guy swore inwardly as the monk stepped backwards onto the high ground. The axe was now raining down heavy blows as the two retreated slowly up the stairs, it took great effort to move and dodge while calculating the next steps. Then Guy saw a break and tried to stab his sword at the monk. Eustace moved swiftly and Guy's sword embedded itself into the heavy brickwork behind him. Guy tried to pull, yanking it with all his strength but it would not budge. His grey eyes looked up at the monk just as his boot hit him in the centre of the chest.

Guy tumbled down the spiralling stone stairs, hitting the hard slabs at the bottom heavily. He tried to rise but felt his sight dizzying instead. Eustace came to stand over him, his outline dark and his voice deep. "A truly skilled fighter would not allow that to happen."

Guy grunted at that, somewhere between a scoff and a laugh.

"I will see you again," continued Eustace, "when I'm fully recovered, and then you'll meet death, swordsman."

With that, a fist came down on his face, sending him to blackness.

Guy woke, his bones aching and his head bleating with pain. For a moment he had no idea where he was, as if a well of wine had been drunk before he slept. But within moments he knew where he was as he looked around the dimly lit dungeon. The memory flooded back to him and he sat up with difficulty. He dreaded to think what chaos had descended onto the town with that group of sorry men roaming it.

Guy rose and slowly brushed off his dark clothes. He went to tie back his hair with the band of leather in his pocket, but as he touched his scalp a searing pain entered him. "Bugger it," he sighed, throwing the band to the floor. He walked up the spiral stairs and halfway from the top he saw his sword embedded into the brickwork. His leg lifted and pressed itself against the wall, pulling with all his might. When it broke free he nearly fell back once more, repeating the same horrendous fall. He shook his head at the stupidity of it all.

As he entered the yard outside the dungeon, he saw a litter of bodies and a deserted wagon, two horses still attached. The men were the Sheriff's, the wagon he didn't know. Arrows were planted in some of the corpses, the accuracy was deadly. Obviously Hood's work, he thought. As much as he hated the man, he couldn't help but appreciate his skill with the weapon. Skill was something to admire in a person, not just skill, but exceptional skill. It shows they've got discipline and that's something to be respected.

Guy didn't know where to start, he figured the whole town must be on the search for them, so what's one more man going to do. So he wandered slowly through the streets of Nottingham. He was sick of it all, sick of the tracking, sick of the killing. He'd made enemies, powerful enemies for a man who he despised. Where was the sense in it all? He was an incredibly rich man after his years of service to other men who wanted blood. Guy pictured himself in a cottage, far away, a fire roaring and hunted venison cooking while his wife and daughter sat near him, carefree and happy. Not in this bloodbath of a town.

That's when he decided, he'd leave it all. Bugger the Sheriff and his demands. Pointless feuds shall be forgotten and he'll go on to live in tranquillity with what he really cares about – his family.

A sense of peace flowed through him making the sword on his belt felt like unneeded weight, so he unbuckled it, allowing it to drop to the cobbled floor. Guy turned the corner towards his house, curiously, he found the front was wide open and a few townspeople were moving in and out of it. Panic rose in Guy and he began to sprint down the street, every muscle in his body pushed to breaking point until he reached the open door.

His mouth dropped open as he saw the carnage, people milling around a figure in the corner of the room drew his eye. Then his gaze was diverted to a different scene. As he moved his head, he saw laid out upon a rug near the back door was the body of his little girl. He ran to her, kneeling by her small frame, attempting to wake her. Panic was set on Guy's face, the realisation was dawning on him. She was so cold and pale, he wanted her eyes to open, he wanted to hear the sound of her laugh and squeal of excitement. His head slumped and he began to sob into the body.

"Guy," an older woman said softly. "Your wife needs you."

Guy turned to see the people tending the figure in the corner of the room had begun to leave, watching him with pitiful eyes.

"Jule!" cried Guy with relief as he saw his wife's eyes open. He ran to her hugging his head into her breast and kissing her face.

Jule's beauty remained, but something there was amiss. Her once bright eyes were dull and life almost seemed absent. "He killed her, Guy," she said slowly.

"Who did, Jule?" he asked desperately. "Tell me!"

"A giant, men were looking for him."

"What did he look like?" demanded Guy, but he already knew, he already knew the man responsible.

A tear ran down her soft cheek. "He broke me, I can't move."

Guy felt desperate, white-hot anger flowed through him, coursing through his veins and revenge ached in his heart like a thirst that could not be quenched. Rising from his wife, Guy stormed from his home and back towards the sheathed sword that lay so peacefully on the ground.

Hood had been wandering the town all day, keeping to the shadows and getting to know the area. He found there were two exits, one was the southern gate, the one they'd entered through, the other was the northern gate. The northern gate looked as though it hadn't been opened in years and had a small barracks nearby, so the place was swarming with soldiers on and off duty. The other option was the walls, except they were built high and now archers covered any areas that could be climbed over. Hood knew they all should have acted sooner, before the sentries were enforced. The bowman shook his head. "Rid yourself of doubts, the past is dead, it's smoke in the breeze," he reminded himself. Hood had never gotten anywhere by focusing on what was, he had an eye for the present and future. The past is dead and never coming back, it's pointless wasting present thoughts on it.

The evening was coming now and the bustle of the day was dying down, the market was packing and preparing to leave the city. Now would be a good time to make himself scarce. But his comrades lingered in his mind, perhaps they were already at the cave, he thought. Hood dismissed it. He couldn't see how that'd be possible right now.

Thoughts trailed through the young bowman's head as he watched the stalls pack away on the square. "Oi," he heard come from behind him, a low voice. A hand touched his shoulder and Hood turned, dagger unsheathed ready to plunge into his enemy's stomach. Scarlett raised his hands, the easy smile disappearing from his face.

"I told him not to do that," said Stutley, shaking his head.

Relief flooded Hood as he saw who it was. "Foolish men," he smiled. "Why aren't you two at the cave?"

"Have you seen the bloody place?" said Scarlett. "It's crawling with soldiers. I've no idea how John and Gilbert will have escaped."

Hood shook his head. "We've no time for negative thinking, Scarlett. A negative thought never once produced a positive outcome in the history of the world. Now, the only real option, and the one they'll least expect is exiting through the gate we came."

The outlaws began to make their way through the streets towards it, still keeping to the shadows. Streams of men and women were making their way there too, but the soldiers were hovering around them like flies, looking at faces and checking their wares.

The three outlaws could see the gate from the

shelter of an alley. There was a large clearing where men and women would line up, slowly edging their way past the guards and out of the main town. They all stared in silence at the scene, there were more soldiers than peasants, lining the walls, huddled around the gate and even checking under marketer's wagons. "What's with the stupid hat?" asked Stutley.

Hood tutted. "It's style, Stutley. Besides, I've come up with a plan. Now, what we need to do is…"

A roar interrupted Hood's words, in fact, it interrupted the whole of Nottingham. The giant Gilbert came into sight, his broadsword swinging with speed, delivering crimson death to any that came against it or even got in its way. Peasants were sliced, soldiers were downed and children were kneed as Gilbert moved like a madman towards the southern gate.

"What in God's name is he doing?" said Scarlett.

"Without guidance, some men crumble. Gilbert, though, he panics and kills," said Hood, smiling.

The crowd had lost control, hundreds of queuing peasants began to scatter. Panic amongst crowds is a strange thing. It's like a spark of fire igniting in a dry field, if it's not extinguished instantly, then it'll spread in seconds, creating an inferno. Gilbert was like a great bull with razor-sharp horns, trampling and goring as he went. Soldiers could not reach the giant and form an efficient attack because of the frenzied crowds and the archers on the walls would not shoot in fear of hitting an innocent. So Gilbert was free to do as he wished and whatever soldiers did reach him lost their lives in moments.

"We must do something," said Scarlett.

"You're right," replied Hood. "Arm yourself and follow the chaos." With that, the bowman unrolled his pack and swung his quiver onto his back, wielding his treasured bow in his hands. Hood shot arrow after arrow at the archers on the wall, downing them with ease, while Scarlett and Stutley entered the fray of people, slicing and stabbing whichever guards they could find. The soldiers weren't aware there was more than one foe until their numbers began to thin.

A bell was rung from upon the wall, it was loud and alarming, a signal to others. Hood recognised the urgency and someone needed to control Gilbert so they could get out. "Gilbert," shouted Hood, while the giant continued to slice. He wouldn't listen, he was in a trance of death, the very same look on his face when he sees holy men.

More soldiers began to stream from the various roads and alleys, filling the area around them. Time started to slow as they were becoming overwhelmed. It was now obvious to the guards that Stutley and Scarlett were outlaws, they were surrounded, backs to each other. Gilbert had a ring of men around him, every time he swung his sword the soldiers would step back out of reach and soon he slowed, realising it was done. Hood had his back to a wall, his bow pulled. Soldiers could have stabbed at him, but they knew the Sheriff would want them alive.

Armoured horsemen entered the scene followed by the Sheriff upon his own steed. He was a hideous man, his body long and thin almost hanging from his mount. There was complete silence in the square of cobbled street, around a hundred soldiers with their weapons drawn and peasants on the outskirts watching the scene before them. The Sheriff's sickly laugh broke the silence. "Are you that arrogant that you think you can come into my castle and rob me? You are nothing, you are peasant thieves with sticks."

Hood realised that the Sheriff was speaking to him and he smiled, lowering his bow to his side and walking casually through the soldiers. Hood gripped the bow tightly, focus and confidence flowing through him. The soldiers moved for the outlaw, but their swords and spears were keeping him at arm's length. He came to stand before his horsemen, the Sheriff practically hiding behind them. "Do you hate me, Sheriff?" asked the handsome bowman.

"Hatred would not come close, Hood, I despise you and I will revel in seeing you die."

"You know, if you go east and I mean far east beyond Europe, there are scholars there, older than any man that we've ever known. They're on a constant path to find inner peace, something that will calm their soul. They study their emotions, discovering why they feel what they feel." Hood paused, looking around, all eyes were on him, all ears open. "Jealousy, they say, breeds fear. Fear simmers, sitting like a terrible taste on your tongue and goes on to sire hatred. I do not hate you, Sheriff, I pity you. I pity you because you are jealous of me and my lads, and because you fear me so much, that you need a hundred men to fell four outlaws."

The Sheriff's face dropped slightly, his expression unreadable. The men around were uncomfortable, the tension unbearable. "Those whom the gods would destroy, they first make proud," quoted the Sheriff, his voice deep, lashing out across the cobbles. "Kill them," he ordered. Soldiers began to move in with their weapons, the outlaws raising theirs once more. Hood looked around him, would this be how it ends? His legend left bleeding on the street, holes in his body.

"Hold your weapons!" came a voice from a

darkened route, only peasants lingered there, getting their fill.

All heads turned and the action halted once more. The Sheriff's face one of utter disgust at being spoke against. An armoured horseman emerged. The man was huge, too big for a normal horse, but this horse was not normal either, the beast was colossal. In front of him sat a woman, slender and dark haired. Hood basked in her beauty and forgot all else existed for a moment. Then he noticed the horseman's arm was raised, a sword held to her throat. The horseman pulled off his helmet and threw it to one side, it was John and Hood's heart leapt with joy. "You'll let me and my brothers leave here, not a man will follow us, or this sword will slice open your sister's throat," said John. His face was one of calmness, but everyone knew he was serious. The outlaws had a reputation of ruthlessness and death, John had no issues with killing one more person before he went to the grave.

Eyes were flickering between the Sheriff and John, the horse creeping slowly through the moving soldiers, the sound of its hooves clicking through the air. All could see the Sheriff was in turmoil, his face hard as a rock, a giant vein almost bursting from his forehead. "Move from the gates," the Sheriff shouted, the order sharp and short.

Soldiers lowered their weapons and moved away from the outlaws. Hood smiled and fell low into a curtsey as they did so. Scarlett and Stutley moved sheepishly towards the gate, close to John's horse and Gilbert stood, unaware of what was happening. "Come, Gil," said Hood, tapping his arm. Gilbert smiled widely at the sight of his friend and began to follow.

As the outlaws gathered outside of the gate they

heard a roar, not a roar of anger and death like Gilbert's, but a roar of hurt and madness. The outlaws looked back and pushing through the horsemen was Guy of Gisborne, an expression of lunacy upon his face. He ran towards the men, sprinting with speed, his sword raised. "Grab him!" screamed the Sheriff, panic overcoming him. Soldiers nearby leapt at him, bringing him to the ground. Guy writhed, stretching out towards the outlaws only feet away from him.

Hood looked back at the blank-faced group and laughed. "I suppose that means Eustace is dead then." The outlaws chuckled in agreement and turned, heading back towards their forest.

Chapter 10

Eustace looked down at Guy as he lay unconscious on the dungeon floor. The fallen man was worthy in skill, but his heart did not yearn to kill. Not yet anyway. This wasn't a bad thing of course, but blood-thirst can be a useful thing in a fight.

Eustace turned, making his way back up the dungeon, edging by Guy's sword stuck in the stonework. The monk half expected a fight as he edged his way towards the doorway, but as he peeked his head around the exit, he saw the back of Hood galloping through the small battalion of soldiers that faced him. The outlaw shot arrows valiantly from his mount as he rode. Eustace watched with anticipation, gripping the haft of his axe tightly, wondering if the soldiers would use their minds and search the dungeon. But they did not. The men stood, looking between themselves in shock that they'd lost Hood so easily. Words were said between them that Eustace did not hear and then they split up, heading down different avenues into the town. Within moments the area was clear, all that remained were a few dead or dying men looking up at the blue sky or face down to the gravel. The wagon was still there, two horses standing aimlessly in front of it and his empty cage sitting behind.

Eustace walked to the rear of the wagon and removed the bolt holding the cage to the back of it. He hopped up, looking into the main of the wagon, bits of food mainly and old priestly clothes occupied it. The monk removed the weapons from it and placed them on the ground, then donned the priest's robe and sat upon the front of the wagon. The horses neighed softly as he prompted them into movement. The wagon jolted and the wheels turned, circling around towards the path they had first entered through. It bumped up and down as the large wooden wheels rolled over the dead bodies below it. Blood trailed for a little while but soon ran thin.

The monk's pale blue eyes watched the terrified men and women around him as he moved down the main road. They weren't scared of him, for he was apparently a man of God and he smiled with kindness as their own eyes fell upon him. He hated that smile, the soft smile mimicking that of an old man to a hapless child, his eyes almost shutting as his mouth stretched wide. Was he mad rolling himself through the heart of the enemy for everyone to see? He didn't think so. Eustace remembered a key rule of trickery, the art of becoming invisible to everyone. His master had taught him that men who were looking for someone would look for the man with his head down, lurking close to the shadows. So walk with your head high, he'd said, they may look at you once, but when they see a man of confidence and comfortableness, you won't warrant a second look.

The dark monk thought back to the last time he'd seen his master. They'd been on the coast in their ships, ambushed by English vessels. Eustace's target had been a cargo ship, filled with supplies and gold. They needed to intercept it and halt any form of sustenance to their enemy. It should have been easy and fast, no casualties. But Eustace's confidence had risen of late and arrogance had started to bloom.

"Wait for it to move out of the cover of the cliffs, Eustace, that way you'll know it's safe and we'll be able to move in freely," said his master. He was older than Eustace, his was hair iron-grey and beginning to thin at the crown, his eyes were dark and his body slender. He dressed in fine silk robes, a short sword at his side.

"If we allow the ship to move out," said Eustace, "we may lose it. It's lighter than us and if it hits a current it'll be out of reach. They can't see us right now and we lay hidden by the land, the time to strike is now."

"Patience, my boy, is all it takes for suspicion to become certainty."

Eustace shook his head and smiled, patting him on the shoulder as he walked by him. "I appreciate your advice, master, but you need to trust me, I know the situation and it will work in our favour."

His master shook his head as he watched Eustace walk through the belly of the ship and climb the ladders to the deck. Eustace was twenty years younger than his master, even though his hair was grey too, it was thick and his face was ageless.

Eustace had stood upon the helm guiding the wheel, while his men below rowed in sync, expertly steering the vessel to their target. Eustace's eyes narrowed and the hot coastal sun beat down on his plated armour, heating his body, warming it for battle. The monk's mind was cool as they rounded the edge of the land and when he saw the huge English battleship waiting, he wasn't overly surprised. His master was never wrong and he knew when he looked down on him that this was it, this was when it was done.

The enemy ship was colossal, it would hold at least four times what his own ship would. The only advantage Eustace had was speed. The angle they were at, the English ship would come close, so close that many of the enemy would board and overwhelm his crew. The monk watched his men, the courageous bunch would die for him in a heartbeat if he wished it so.

"Angle her close!" Eustace called, as he prompted his master to take the wheel. Eustace climbed the rigging of the ship, moving higher and higher towards the mast. The enemy ship was large, the decks much higher than his own. The two vessels neared and one dwarfed the other. Eustace could just see over the enemy deck now, the English soldiers readying themselves on their boarding ropes. The dark monk took one last look down at his master, the old man nodded at Eustace, his head lowering in understanding. "I'll see you at the bay!" Eustace shouted at the top of his lungs before leaping onto the decks of the English, scattering the soldiers.

It seemed like time paused as Eustace pulled his axe. He looked around the ship, the deck was huge and then men lightly armoured. They were all edging closer, their swords pulled. Curiously behind them, leaning casually against the mast was a handsome man garbed in black, his dark hair was tied back and his beard was short and neat. The man watched Eustace, his sword still sheathed at his side. He was the only man there who didn't hold a weapon in his hand. "Take him down," said the leader. "I want him alive."

Eustace disliked him instantly and the manner of him fuelled his fury. His axe swung, cutting into his enemy. The first man fell with a gaping hole in his chest, screaming. The second and third were swatted like flies. The fourth ran at him with speed, attempting to catch him off guard, but Eustace parried and the enemy was thrown from the ship with a wound in his back. The fifth man who came at him was how he came to be in chains. The soldier had thrust carelessly at Eustace, in return his axe had swung for his neck, delivering a fatal blow. It was a hard thing to decapitate a man in one swing, even heavily stacked executioners often took two tries. Unfortunately for Eustace his axe was caught halfway, embedded into the man's cartilage and spine, pumping blood onto half the crew.

That's when the soldiers pounced and pinned the monk. The man in black had come then, looking over Eustace while six men restrained him. "You're a talented fighter, pirate," Guy of Gisborne had told him.

"Hand me my axe and I'll give you a lesson or two," said Eustace, his voice strained as the soldiers held him.

Guy laughed. "You don't deserve to cross weapons with me after that. Fancy getting your axe stuck, a truly skilled fighter would not allow that to happen."

Eustace's mind came back to the present, he smiled at the memory and patted the axe that lay under his seat. His wagon continued to roll slowly, teetering over cobbles and towards the gates. He moved past the marketplace and joined some of the leaving traders that were queuing for the exit. The line was long to the gate and guards were everywhere, checking wares and under robes. He started to feel the pressure as the soldiers made their way up the line. Another wagon, three places in front of himself had been thoroughly searched and Eustace had no doubt that they'd find his axe. He knew it would certainly raise some questions, at least enough questions to warrant detaining him a little while.

They finally reached him after briskly moving by the farmer in front. "Afternoon, Father," said one of the young guards.

Eustace smiled warmly, not wanting to give away

anything with his accent.

The guard signalled two of his comrades to begin the search, one climbing in, looking through the cloths and food, the other checking beneath the wagon. "I'm not sure if you're aware," the young guard continued, "but there's been some trouble and we can't be too careful."

Eustace smiled again, spreading his ankles so the back of his robe covered some of the axe. The guard at the front was checking the flanks of the horses and then began under the cargo hold at Eustace's feet. The guard's hands moved the axe and it slid, prompting his attention. Just as he dipped his head to search further, there was a wild roar coming from the top of the square. Everyone's attention was stolen and Eustace saw the massive form of Gilbert swinging his sword into the crowd, downing whatever he faced.

The queue soon dissipated into a frenzy and Eustace saw his chance. His horses began at a panicked trot that turned into a gallop towards the gate, the wagon almost spinning from his control. The soldiers didn't even try and stop him as Eustace came hurtling towards them. They moved gratefully, accepting it as backlash from the attack, then moved back in to cover the gate.

Eustace could scarce believe his luck as he faced the open fields and hovels scattered around him. Behind, he could hear chaos and couldn't help but feel thankful he was not a part of it. His journey back was peaceful from then; he took the main road through the valley and into the forest where he'd first met Hood.

Halting the wagon at the blood-stained road where he'd seen the priests butchered by Gilbert, he hopped into the back, filling his stomach with food and downing what water he had. The sun began to set and

Eustace wondered if he should leave. Hood owed him gold and the outlaws would prove useful in the days to come, however, they were not essential to him and not even a guarantee.

Sundown, he thought, that's how long he'd give it. Then, just as he was about to move off, he saw on the horizon of the road silhouettes moving slowly towards him, a low orange sun behind them. Eustace smiled. A stubborn group, he thought, who bat away death like an irritating fly.

Chapter 11

The Sheriff had sat upon his horse in the square behind the gates, watching as the outlaws left with his only sister. His loathsome sister, but his sister nonetheless. Family was an odd thing, it was the only time both hate and love could find themselves entwined so tightly.

He shook his head as he watched Guy of Gisborne thrash like a madman on the ground, almost breaking his bones to reach the outlaws. The Sheriff knew all about his wife and child, a soldier had informed him as he'd made his way through the town. "Shall we remove them from the house so Guy doesn't find them like that?" the soldier had asked the Sheriff.

"Leave them," the Sheriff had told him, as they veered away from the house of Guy. The Sheriff wanted Guy to see it, he wanted the need for vengeance to boil from his every bone. Guy was a gifted killer and tracker, but he had always lacked a certain drive. The Sheriff didn't want to tempt fate, he wanted his sister alive and he needed Guy driven. He turned on his horse and began to head back to his manor. "Send Guy to join me for supper, have him at my home by sundown," he said to one of his guards casually. The guard nodded and swung back to the fallen figure of Guy, assessing the broken man carefully.

The Sheriff sat in his long dining room, his body half slouched in a firmly padded seat. The sun was down and the dark-oak room lit by long dinner candles spaced out across the table. The corners of the room were gloomy, shadows lurking on the paintings hung on the walls. The aromatic food made the Sheriff's stomach grumble. There was glistening duck, roasted vegetables, glazed fruits and cakes. By the time Guy was finally announced, some of the food was cold, the Sheriff would usually be irritated by this, but the jug of wine he'd sunk had eased the tension in his head.

Guy had been sat opposite the Sheriff, at the far end of the table. A servant appeared from the shadows, placing food in front of him. Guy's head was in his hands and his clothes were unwashed, stained with blood and dirt. "Eat, Guy," said the Sheriff, calmly.

"She's crippled," said Guy, simply.

"I'm sorry to hear that, but don't you worry, we will look after her. You've served me well these past few years."

Guy looked up, fire in his eyes. "She can't move, she can't go to the toilet, nothing. She just lies there, doesn't even cry."

"We'll look after her, Guy, the best help we can provide," reassured the Sheriff softly.

Guy slammed his fists down onto the table, the cutlery shaking and the candles nearly toppling. "There is no helping her!"

The servant standing close by looked uncomfortable and the Sheriff dismissed him. Rising from his padded seat, the Sheriff went to the corner of the room and pulled an old bottle from a cabinet. Two fine glasses were next to it and the Sheriff poured a little in each, placing one down in front of Guy.

Guy looked up, his face seemed to have aged terribly since the last time he saw him. "Why did you let them go?" he said, pitifully.

The ugly Sheriff looked down at him, his face stern,

his voice deep. "Because, Guy, she's my family, the last of my family. As much as the bitch fuels a hate in me, I can't just let her die."

"They wouldn't have killed her," said Guy, sipping on the strong alcohol in front of him, the liquid warming his body.

"John is not known for the butchering of women, that's true, but I can't speak for the rest of them. You know yourself that Gilbert's a ruthless one."

Guy tensed at that and his eyes dropped to the table. He took another sip.

"Sorry," said the Sheriff. "I do mean that. I know I'm not the most merciful man, but I've felt loss before, deep and painful loss. The type of loss that rips part of the soul from the body, leaving you only a fraction of the man you were." The Sheriff sat on the seat nearest him, pulling it in close. "But you mustn't give up, I've got scouts out and we're setting off at dawn, I'll be part of the party. We'll track them to the edge of the world if we have to. I don't know when we'll get them, Guy, but you have my word that we will." The Sheriff stuck his hand out at that, waiting for Guy's grip.

Guy stared at the bony hand stretched out in front of him. He knew he was just a pawn and he was more than aware that the Sheriff wouldn't be able to catch the outlaws without him. Guy was being used and he didn't care. All he wanted was revenge, the Sheriff's resources would help, perhaps even the King's guard will be able to be summoned at this rate. Guy's hand gripped the Sheriff's, it was cold and clammy. He let go and held out his empty glass, gesturing it towards the bottle next to the cabinet.

The Sheriff nodded, a forced smile on his face. Being made to pour another man a drink in his own home was unheard of. If he weren't so useful, thought the Sheriff, the bottle would have been used to gauge his throat.

The darkest hour was that before dawn, that's when the Sheriff rose. He slowly donned his travelling garments while his servants cooked him an early breakfast. As he came down his stairs, he saw Guy was still sitting there awake, his eyes out the window like a hound. "They stole from here, you know?" said the Sheriff, his voice a raspy hiss. "It was John just before he took my sister."

"What'd you do to the men who saw it happen?" asked Guy, his weary eyes turning on him.

"Well, they tried to keep it from me, as if they didn't see anything. An hour with the torturer got the truth out of them." The Sheriff's thin lips stretched into a smile. "They're due to hang today. Shame we'll miss that."

"Aye," said Guy, turning away. "Shame."

"We'll be setting off soon, Guy, join me for food."

Guy didn't feel like eating, but he knew it was necessary before a day of tracking. Losing focus was detrimental to tracking, one missed print or broken twig could cost them hours, if not the whole endeavour. So Guy rose slowly, heading towards the dining room.

The two men sat and ate together, breaking fast and watching the orange sunlight fill the room. "It's time," said the Sheriff, leading them to his stables where their mounts were waiting. The horses were huge, their breed built for stamina and strength. Servants had woken early to fill their saddlebags with the necessary provisions.

The two men rounded to the front of the manor, there were fifty men on horses waiting, each of them ready for the hunt. "Let me lead once we're out the gates," said Guy, turning to look at the Sheriff. He sat on his saddle, his back straight and his face strained. The Sheriff was not a man who enjoyed riding and his body would ache in the days to come.

"I'm leading, Guy, it's my sodding sister they've got."

"And it's my daughter they killed," said Guy sharply, his tone cutting into the Sheriff.

The Sheriff reddened with anger, fury almost engulfing him. "Watch it, Guy, I know you're grieving, but if you speak out of turn again it'll be you we are hunting."

Guy took a deep breath, calming himself. "My apologies, but I'll need to go further in front at times, you can follow me from a distance. It's a matter of tracking, fifty horsemen can make wildlife scatter, ruining valuable tells, or they themselves can do that. This takes time, you understand that."

The Sheriff nodded, his dark eyes calming. "Understood."

"Do surrounding villages know to look out for them?"

The Sheriff smiled at this. "I've sent out riders to every corner. They've kidnapped my sister of royal blood and killed my other. The King will have no choice but to issue a warrant. Every town, city and village will hear of this in days to come."

"What's the reward?" asked Guy.

"A thousand in gold for Hood, three hundred more for each of the others. And before you ask, this does not include you, Guy, you're technically in the employment of the King, so you're exempt."

Guy frowned. "Gold bothers me not. I just want

them for myself, others will only get in the way."

The Sheriff continued to lead the soldiers through the city, men and women who were rising early watched from their windows at the sight. They knew from the events the previous day what their mission was and who their target may be. The Sheriff led them tactically past Guy's home, he wanted to watch the man's fury smoulder a little more. Instead, Guy turned his head, unable to look at the place that he once held so firmly in his heart.

Death and hurt bring out the best of men, thought the Sheriff, it destroys a person's weakness and burns the ropes that hold them back, or dismantles them completely. Either way, to him the gamble was worth it.

Once the gate of the city was reached, the Sheriff stuck to his word and let Guy ride ahead. In truth, Guy was thankful for it. He knew the Sheriff was playing him, he would do anything to have control over a man's mind or watch him squirm during his darkest moments.

The tracker was tired, his bones were weary but his mind was focused. A coldness that he'd never felt fuelled his motives. He'd been up all night in the Sheriff's home, watching through the window, considering making his move and leaving the Sheriff behind to hunt for the men himself. Only common sense had stopped him, for he knew his chances of catching them would rise with the awful man's resources.

Guy had only been interrupted once through the night, a heavy-set older woman had approached him, her face soft and her eyes kind. "Why aren't you with your wife, sir? I believe this will be a time just as trying for her as it is for you."

Guy had turned, at first he was shocked by the woman's directness, perhaps he was angered, he couldn't decide and realised he just didn't care. "Tell me, were you beautiful before you were old and sagging, Kathryn?"

Her cheeks flushed and her eyes narrowed with anger. "You know this, Guy of Gisborne. Men still speak of my past beauty with great fondness. Why would you ask this?"

"And how often do you look in mirrors now?"

"I avoid them," she said simply. "Now what's your point, you bitter man?"

"To look upon something that once meant everything to you, that was your complete existence, defining who you are…" he said, taking in a shuddering breath. "To look upon what was once your life, seeing it broken, well, it feels like losing it all over again. That woman meant everything to me, that home, that little girl. My heart breaks every time I think of the memories, if I were to walk in there again, I believe I would drag a dagger across my throat." The dark-haired man turned away, facing the window once more. "And before I do that I need to collect some souls to take with me."

Guy looked back at the Sheriff and his men; they looked like a dark swarm moving over the land, filtering through the hovels of the lower town. They would keep their eye on Guy, making sure he was only just in sight as they moved.

Guy was told which direction Hood and his men had been seen going, so he ignored the many boot prints of hunters and tradesmen, until he reached an open gate in the distance. The gate was solitary and it was the only route that would lead back to the forest without drawing attention to themselves. Guy knelt and inspected the ground, it was still soft and imprints visible; four sets of boots and a set of hoof prints.

The tracker left his horse for the Sheriff and his men to pick up. From now it would require closer inspection on foot. There were many avenues into the vast forest of Nottingham, so he moved on, his eyes scanning carefully. Finally, the tracks became churned and messy, his instincts making him half draw his blade. Guy spotted blood, trickles at first which then led to a small pool at the base of a thick tree.

Guy froze and he stared hard at the tree trunk, moving slowly to see where the origin of the blood was coming from. It came as no surprise when he rounded it, seeing one of the Sheriff's scouts sitting with his back against the trunk, the blood saturating the bottom of his leggings along with the ground. What did surprise him was to see the scout's eyes blink and his head turn towards the tracker. Guy's stomach turned as the scout's head came to face him, the right side of it was completely caved in, his scalp misshapen and part of his skull protruding. Blood flowed freely from the head wound and Guy sheathed his blade, kneeling down next to the man. He reached his hand out, resting it on the scout's shoulder. Guy didn't know what to say, to ask the man if he was alright would be ridiculous.

The scout was young, his hair was tufty and brown, his eyes half glazed and green. His stare landed on Guy, focusing for a moment. The scout began chuckling quietly, but soon it transformed into manic fits of laughter. The Scout tried to stand and Guy removed his hand, backing off and resting it on his hilt. The laughter then turned to screams, the scout's eyes filled with frenzied fear. He ran for Guy, his arms outstretched.

Guy pulled his weapon ready to take him down, but to his surprise, an arrow slammed into his body, another three quickly downing the scout. The tracker turned and saw the Sheriff and his men not far off, a few of them with bows in their hand. The Sheriff dismounted and walked towards Guy. "What the hell happened to him," he asked casually, kneeling and inspecting the caved in head. Guy watched with revulsion as the Sheriff's long fingers reached out and touched the indented head, running his fingers slowly over the ruined scalp then tapping the exposed skull.

"I'm not sure," said Guy. "I've only seen a man's head once like that before and that was when he was kicked by a horse. Died instantly though, not like this one."

"Intriguing isn't it?" said the Sheriff, his dark eyes still staring at the scout.

"Disturbing is more suited I believe."

The Sheriff looked up at him in disgust. "Disturbing? Death is not disturbing, it happens to us all, it's Mother Nature's fairest gift."

"That death was far from fair, his mind was unhinged to the point of insanity."

The Sheriff rose, absently brushing the dirt from his knees. "Where now?"

"Follow me, keep the men back though, their horses are too much. Bring one man with us and we'll send him back if we need horses."

"You expect me to follow you with one guard? After what I've just seen? Hood could be hiding in the next throng of trees for all I know. I'll have a man trail you and we'll wait. Send him back for us when you have a sure trail."

Guy nodded and moved on. From there it was no

trouble to follow the trail and Guy knew Hood would not be close by, not now, he just wanted time alone.

He found himself moving through a small thicket of trees then onto the main road running through the forest. There were numerous wagon trails leading back and forth down the road as well as hoof prints. The outlaws' prints he managed to follow to a point, then they all dissipated, separating off into different avenues of the forest. "Sneaky bastards," Guy whispered to himself in frustration. The outlaws had created separate trails into the trees, knowing they'd be followed. He knew they'd all lead to the same place eventually, but it meant the horsemen could not follow, they'd need to meet them later.

Guy called for the soldier following him close by. "Tell the Sheriff I need ten men and one runner, no horses. We'll send for the horses when we're out the forest."

The soldier nodded, moving off. Guy then sat on the ground, his lids were heavy and sleep whispered his name. But sleep, he decided, would not come, for rest was only for those who deserved it.

Chapter 12

Hood was ecstatic as he looked back at the castle and its walls from a distance. He had faced certain death in the square, his men fighting valiantly against the Sheriff's own until the last moment they could. Then John had come, rescuing them all while upon his horse he had carried something more valuable than any amount of gold – Athella, the Sheriff's sister. He'd watched her as they travelled, sitting atop John's horse. She did not complain and avoided their stares like the plague. The bowman would say something to her, he knew, something charming and witty, but he had not decided what.

"Where do we go now?" asked John, looking down to Hood.

"We'll make our way back to the cave, pack what we can, then move off," he said positively.

"Move off?" John said. "This is our home."

"And before this, somewhere else was. Things change, John, circumstances change and if you remain complacent and don't adapt, then the change will consume us."

"We've lasted this long," argued John.

"Christ!" said Stutley, irritation on his face. "Will you just listen to Hood, it's because you didn't listen to him that we had to break in there and free your clumsy arse."

Anger burst from John and he drew his sword atop the horse, turning it suddenly to face Stutley, who in return drew his long dagger. Scarlett pulled his own weapon then, edging around the side of John. Gilbert watched in confusion, as his mind hadn't been following the conversation, he went on to draw his own long sword, twisting his head and looking for soldiers.

Hood's laughter broke the strain and all looked at him – except Athella, her eyes were on the ground. "Brothers, put your weapons away. Have we ever gotten anywhere without each other? Before we all met, we were nothing, nobody, poor sods with nought but ambition in our hearts. Recognise that we've just come from a highly stressful situation, where we all more than likely faced death. After such instances our thoughts are not straight, panic and elation merge creating a feeling we cannot understand." Hood looked between them, tension was dissipating and Stutley put his dagger away. Scarlett followed this and sheathed his blade, as did John. Gilbert stood, his long sword hefted and a smile on his ugly face, staring at Hood. "Away, Gilbert," the bowman commanded sternly. Gilbert's sword was sheathed in an instant.

"What do we do then?" asked Stutley.

"A vote," said Hood. "Hands up if you'd like to leave Nottingham?" Hood's own hand went up, as did Scarlett's and Stutley's, Gilbert copied Hood and John sighed, slowly raising his hand. "And who votes we should stay?" Athella's hand rose slowly and the men began to laugh, the tension easing from the men. "My lady, I'm afraid you have no choice in the matter. But, if you manage to escape before either my arrow finds you or Gilbert sniffs you out, then you're free to go."

The outlaws shook off the disagreement and began to move once more. Their pace had quickened and the sun was getting lower, the scent of the forest was wafting their way and Hood revelled in it. The smell of the town had been one of filth. Piss and shit lined the alleys and rotting butcher's meat was overwhelming in the poorer sects. The forest had a way with Hood and he had a way with it. There was everything a man needed in nature, look after it and it will look after you. The very sight of the distant treeline calmed his soul.

A new forest, he thought. The notion galled him, for Sherwood Forest had been kind to him, he'd grown richer than most men and women as he sat in that mass of trees and rocks.

"We've got company," said Stutley to Hood, his voice low as they walked.

"Where and how many?" asked Hood, his voice equally low, not to alert his outlaws.

"Just the one, behind that small rise in the earth, I believe he's lying down."

Hood squinted. "God's," said the bowman. "You must have the sight of a hawk."

Stutley chuckled. "No, lad, Scarlett pointed him out. What shall we do?"

"If we walk towards him, it'll surprise him, he won't rise to run as we'd see him and John would run him down on the horse, or my arrow will find him. His only option will be to hide within the bushes nearby. That's when we'll get him."

The outlaws slightly altered their direction and the men were informed of the situation, except Gilbert, he's not one for subtlety. So they walked, closer and closer to the spot of the hiding man. There was no movement, which was good, it meant he was hiding, waiting for them to pass. Soon, they were close enough for him to be within earshot and stopped where they were. "Come out, man, come out and play Hood's game of chance," said the bowman.

The outlaws looked about each other, grins on their faces at Hood's proposition. Athella's expression was one of intrigue, no man she'd known would approach the situation this way, especially not the Sheriff.

Gilbert's attention was roused by the mention of Hood's game. "Who we talking about, Hood? Who's playing?" asked the giant, plastered with enthusiasm.

"Why, Gilbert, there's a man lying within those bushes, fetch him for me will you?" asked Hood, loud enough for the hidden man to hear. The bushes nearby began to rustle and a young man emerged, garbed in greens and armed with a sword. His green eyes fell upon the outlaws, moving from one to the other, until they came to rest on Gilbert. The huge man's jaw was slack, his mouth had fallen open and his eyes were wide with excitement.

"Fetch him, Gil," said Hood, his voice quiet but commanding.

Gilbert charged at him and the scout instinctively began to flee. There was a long stretch of grass ahead of them, forest far beyond that. "It'd be best to have him alive, wouldn't it?" said John, looking down from his horse at Hood.

Hood shrugged. "Gilbert knows that when I say fetch, it means to bring them back alive. He'll knock them unconscious. He likes the game too much to kill him.

The group watched with anticipation. It was like a hunt, the dog catching the hare, they all knew it would happen, it was just a matter of when. Although, every now and then the hare found its freedom. Not this time though, Gilbert dove, his massive arms grappling onto the prey. The outlaws gave a cheer at the sight and began to move towards them. The scout was struggling, wriggling to be free. Gilbert lifted his fist with frustration and let it fall with power onto the man's skull. There was a loud crack that echoed through the glade and the outlaws winced. At first, they thought it was Gilbert's hand that had broken, for he was rubbing at his knuckles tenderly. But as they moved in, they saw it was not Gilbert's hand that was broken, it was the scout's head.

The outlaws stood back, keeping their distance as Hood moved in close. The scout was reeling in pain, his eyes circling the sky in motions. Blood was slowly trickling out of a small wound where skull had pierced the sunken scalp. "Good lord," said Hood under his breath. He turned, a boyish grin on his face. "Lads, you must see this."

The outlaws slowly moved in and John leapt from his horse, bringing Athella with him. They all looked at the man's wound closely as he lay on the floor, saying nothing. "Is he alive?" asked Stutley.

"I believe he is," replied Hood, astonishment in his voice.

The scout began to mumble something under his breath, then it became louder and louder, his green, wild eyes fixed onto Hood. "*Eritque arcus mortis, eritque arcus mortis*," said the injured scout, over and over.

"What the bloody hell is he saying?" said Hood, the grin slowly falling from his face as the scout spoke so urgently at him.

"That's the old language," said Scarlett uncomfortably, his hand rubbing at his stubble.

"Just kill him," said John. "The man's half dead anyway."

Hood still stared at the scout, and the scout stared back. "Nah, leave him to rot."

The outlaws turned and left the scene, the scout had stopped talking and began releasing intermittent screams. The experience left a bitter taste in Hood's mouth and the group could tell. He had trudged on in front, not saying a word until they reached the main road that led through the forest. The sun was setting behind them and the sky was almost orange. In the distance they saw a stationary wagon in the middle of the road. "I can't believe we'll be leaving this place," said John. "I mean, look at that, as soon as we're here I see a wagon ready to be looted right in our line of sight. I tell you, we won't get it that easy elsewhere."

"Calm yourself, John, we've already looted that one," he said, excitement rising in his voice.

"What do you mean?" asked Stutley, puzzled.

Scarlett smiled to himself as he recognised the man with the cart. "That's our friend Eustace."

Hood took the lead and reached out his hand, gripping onto Eustace's as they met. "It's good to see you, axeman. Come for your gold?"

The rest of the men greeted Eustace in a similar way and John nodded sternly from his mount. "That and more," said the dark monk. His long grey hair was tied back and his clothes were filthy, stained with travel. "Where are you headed?"

"We're heading back to our camp and then we're off. As you can probably understand, the whole of Nottingham are after us."

"Yes," said the monk, looking up at Athella. "I can see why."

The men travelled through the forest until well into nightfall. Hood had taken the horses from the wagon then rolled it off into a ditch further up the road. Scarlett and Gilbert had been sent out to set fake tracks in an attempt to slow down any men following. Eventually, they reached their familiar cave, the area cleared and stones already laid out for a fire. John laid down Athella and got to binding her hands and feet, while Stutley set about making a fire.

"This is our home," said Hood, brightly, looking between the displeased Athella and Eustace the monk.

"Was our home," muttered John.

"About that," said Eustace, sitting his lean body down next to the almost lit fire. "I have a proposition for you all. I was going to wait until the others came back but—"

Hood cut him off. "I speak for them mostly, out with it."

Eustace nodded and continued. "I have a ship, far north of here on the coast, I'd like you all to accompany me there."

"Why would we do that?" asked Hood, engaged at the thought of a plan.

"Well, I'm a rich man and my crew are loyal. They wait for me with plunder and I have even more of it across the sea. If you all help me there, you can join my crew and with that, comes your own weight in gold."

John's eyes widened at the mention of riches and Hood saw the desperation in his eyes.

"Why do you need us?" asked Hood, curiously.

"I'm a wanted man, the King had put a warrant out for me, if someone hears my accent or looks at me too hard, they'll know. A man walking the country by himself is doing it for a reason," said the monk.

"But we're wanted men, you think he hasn't got people looking for us? She's kin to the King," said Hood, pointing at Athella.

"Ah, Hood, but you are loved by the commoner, a

foreigner is despised."

"Aye," said Stutley, stacking dry wood on the fire. "But trouble seems to find us wherever we go."

"And yet, here you all are," replied Eustace, smiling. "You have proven yourselves survivors, apparently immune to death. It works in a man's favour to travel with such people."

Hood's face was one of thought, trying to weigh the options. There weren't many.

"If riches don't tempt you, Hood, what does? For you're not a man that strikes me as someone who will run from here with their sack of gold and settle down. You yearn for action, you take pleasure when your name is heard. You want fame, a legend? Then your path lies with me. No one remembers the men who do nothing."

Hood smiled at that, his teeth glowing in the firelight. "We still want the gold though."

Athella hadn't been scared at first when John had taken her, in fact, a tiny wave of relief had swept through her as she realised she was to be taken from the castle. Even more to her surprise was when the Sheriff had let the outlaws leave with her, when all it would take was her life to have theirs. Part of her was happy to see that side of the Sheriff, she hadn't seen an ounce of humanity in him since he was a very young man. That had disappeared with each atrocity he committed, with each man's wife he slaughtered or raped or with every child he had mercilessly flayed.

She'd heard stories of Hood and his men, the common folk at the market spoke about him constantly. They'd made him out to be invincible, but Athella hadn't believed it. When she first saw him, facing down the Sheriff, a score of soldiers around him, he had seemed like the demi-god that all had spoken of. Her expectations had died soon after. Once all the excitement had worn off, that's when the worry started to slither into her soul. How little the group cared for the life of a man as they had gathered with boyish amusement at the scout's crushed head. The group were barbaric, life meaning little to them. The scene had made her question her own worth to them, it made her picture herself dying, the men laughing as the life drained from her. Strangely enough, John, her kidnapper, had been the one who'd made her feel most safe. Perhaps he felt responsible for her as he'd snatched her from the manor. Despite this, the man remained a brute in her mind, for what kind of person would choose to have the outlaws as their company.

She looked down at her bound feet and wrists and then to the snoring figure of John next to the fire. They'd travelled far that day, further than she ever had before in such a short time. It'd taken three hours or so to walk from the road where they met the dark monk Eustace to the cave deep within the forest. Hood had sent Scarlett and Gilbert off with one of the wagon horses to make fake tracks and they hadn't arrived at the camp yet.

Athella stared at the monk from across the fire, for a while she had thought he would never sleep, but eventually, he dropped off, snoring lightly. As for Hood, he sat with his back against a tree, his strange hat dipped over his face and his arms crossed. Stutley, the old man, had decided to sleep in the cave with the blankets away from the noisy forest. They'd openly spoken in front of Athella about escaping. This confused her, did they plan to kill her or take her all the way? Letting her go would only uncover their plans. She cast the thoughts from her mind, it would do no good to ponder on such things.

The group had roused slightly as Scarlett and Gilbert returned with the horse. Scarlett spoke briefly to Hood, outlining their route, then the two dropped off quickly, sleep coming easily to them.

Athella sat in her binds, she was not tired, there was no way sleep would touch her in such a circumstance. She needed to escape and the perfect moment would be when all men fell to their slumber, but only one remained, it was the giant, Gilbert.

He sat near the cave mouth, the fire illuminating his massive figure, his dark eyes staring at her unblinking. She felt uneasy and wanted to wake John, but the thought made her feel stupid, what would her kidnapper say if she voiced her concerns. Dread swept over her when she saw Gilbert stand, his stare still on her. He came and sat next to her, his legs crossed and his knees slightly raised. She could feel his body breathe in and out, the side of him scraping against her. Athella slowly twisted her head, looking up at the brute. He was ugly, his eyes far apart and his nose flat. His mouth opened, a great smile showed broken and stained teeth.

Athella held her breath, for fright was holding onto her body as his huge finger reached out towards her face. It stroked her cheek and she shuddered, the finger was caked in dried blood from the scout's crushed skull. Gilbert rose suddenly, the movement incredibly fluid and swift for a man his size. His hand opened and shut, raking in the full head of Athella's hair. She yelped instinctively at the pain, but the rest of the camp did not stir as she was being dragged away from the fire towards the confines of the forest. "Help!" she managed to shout. And just as the trees were about to engulf her, Hood was there, standing before them.

"Gilbert!" his voice rang out, deep and commanding.

Athella felt the dirt and twigs halt beneath her and the grip loosen on her hair. Gilbert moved away, backing towards the fire with his hands raised in submission. "Sorry, Hood, I thought…" stammered Gilbert.

"You thought what?" exclaimed Hood, slamming his fist into the big man's jaw and then another into his stomach.

Gilbert wobbled and Hood sent another right that sent Gilbert crashing down, almost into the fire. Gilbert lay there, his colossal body shaking and his eyes squeezed shut.

Stutley rose and stood between them, the old man placing his hands on Hood's shoulders. "Come on, Hood, you know what he's like."

Hood shook his head with frustration and looked back at Athella. "Will someone keep an eye on her? I'm going for a walk." He began to storm from the camp and turned to Gilbert. "You keep your hands to yourself!"

Athella was in shock at the events that unfolded. The young bowman had saved her from the brute, attacked him even. Hood was a man unexplained, his actions contradicting. She watched as he disappeared into the dark forest, his bow gripped tightly in his hand. Stutley had helped up Gilbert and led him back to the cave. The dark monk Eustace rose from his place and came to move her back to the fire then sat a body away from her. "You're not going to try anything are you?" asked Athella, failing to hide the distrust from her voice.

The grey-haired monk laughed warmly, amusement on his face. "Trust me, lady, you need have no fear in that."

They sat for a while in silence, neither finding sleep, the crackling fire taking their weariness. "You are from across the sea?" she asked.

"Yes," he said simply.

"Do you miss it?"

The monk took a deep breath and threw a small rock into the fire. "Always."

"Do you know Latin?" she asked, curiously.

His eyebrow raised at the question. "I do, it's a language of beauty and grace."

"*Eritque arcus mortis*," she recited. "What does that mean?"

The dark monk smiled once more, his pale eyes turning back to the flames. "The bow of death."

Chapter 13

Ten years earlier

Hood lay on his cramped bed in the keep, the chest at the end of it whispering out to him, urging him to open it. His eyes were on it and he was pushing closer. Nimble fingers flicked open the clasps and there it lay, covered carefully in oiled cloth, waiting for him.

A knock at the door startled the lad. "Lord Fitzwalter wants to see you; he's at the top of the keep."

Hood closed the chest quickly and donned his tunic, making his way to the top of the keep. The stairs were many; numerous arrow slits placed throughout and soldiers constantly moving around. They smiled kindly at Hood as he passed them. Reaching the top of the stairs, his muscles burned with strain but he enjoyed the release.

"There you are, boy!" said Lord Fitzwalter warmly. He was without his armour today, yet his sword still scabbarded and his colours of red and yellow were draped over his torso. "Come and see this," he prompted.

Hood stood upon a stone next to Fitzwalter and peered over the battlements of Rochester Castle. Thousands of men travelled over the distant hills towards them, weapons gleaming in the sunlight.

"Are they our friends?" Hood asked, naively.

Fitzwalter turned to him, his heavy brows fixed in a manner of concern. "They are not. What would you have us do?"

The young man tried to think, but his thoughts could not solidify.

"Think, boy! You're almost of sixteen years; your father could have come to this conclusion in moments at your age!"

Hood sighed. "I can't think clearly, that's all."

Fitzwalter's eyes narrowed. "You've still got it, haven't you?"

Hood looked up, his young face blank of expression. "No, of course not. You said to get rid of it."

"Don't lie to me, dammit!" roared Fitzwalter, heaving Hood up by his tunic. "I've seen that look before, years ago in your father."

Hood was held close to the battlements, the strong wind blustering against him. He thought for a moment he would be thrown over. But Fitzwalter's face softened and the big man slowly let him down. "Your father favoured war, you know? Violence and glory ran thick in his veins, but you saw where it drove him in the end."

"It's just a bow!" urged Hood, anger beginning to rise.

"You've got natural talent with it, there's no question to that. As did your father, he was the best I've seen. Alas, arrogance and thirst for recognition humble even the best," said Fitzwalter, his voice trailing off and his face showing its age. He turned away from Hood to look back over the battlements. "You get rid of it tonight, or I will tomorrow. And if you leave me with that choice, then you must face the consequences."

Hood glared at Fitzwalter with malice. The lord had taken care of the young boy since his father was killed and he'd promised himself that he wouldn't let his best friend's son meet the same end. Hood had turned away, heading back down the stairway of the keep, soldiers rushing up and down, more urgently this time. He made his way out into the courtyard and sat upon one of the watch walls, looking out over the forming army before them. He studied the landscape, trying to conjure battle plans and tactics his teachers had attempted to drill into him. Concentration had found its way to him and tactics blazed into his mind, but as did the lust to fire his bow, to display his grandeur to doomed victims.

"Hello, Robin," came a sweet voice.

Hood's heart sped up as he recognised it. He turned, his eyes drawn in by the beauty before him. Fox-red hair flowed, her skin pale and unblemished.

"Marian," he said with a genuine smile. "A lady should not look upon such scenes of potential violence."

She rolled her green eyes. "You sound like my father."

"I've just been speaking to him."

"And what are his thoughts on this?" she asked, gesturing to the army gathering before their walls.

"He seemed… untroubled by the army. I imagine he'll have some sort of plan forming in that head of his, he always does."

There was silence between them as they watched the land beyond. "What are you thinking, Robin?" she asked curiously.

He sighed, watching the army. "Those men, everyone there will be forgotten. I will be forgotten. However, your father will not, he's a great man, you know? His name will be etched in time."

"Father once said to me that the fear of not being remembered is a dangerous thing, for it can make a person act reckless and do more harm than good."

"Your father may be wise, but that doesn't mean he's always right," said Hood, grinning at Marian.

Marian smiled, her large green eyes upon him. "I shall see you tonight at dinner?"

"Yes, I'll see you then."

She rose and kissed his cheek lightly then moved off with grace. Hood turned to watch her. The young lady had a way with him and his heart had long belonged to her, if she was wise to it he did not know, he did not care either. The only matter that bothered him was Fitzwalter's wrath.

Dinner had not come that evening for Hood; the siege on Rochester Castle had begun sooner than anticipated. Hood had watched Fitzwalter defend the walls of the castle like a god of war. With his men beside him, he stood in full armour, a chainmail hood that only left his pointed beard on show. His sword and shield worked together in sync and Hood studied him with a keen eye.

Hood stood with the old generals that Fitzwalter wanted him to learn from. His goal was to have Hood behind the lines, away from the battles and unarmed. A strategist. Hood spat at the thought. Fitzwalter would have Hood plan the battle and carve the heroes that would be remembered while his own name was forgotten.

The young man felt a pull at his thoughts, an urge that needed to be met. He moved away from the generals that stood close to him and back to his small room in the keep. Hood lit a candle in his tiny room, illuminating the dark, stone walls. The young man's hands reached out for the chest, flicking the clasps open. The sound of dying men and clashing swords echoed through the walls and surrounded him as he reached for the bow. Hood unwrapped it carefully, and laid his hands on the wood, holding it in both hands. He felt his heart quicken and elation swept through him.

Hood strung the bow with speed and ran to the small armoury within the keep. Swinging a quiver of arrows onto his back, he set off, making his way back to the courtyard. As he stepped out, the young man saw the walls becoming overwhelmed. More and more enemy troops making it past Fitzwalter and his men.

Hood began to loose his arrows with deadly accuracy where the other archers would not have dared, for the shots would be too close to their own men. The other generals took note of the boy and his bow, but did nothing to stop it, the aid was required more than their curiosity needed to be satisfied. Fitzwalter watched the men fall around him, not needing to look back to know who it was, for he had known only one other man who could shoot like that.

"Gullies!" Fitzwalter shouted as the enemy on the long stretch of wall were mostly cleared. All around fire gullies were emptied onto the forces below, tar and coals rained down, the opposition screaming in pain. "Fall back!" ordered Fitzwalter, making his way down from the walls. The man didn't see Hood within the swarm of soldiers moving back from the battle.

Their plan was clear, they were overrun and it was time to leave. Fitzwalter never did see any point in dying to hold onto stones and mortar. He knew when a battle was lost and that's why he didn't ever lose.

Marian and her mother had been brought from nearby, horses saddled ready for them both to move out. Fitzwalter's remaining force moved from the northern gate, where the enemy had not besieged and began to make their retreat. Hood lingered, he wanted to say goodbye to the girl himself but was waiting for her father to leave. Hood's ears pricked as he heard the sound of hooves, then his sight focused on a small group that had made it beyond their force. They were heading for Fitzwalter and his family.

There were ten in total, galloping at speed towards the leader, their swords unsheathed. Fitzwalter released his wife and turned to see them, they were but a few seconds away when Hood decided to intervene. His first arrow caught the lead horse in the neck, causing it to fall to the ground, tripping four others. Fitzwalter ran to them, his sword stabbing down into the enemy horsemen as they writhed on the ground. Hood began to pick the rest off with incredible speed, one arrow flying after the other, his eye never faltering.

Within moments the remaining horsemen were dead in their saddles and were trotting past Fitzwalter's family. He turned to look at Hood, frustration in his dark eyes. "Leave the bow, boy!"

"I just saved you, I saved your family!"

"I promised your father this would not be your fate!" urged Fitzwalter, pleading in his voice.

Hood looked down at the bow in his hand; it was simple, perfect and promised him his glory. Then the young man stared up at Marian, her beautiful face an expression of worry, her mother's one of confusion. Hood turned from Fitzwalter without glancing back and mounted one of the horses he'd shot the enemy from. "You come back here!" shouted Fitzwalter, Hood could not see him, but he could hear his heavy footsteps coming towards him.

The bowman kicked the horse into a gallop, speeding past his former comrades and onto the land beyond. He reached a crest in the distance and looked back at the besieged castle. The enemy had swarmed it now and he could see Fitzwalter's men had safely retreated. Hood felt sadness in his heart for a moment. But only a moment. Warmth grew in his grip and he looked down at the simple bow, Hood smiled to himself contently and rode off without a second thought.

Chapter 14

Hood pulled a knife down his young face, cutting away the bristles of the previous day. The blade was then ceremoniously dipped into a stream, yesterday's hair washing away. It'd been a tense few days since the night at the cave, Gilbert had stayed away from Athella, and Hood had stayed away from everyone. Only Eustace had communicated with the bowman, discussing plans and resting points.

They'd packed their most valuable assets into the saddlebags of the horses. They were laden with gold and trinkets, slowing them slightly but not too much. It had cut John deeply to leave some of the treasure behind; the man loved loot more than he loved his own mother.

Darkness had settled on Hood during the night. He enjoyed being wanted, but not hunted. Having Guy of Gisborne on his trail was a dangerous thing. The man had seemed possessed when he'd run at them in Nottingham, something in his eyes that surpassed hate. Insanity? Hood had seen the look somewhere, perhaps it was in himself. The thought galled him, for to be hunted by a man such as himself would be tiring, relentless even.

Sunrise came on the fourth day since leaving the cave and Hood felt the rare warmth of the sun at dawn, followed by the fresh scent of nature. His hazel eyes stared around the camp and he found them resting on Gilbert. The man had a gentle face, not so unlike a child. Perhaps, Hood thought, that the perception was exclusive to himself, for in reality he was a brute. A ghastly one at that. It had always surprised him how silent such a beast slept, not even the tiniest snort left his mouth.

Hood knelt beside him, the slender man looking over the giant, his hat on his head and his knife in his grip. The big man was a child, a child that needed taken care of. A burden in some ways. The blade touched the dirty skin on his neck and he pressed ever so slightly. Gilbert didn't even stir as the tiny trickle of blood stained his knife.

Hood stopped when he felt a hand on his arm. Gentle, yet firm, warm, yet cold. His head lifted and his eyes rested on Athella, her dark gaze saying something to his, but he could not understand the words, or even the language.

She pulled him gently, breaking him away from his dance with death. At first, he was sceptical about leaving the chains off her, due to Stutley being adamant she'd run back and get them caught. Hood said he didn't care, but somewhere in his blood he knew she wouldn't. Now he was glad the chains were off, for the moment would not have come otherwise.

The two walked from the camp in silence for a little while, a steep hill was in front of them, sheep dotted here and there. Hood began to veer from the incline, wanting to save his legs from a climb in the morning, but she guided them up the slope, smiling as she noticed his reluctance. "Were you going to kill him?" she asked, harmlessly.

"Would you have cared?" Hood replied, stepping around an unmoving sheep.

"I would not have. What would be your reason? I know it would not be for me."

Hood smiled. "He's an oaf, a man who causes trouble, the wrong kind of trouble. Common sense tells me to slit his throat and leave him to rot, stupidity with a dash of pity stops me." Hood laughed then. "The skin on his neck is as thick as an elephant's, he'd wake and kill me before I reached anything vital."

Athella had a look of confusion. "Elephant?"

Hood grinned. "A great animal the sultan countries use for both war and parade. Gentle, yet destructive. I'd say Gilbert compared to one, but he's far more stupid than one of those."

Athella almost laughed at that, and they continued to walk.

"Why have you not run yet?" asked Hood, breaking the silence.

"I'm curious."

"Curious about what?" Games displeased Hood, playing them was one thing, but to be played was another.

"To see what happens when Guy finds you."

"What makes you think he'll find us?"

She did laugh then and Hood didn't blame her. "Because Guy of Gisborne finds whatever he wants to find."

It was a fair answer, Guy probably would find them, but with them he'd find death and more misery. Hood was a man that promised it to any that dared to seek him.

They stopped at the crest of the hill and found themselves overlooking a sizable village. There was definitely an inn there, which would boost the lads' morale. His calculating eyes took in the areas of more wealth.

Athella noticed the direction of his gaze. "Does an outlaw's mind ever stop?"

"What can be achieved when the mind ceases to

think? Imagine if I were to sit and do nothing, relax and look at how picturesque life can be. What would ever be achieved if people did such things?"

"Contentment," the girl said simply.

"Contentment, Athella, is not achievable while ambition holds onto the reins of your mind."

Hood and Athella made their way back down the hill towards their camp. All were sleeping except John, he was up, his narrowed eyes on them. A sword was next to him, a sword Hood had noticed more than once. It sat in a fine scabbard, only its handle on show; it was polished silver, inlaid with blue stones that glittered when light hit them. It didn't suit John, it was far too short and as regal as the man looked, he didn't have the makings for a weapon like that.

"Where you two been?" John asked, the words were the first he'd spoken of the day, deep and husky as they always were following a night's sleep outside.

"A stroll," Hood answered, loud enough so the others began to wake.

"What's for breakfast?" asked Gilbert, it was the first thing he'd said to Hood since the bowman had hit him.

"Well, Gilbert, my fine man," said Hood, vigour entering his voice. The group were roused by the tone, that's what they loved the bowman for most – his presence. He bled life and made life bleed. "We've found ourselves a town not a mile away over that hill. It's no Nottingham, but I see an inn that can fix us breakfast."

Gilbert grinned at this, his eyes shining, Hood knew what he'd ask next. "You think they've got whores?"

"I bloody hope so," put in Stutley, using the broad, bearded Scarlett as a hoist. "It's been a while since this old man's had his end away."

"I promise you, lads, I'll have you all fed, drunk and milked by whores by the time the Sheriff even catches scent of this place."

The outlaws had stood on the hill overlooking the bustling village beyond. At least four hundred would be housed there and others would visit daily. Soldiers would be present, but they'd be few and far between in a place like that.

John clapped his huge hands together and gave out a great laugh. "That house at the far west, Hood, that will have some fine loot there."

The outlaws turned their attention to the house; it was grand, bigger than any they'd looted before. Even Eustace seemed impressed by it.

Hood changed his tone, deep and authoritative. "Now, we have all the loot we can carry, any more will slow us. Don't forget we're on the move and this is but a short stop along the way. We need as little attention brought to us as possible."

The notion of that was laughable, they all knew it, just one look at the group would raise more than an eyebrow. Probably a sword.

The outlaws walked hastily down the slope as the sun began to rise higher in the sky. Old Stutley and red-bearded Scarlett trailed the back with the horses, John and Athella spoke quietly between themselves, just in front, while Gilbert marvelled at the village before them. Hood walked with the tall monk at the front. The two often walked together and despite the silence, Hood enjoyed his company. Maybe the silence is what he enjoyed. When words are spoken too much they become meaningless, just irritating noise on the wind.

The monk turned to Hood as they reached the edge of the village. "I shall meet you at the inn before dusk, I wish to look over this place myself."

Hood furrowed his brow at first, struggling to comprehend why a foreigner would wish to explore by himself. But foreign men sometimes have a foreign mind and do things differently for one way or another. He smiled and slapped the monk's shoulder. "Use that axe if you need to, farmers can be vicious bastards if they see something they don't recognise."

The monk nodded and walked away from the group, making his way through the streets ahead.

"Where's he off to?" asked Scarlett, the burly man never liked things that didn't make sense to him.

"To clear his head, I suppose," said Hood, looking over his men. He walked further through the village. Men and women had started to appear from their homes, not one friendly eye amongst them as they looked upon the dirty bunch of outlaws. Even Athella was getting a curse or two thrown at her.

They reached the inn, a small wooden sign hung from the front with crude red writing, peeling off, the ageing script showing remanence of 'The Pilgrim'. Despite the rotting nature of the sign, the inn was large and well built with stone, a sturdy door stood in the centre and Hood looked at with happiness. It'd been a while since he'd sat down in an inn for a jug of ale never mind a meal. The forest had been good to him, he thought, but there was nothing quite like a drink in a well-kept inn.

"Take the horses to the stable across the street and let them know that if anyone goes near those mounts, Hood will have their eyes," said the bowman to Stutley and Scarlett, a smile on his face. The outlaws enjoyed seeing that their leader wasn't afraid of his name being heard, his confidence in their safety solidified their own.

The door was pushed open and wooden tables were dotted around the open space, with sturdy stools and chairs surrounding them. Stone slabs lined the floor and a huge fireplace was built into the wall. Stairs led up beside the bar and the innkeeper came down from them, his hair was yellow with streaks of grey and his stomach was bloated to an unnatural size.

"How can I help you…" the innkeeper paused as he looked over the group, his gaze lingered on Gilbert the longest. The smile returned to his fat face and he started his sentence again. "Breakfast and ale, is it?"

"Yes, we have two more due to arrive so bring plenty," said the bowman, gesturing his group to sit at the biggest table. Hood tossed the innkeeper a gold coin and he caught it clumsily. "You see an empty jug, you bring another." That was a command, not a request, the innkeeper understood that and Hood liked him for it.

Old man Stutley and Scarlett joined them soon after and two jugs of ale were gone by the time the breakfast arrived. Each of them had a plate stacked with meat and roasted vegetables while loaves of bread with butter sat at each end of the table. Food that was cooked for you tasted far better than cooking it for yourself, even if it was the same thing, it didn't matter. The effort of preparing it yourself takes away the glory of the taste.

Hood looked around the table, his men were merry and even Athella seemed content; she laughed with John and downed her ale like the rest of them. He felt something creep into him as he watched John and Athella, her sweet laugh ringing out above the rest, his eyes looking at her with something other than lust. Was it jealousy? Hood asked himself, he dismissed it, it was something more primal. You could be the sun and still be jealous that the moon gets to shine in a dark sky, he thought to himself.

The bowman went on to pour more ale, but the jug was empty. He turned to look about the inn and the keeper wasn't in sight. Hood cursed and rose from his seat, looking to fill the jug himself. The keeper came from the entrance then. "Sorry," said the fat man. "Just been cleaning up outside, I'll get that for you." He took the jug from Hood and the bowman sat back in his place. The outlaws continued to speak amongst themselves, emptying the new jug of ale quicker than it took to fill it.

Something didn't sit well with Hood, something had changed in the keeper when he'd come back in. Then he heard the door of the inn open once more and three finely dressed men entered. The leader of the three men was clear, he was dark-haired, a pompous look on his face and the finery of his clothes was more notable than his companions'.

Conversation ceased and the outlaws turned their heads. Hood didn't, he didn't need to, he had an extra sense for trouble. He used his brothers as that sense. Just from the look on their faces he knew everything he needed to. They weren't armed, or John would have his sword in his hand. They weren't soldiers of any type, or Stutley's gaze would have been swimming with hatred. And if they were holy men, well, Gilbert would have blood on his hands already.

No, no one recognised them and they were unarmed, no armour, so Hood had them down as locals, probably noble ones at that with a sense of entitlement. The bowman heard footsteps make their way towards his back, well-spoken words followed. "I believe you've outstayed your welcome in this inn, man of the road," the speaker was addressing Hood and the sip of ale became sweeter in that moment. Hood's hazel eyes looked up at his men once more, none of their faces were of concern, in fact, Gilbert had a look of excitement etched into him. "You," said the high voice once more. "I'm speaking to you, road scum." A finger prodded Hood's back and Gilbert almost fell from his seat.

Give them an inch, thought Hood, and they'll take it all. Bend, and they continue to flex until you break. Hood's rule was not to bend and not to hesitate. He rose and twisted all in one motion, grabbing the blunt butter knife from the table on his way up. The cutlery was firmly embedded into the noble's eye, there was no doubt that butter would be upon his brain.

Gilbert roared with laughter and the outlaws joined him. The two companions of the dead man that was still wobbling upon his feet were unmoving. Stutley was caught up in the moment, the old man got vicious when he'd had his fill of ale. A knife was flung from his belt and stuck itself into one of the visitors' chests. The other ran, quick enough to flee the inn before Stutley's other knife found him.

"Innkeep!" shouted Hood as butter-brain finally dropped and the outlaws gave another cheer. "Where were they from?"

The innkeeper was frightened, fear of death overcoming any other thought. He stammered and Hood gave a look of annoyance. "The big house on the west of the village, he owned the estate around it," he finally said.

Hood nodded his thanks and turned back to his

outlaws. "Let's get us some loot."

The men all stood at once and Athella stayed seated for a moment then rose with the rest of them, a smile on her face. Hood swept up his bow and swung his quiver onto his back, leading the group from the inn.

The sun was bright, but the ale had made it seem brighter. Hood squinted as he moved across the street, allowing his eyes to adjust. Now the streets were busier and many of the villagers focused their stares at them. Some people even made their way for the inn, finally seeing the famed Hood and his brutes were cleared of it.

Hood took great pleasure as he strode with the group behind him, people parting with gasps as they neared. A guard of the village came alongside them as they walked, attempting to get whatever he had off his chest. Gilbert took care of him. His huge hammer of a fist upper-cut the guard into a set of stalls at the side of the path, the structure breaking under the weight. Shrieks followed gasps.

Another guard, much further ahead, was making his way through the throng of people. Hood stopped the group and bid them to watch. The intoxicated bowman pulled an arrow from his quiver and moved his tipped hat to shade the sun from his eyes. The shot would be impossible even for an accomplished archer. The guard weaved in and out of villagers, his pike in the air being the only constant.

Hood loosed his bow and the arrow seemed to zig through the crowd, the men and women strolling from its path. Then the pike dropped and screams tore through the air. He smiled inwardly, perhaps he allowed his own pride to control that man's death, his old teachers always said pride was dangerous.

Hood continued to walk and his group followed, the villagers resuming to shift as they did. The bowman stepped by the fallen guard, plucking his arrow from his neck as he moved by.

It was a mystery to Hood how trouble always seemed to find him, he never did spark the fire, but he would always fuel it.

Not much time had passed for them to make their way from the inn to the dead man's estate, for the span of the village could be walked in a quarter of an hour. More trees were present here and no poor dwellings were in sight. The house came into view, it was huge and stained glass windows were in the centre. Gilbert wouldn't like that; stained glass reminded him of the church. A fountain stood in the middle of the courtyard, no water came from it, although there would no doubt be a pump house nearby. Black wooden beams lined the white body of the house and dried out ivy covered half of it.

"It's beautiful," said Athella, in awe.

"Aye, and it's ours now. Well, whatever it holds," said John.

They were about to move in closer, so they were in full view of the house. Then Hood stopped them, they could smell the smoke before they saw it. There was an orange glow behind most windows, brightest in the centre. Fire was furiously eating away at it from the inside.

Then they saw a figure coming towards them and the group knew it was their time to leave.

Chapter 15

Guy of Gisborne had sat in the cave of the outlaws, he could feel the old heat off the campfire they'd not long left. He stroked his black stubble as his grey eyes stared around the camp. There had been a struggle, he could see the indents on the ground. He felt sorry for Athella, it would be a greater kindness for them to kill her, he thought. Carcasses stripped of their meat lay to one side and Guy could see the men must have been staying there for many months.

The cave was dark and the floor was cleared, he moved to the back where there were some old cloaks, worthless trinkets and the like. There's no doubt the outlaws would have buried their loot. Guy cared nought for loot, he wanted blood and that was it.

Ten of the Sheriff's men and the runner caught up to him. They looked exhausted and lack of sleep would make them reckless. Guy sighed. "Go back to the Sheriff, tell him to meet me at the far road of the forest, then follow the track north-east, I'll see him there. There's no need for you all here."

"What if you find them? You can't take on them all," said one of the soldiers, tiredness had made his tongue loose and the soldier knew it.

Guy's hand twitched for his blade but releasing his fury on this man would not quench the thirst. "They're long gone. Their aim is to lose us, not fight us, and they'll have more chance of losing us with you useless bunch of arses slowing me down." The slight was enough to turn them away.

The Sheriff would make them pay, he knew, watching them walk from the camp disheartened. They probably knew as well. The Sheriff wanted to lead this thing, not be led.

The leader trailed through the forest, following whatever he could find. Hood's group were messy. Gilbert, being the least aware of his own size, left the biggest tracks; trampled bushes, snapped logs and prints double a normal man's own. They even led two horses and kept to the parts where the spaces were widest. But they moved fast, too fast for Guy. His tired legs did what they could to keep moving, energy being forced from places unknown in his body. The lack of almost three days' sleep combined with the dullness of the evening would eventually get him to rest, one way or another.

Bog – that was how he slept. Guy's boot slid on the soft outskirts of a bog, his hands reaching out for whatever branch they could find. To his disappointment, he found no such branch. He was sliding and not stopping, his body heading down a steep slope in the forest where no end could be seen. Then the inevitable tumbling started and somewhere along the line his head struck the trunk of a tree, bark sticking to his head. Guy could have held on to consciousness under normal circumstances, but he let go and allowed the sweet grip of darkness take hold of him.

Guy lay in a trench of the forest, dirt, leaves and twigs surrounding him. Was this the only way Guy of Gisborne could find peace — unconscious, the dark forest air taking his warmth, slowing his heart? No, peace couldn't be found even that close to death.

Dreams of his dead daughter and crippled wife haunted him, fuelled whatever life was left. Was the death of another the only thing that could bring him peace? His heart doubted it, but he had to try.

Guy's grey eyes fluttered open, dirt making them flutter more. His body felt as if it had sunk into the spongy ground. It was soft, comfortable. The man felt like staying but knew it was a bed of death. He had his death in his own hands, not the forest. The darkness of the night made him question whether he truly had his eyes open. They weren't adjusted and only when he sat and stared at the darkness did shapes form. A man's imagination can play tricks on him with forms of the forest. When the sun goes down, suddenly dead men and witches roam the trees, but that's not true. Fear plays a big part in what a man can see. Too much fear and you see everything, even things that aren't there. Not enough and you don't see anything, you become blind and arrogant.

Guy's head pounded. He was thirsty and the trunk had caused somewhere to bleed. His hand snaked to his belt and grabbed his water-skin, he drank deeply and pulled his sword. The moonlight etched through the trees and bounced from his blade. He rolled his sleeve and rested the sword to his wrist. All it would take to end the pain, he knew, was to lash the sword back and open his veins. A voice in his head spoke against it: 'Finish your business,' it said. And he listened. Guy's sword was away and he knew that any inward doubt he felt meant the choice was the wrong one.

Guy thought back to when he was a child, he'd walked in on his uncle with his wrists open, a dagger by his side. The man had lost his wife and felt there was no need to live any more. In his last moments, the uncle had told Guy that as soon as he saw the blood gushing from him, his life spilling onto the floor before his eyes, that was when he had realised he wanted to live. In the moments before death, clarity had hit him and he knew that nothing was ever bad enough to take your own life. Pain would dull and meaning would find itself once more. Guy tried to remember that, but through a heavy fog of anguish it seemed like a fairy tale rather than fact.

The tracker carried on, as he always did, as he always would. Miles of forest seeming like nothing to him, seeing the tracks through the darkness of the night was easy enough when they were of a group. He wasn't sure how long he'd been unconscious for, perhaps it was an hour, or ten hours, the dark-haired man didn't know. Despite it, he felt rejuvenated, his mind was clear and peace settled on him as the sun began to rise through the trees. His mind closed off then, it was blank and he allowed instinct to take over. He ate, pissed, drank, slept, walked and ran until he found himself at the edge of the huge forest, the outlaws' trails leading off over fields and through brushes.

Guy veered for a few miles to the east, that was where he'd said that the Sheriff would be met. Sunlight warmed his skin as he walked over the grassy verges towards the road. A mile off he could see the troop of cavalry waiting in the distance. The Sheriff wouldn't be happy about that, the spoilt man-child didn't warm to waiting for anyone.

Guy approached and the soldiers looked uneasy. The tracker strode through, thick of mud, blood smeared on his face and his black hair stuck to his head. Guy leapt up onto the spare horse just feet away from the Sheriff. The Sheriff's face was twisted, it was always twisted, but this day more so than normal. "Where have you been?"

spat the Sheriff.

"Why are there three less men than we started with?" asked Guy. As a man of battle rides towards a group of people, their mind will calculate the mass almost instantly. It's the way of a strategist, to know your plan is to know your enemy by number and nature.

The Sheriff wasn't impressed at his question being answered by another. "The group was told to stay with you. They didn't, so some died." It was said casually, bouncing off the tension of the guards.

"I'm sure that taught them a great deal," said Guy, urging his horse back through the soldiers.

The Sheriff followed, his men following behind. "Do you know where Hood went?"

"Aye, the trail is a few miles west, but I know where it leads. There's a small village that way and I know a quicker route to it without following their tracks."

Concern entered the Sheriff's voice. "What if they avoid the village, just go through it or around?"

Guy looked back, his expression blank. "Their breed is predictable, they see peace and they wish to disrupt it. We just follow the chaos."

Guy stood next to the Sheriff, their horses dismounted behind the crest of the hill with the forty-odd horsemen. Guy's gaze leered on the Sheriff, the sun was hitting him in the eyes making the foul man squint. "You think they're in there?" asked the Sheriff, looking over the town.

"Aye, their tracks disperse down at the bottom," replied Guy looking over the main buildings of the village.

The Sheriff was stuck, his focus on something at the

far end.

"A grand house, is it not?" said Guy, noting his discomfort, the envy in his dark eyes.

"Too big and open, only a fool would live there."

"A rich fool," said Guy, with a smile.

"Indeed. How are we going to find them?"

"I believe I might have already. You see the large inn, with a sign hanging outside?" Guy pointed, he shouldn't have needed to, but the Sheriff was still focussed on the rich man's house.

"What about it?"

"The only two horses in sight are stabled across the road from there. The outlaws had two horses with them. My guess is they fancied some ale and thought they had a start on us."

The Sheriff grinned, his long, bony hands rubbed together. "Then we surround it and take them that way." The leader turned, about to signal his men to move out.

Guy's hand reached out and stopped him, the Sheriff's face twitched at the touch. "Fighting in a place like that would be a death trap, they could defend it. Their lot may be outlaws but they're fighters, they would take down a good few of us before we got them."

"We could burn it?" suggested the Sheriff.

"They have your damned sister," scolded Guy.

The Sheriff squeezed his eyes shut in annoyance and ran a hand over his face. "What do you suggest?"

"You want to catch a moth, you light a flame in a dark room and wait." Guy was looking at the large house at the far end of the village again and the Sheriff nodded in understanding.

The Sheriff led them this time, they didn't move through the village, but around it, far out of sight. The soldiers were bid to leave their horses close by, two men ordered to watch and tie them, then the whole group made their way to the house.

It looked even bigger from the back end, huge black beams lining it and white painted wood made up the main body. Dry, dead ivy covered most of it; too much shade and not enough water caused that. The gardens to the rear were beautiful, but the Sheriff didn't notice. The tall figure trampled through flower beds, carelessly flattening beautiful bulbs.

A well-dressed man stepped out of the back door after seeing the large group approach through the windows. Guy laughed inwardly as he saw the man, if he ever had seen perfect bait, this man would be it. When he opened his mouth it was even better.

"Who do you all think you are? Each and every one of you will be paying for the destruction you've caused my gardens," said the young man, his hair was light and receding, his features curving with nobility. He stuck his finger out at the Sheriff, digging it into his chest as he spoke.

The Sheriff ached to kill him, to pull off his limbs and watch him writhe. Guy was impressed at the self-control, he'd never seen the Sheriff withhold himself from blood. "We're here on the King's business," he said coolly, soldiers around him standing with drawn swords. "And as you know, any man that attempts to obstruct the King's business will be sentenced to death."

The nobleman stood back at that, his stare softening, his aggression castrated. "Why do you need my home?"

The Sheriff placed his hand on the man's shoulder, turning him and walking towards the house. "My man Guy here will brief you on the plan and you will be an integral part." The Sheriff knew his fate was sealed, that's why he didn't kill him the instant his finger touched his chest.

The men had gone inside the luxurious home. Guy ordered the soldiers out of the hall and into the surrounding back rooms. This way, when Hood was inside, he would be stuck, and the stately furnishings would become crimson with outlaw blood. Servants prepared food for the Sheriff. Guy didn't understand how he could eat before a plan was executed, food disturbed his focus in such instances.

Two soldiers were stripped of their armour and given servant clothes, these were to stay with the nobleman. If he were to divert from the plan, he'd be dispatched. "You," said Guy, sitting with the homeowner in one of the back rooms, staring into his nervous face. "What's your name?"

"It's William, William of—"

"You're not William of anywhere today. You're one good man, going in there and bringing a bad man to justice. You're going to coax the outlaws, not enough to make them kill you but enough to make them want to hurt you."

William nodded, his face hardening, mimicking what he thought was bravery.

"You're going to put an act on, speak to them like you did the Sheriff when you saw him. You'll tell them you want them to leave, speak to them like the dirt they are."

The two men rose and Guy felt sorry for William. It would not end well for him; if he survived the outlaws then the Sheriff would no doubt seek him out sooner or later. No one had ever insulted the Sheriff and lived. Guy had no doubt he himself would be hunted once he'd served his purpose. But he'd be gone by then, or slain the monster himself.

Guy, William and the two disguised soldiers walked through the village. It was a peaceful place, no trouble or drunks. The roads were wide and clean, people stood chatting and children weaved laughing. The sound was sweet and untainted. "Do I get a weapon?" asked William.

"No, it would give them more reason to kill you," replied Guy. They stood waiting outside the inn until the keeper came out. Guy told William to wait while he spoke to him.

"Afternoon, fella," said the keeper, as he saw Guy approach.

"I'm on the King's authority and I'm led to believe you're harbouring outlaws in your inn, is that correct?"

The keeper was taken aback, his fat face filling with worry. "I'm just feeding and watering some customers, that's all I do."

"I appreciate that, but if you get in our way then you'll be getting in the way of the King. That carries a sentence of death."

"What do you want me to do?" stammered the keeper.

Guy turned, pointing to William. "Do you know who that man is?"

"Yes, everyone knows Sir William, he's the—"

"I don't care who or what he is. When the outlaws ask about him, you tell them which house he lives at." Guy took a deep breath; he looked the keeper up and down. There was too much fear in him, he oozed it and a man like Hood can smell fear a mile off. "Don't you worry now, do your part and it's the last you'll hear from us."

The keeper nodded and moved back into his inn. Guy walked over to William and the two guards. "When do I go in?" asked the nobleman, anxious to get the deed over with.

"Just wait a little while then go in. Once you're out, don't come back to your home until after sundown, it's best you keep your distance from the Sheriff." William nodded and Guy stepped away. The tracker stopped, he turned his head and set his grey eyes on the man. "Remember, get under his skin, but not enough to make him kill you."

Guy headed back through the village at pace. More people had emerged, taking advantage of the fresh bread and meat at the market stalls. A place like this, he thought, would have been a fine town to settle. A dull ache entered his chest as quickly as the thought came, the pain of his loss still fresh, still weeping with misery. The dark-haired man cleared his mind and looked upon his surroundings with fresh eyes. There were too many people, a riled group of outlaws could do some damage. Guy knew they would not head straight for the house, there would be some collateral damage. Perhaps the cooler-headed ones would, but with an animal like Gilbert and a vicious old killer like Stutley, there was no doubt blood would spill.

Sir William's huge home was in his view, massive trees lined a dirt road that carriages would roll to and from the house. The home was a beautiful one, without a doubt the most splendid he'd seen. Guy knew the soldiers standing within it would be pocketing a trinket or two, in fact, the Sheriff would most likely be encouraging it.

"How did it go?" asked the Sheriff, a smirk on his face and a cup of steaming liquid in his hands.

"It's in motion, we shouldn't have to wait too long. We need all the men in the back rooms though, we can't risk them looking through the windows in the front and seeing anyone."

The Sheriff nodded, his dark eyes shining, they always seemed to when death was near. Then, when death itself was close enough to smell, his gaze would begin to gleam with insanity.

The men were spread out across the house in tactical positions. Guy himself stood in a room with eleven other men, including the Sheriff. All weapons were drawn and they waited silently. There was one small window in the room, it was around head height and stained green and red. The window wasn't big, not much wider than a child's shoulders. Nevertheless, it allowed warm colours to drown the room, the paintings on the walls becoming something else entirely. Light can do that sometimes; make things seem what they aren't, underneath the guise though, they're the same as they've always been.

"When will they be here?" whispered the Sheriff, his knuckles were white from gripping the sword so hard.

"Soon, be quiet, we need to listen for the door," said Guy, irritation laced in his tone. The house was too noisy, too creaky to detect one noise from another. Soldiers around the house could not stay still. Then he heard a click at the door and the soldiers looked between themselves in confusion.

"Was that a lock?" asked the Sheriff, his voice rising now, concern etched on his face.

Confusion ran through Guy and he reached out to grab the metal handle of the door. It was warm as he held it and wouldn't budge in his grip. "We need to get out of here," he said, panic rising.

"Why? What's wrong?" the Sheriff asked.

"We're trapped," he said, rushing around the room, searching in drawers and pockets of coats for the keys.

Too many thoughts entered the Sheriff's brain for him to voice any, the information was attempting to process. His face dropped and his long nose twitched. "Is that smoke I smell?"

"It is," said Guy, turning and pointing to the three biggest of the soldiers. "You three, help me break down this door." Two at a time they heaved their shoulders into the heavy wooden door. The room was hot and black smoke filled it, choking the men inside. The small window was smashed to let out some smoke; it hardly helped. One soldier collapsed after coughing violently, his back against the wall and his eyes closed. The thick wood began to splinter and the weakened, charred door broke in two.

The sound of roaring flames burst into the room and an intense heat struck their skin. The soldiers who were still able ran into the hall, fire lining the corridor. Guy looked back, the soldier who had laid down had been taken by his comrades. Only one man remained unconscious on the ground – the Sheriff. Guy urged his body to step from the room and into the hall before it was too late. He could see light shining from the kitchen where the back door was, an exit beckoning him.

Guy shook his head at his own stupidity as he hefted the Sheriff over his shoulder. He didn't know why, but leaving an unconscious man to burn was worse than killing them in combat. The Sheriff was heavier than expected and the smoke was making Guy dizzy. One step at a time he made his way through the burning house. Something exploded to his right causing pain to sear through his face, it burned and stung, but the pain was dulled by a sense of survival overcoming him.

He reached the light through the tunnel of flames and then the smoke ceased to be as he stepped outside. Guy dropped to his knees, letting the Sheriff tumble from his back and onto the floor. The few soldiers that had escaped crowded Guy as he fell face first into a bed of trampled tulips. The petals were cool but the scent was not pleasing, he smelt cooking flesh and tasted the iron of blood.

Chapter 16

"I shall meet you at the inn before dusk, I wish to look over this place myself," Eustace had said to Hood.

Hood looked as though he would protest, the man was a natural leader and was unused to men with singular motives. Then the bowman smiled, his expression softening. "Use that axe if you need to, farmers can be vicious bastards if they see someone they don't recognise."

Eustace took his words and parted. The others didn't say anything, he didn't care much for them, especially John, the man was a brute and hid behind charm. Hood, however, had grown on the monk. More often than not the bowman spoke with sense, but every now and then he'd let his pride get the better of him. This would be his downfall. He took no orders, though he considered men's ideas. Men with pride are a strange breed, you can't tell them what's best, you need to quietly plant the seed in their mind. The seed will bud and sprout and then they'll say it was their own idea, even if deep down they know it was not.

Eustace walked, his axe hung upon his back and his grey hair tied. He looked different to the folks around him, men and women could see he was foreign from the moment they rested their eyes on him. He'd found small villages to be unfriendly to men such as himself. He couldn't blame them. If he had seen a foreign man walk through his village with an axe hung on his back, he'd be wary too.

He stayed to the edge of the buildings, not venturing

to the centre of the village, but still, he managed to draw attention to himself. "Morning, foreigner," said a large man, his clothes were ragged and his head was bald. Three younger men were behind him, his sons probably. "What do you want in a peaceful village like ours?"

"I'm just passing through," said Eustace, agreeably. His accent not helping the situation.

"Then pass through, be on your way."

"I'm afraid that's not going to happen, I'm waiting upon my group and we'll be leaving at dusk."

"You're not listening," said the older man, he drew a knife and broadened his shoulders. The younger men behind him looked unsure but moved forward with him anyway.

"I do not wish to kill you in front of your sons, but trust me, it will happen. And if they come for me, their fate will be sealed too." Eustace didn't need to draw his axe, they could see it, peeking over his shoulder.

The man's face hardened and he was about to lunge. A voice cut through the tension, stopping the man in his tracks. "Enough of that, Gerald, the man's looking for rest, that's all." It was a woman's voice, strong and commanding.

Eustace looked to her, his eyes widened at her beauty. The woman's hair was red and her eyes an emerald green. She was young, not yet in her thirties. Despite this, she commanded authority. The woman stood in the doorway of a large, wooden building connected to a row of others.

Gerald didn't speak, he sheathed his blade and walked away with his sons, not bothering to glance back at the grey-haired monk.

"I thank you, lady," said Eustace, turning towards

her.

"Come in and rest a little, you look like you need it." The woman had a smile on her face, the type of smile that makes a man's blood quicken in his veins.

Eustace was curious, but he didn't doubt a woman like that made a lot of men curious. He followed her into the building cautiously, the smell of perfume swamping his senses. Eustace saw a man being led down the wide staircase by a painted woman in a robe of silk. The ageing monk smiled at himself as he realised where he was, he'd mistaken the woman's interest for desire. Arrogance will always find a way to emerge from a man, no matter the age or experience.

The monk was led by the woman into the main room, a lobby of sorts. There, he took a seat in a deep leather chair. The woman handed him a glass of liquor, it was good quality stuff. He could smell the smoothness as he held it to his nose. "I didn't think this standard of drink was available in these parts."

"We have the highest quality of everything in this house." That smile again, prodding into his soul.

"Are you the owner?" asked Eustace.

"How did you know?" Surprise ignited those green eyes, polished emerald emerging once more.

"You don't seem like a whore."

"A plain speaker, aren't you. What *do* I seem like?" she asked, curiously.

"Respectable."

The woman stood, she was dressed in a yellow tunic, leggings of the finest quality. She moved to a cabinet and poured herself a drink. "These women are respected, they respect themselves and they respect the customer. There's not much a woman can do in this country to earn themselves a living. Does money earn a person respect? If so, then these girls are richer than most of the men in this village." She turned then to face the monk. "Does that axe earn you respect? Or the blood that stains it?"

"There is honour in fighting," said Eustace simply, putting his glass down onto the table in front of him.

"Fighting's a broad term. It all depends what the cause is. There's a difference between cracking a skull over a spilt drink and duelling for honour. The fact is, these girls fight every day. They fight for survival and they do what they can to give themselves a good life without bringing anyone harm." She poured him another.

Eustace grabbed the glass and raised it to her. "You stand up for what you think is right; you have a good head on your shoulders."

"Have I changed your mind?" she asked, grinning at the older man.

"You may have."

The red-haired woman looked towards the doorway of the room and nodded towards it. Eustace's head turned to see another woman, she was beautiful, her hair long and dark, her eyes wide. "I bet Hannah can change it."

"I bet she could."

Hannah stepped from the doorway and grabbed Eustace by the hand, leading him through the house and up to her room.

Hannah hadn't exactly helped Eustace rest, but she'd certainly relaxed him. She'd made him feel at ease at first, speaking to him, trying to know the man before her. It didn't take long to realise Eustace was not a man who partook in much small talk, so she soon quieted and tended to the man's more base needs.

When Hannah had left, Eustace stood at the bedroom window, staring out over the landscape he and Hood had come from. The monk heard a knock on the door and the red-haired woman entered. She stood beside him, looking out over the quiet scene. "Where are you headed?" she asked.

"To my ship far north, I have friends waiting for me."

"Are you going to the Holy Land?" curiosity piquing in her.

Eustace shook his head. "No, those lands are dangerous now. Blood and death are rife."

The woman's head bowed as he'd said it. "My father's over there."

"A crusader?" he asked, he wouldn't usually, but he felt he had to.

"Yes, he's a brave man."

"Any man who goes over there is brave," agreed Eustace.

There was a moment of silence, a comfortable silence. "You're here with those outlaws, aren't you?"

"Word spreads fast around here, doesn't it?" smiled Eustace.

She gestured out the window, across the glade. "It does."

Soldiers were emerging, around forty upon horse and Eustace saw the familiar figure of Guy at the front. He sighed heavily and picked up his axe. "I thank you for your hospitality."

"And Hannah thanks you for her coin."

The monk dug into his pocket and dropped his money onto the bedside, then turned towards the door.

"What's your name?" she asked.

"It's Eustace, and yours?"

"It's Marian," she said softly. "Tell Robin not to be a stranger."

Eustace emerged from the whorehouse slowly, his eyes scanning the area. The tracks were easy to follow, a herd of horsemen travelling anywhere is a simple feat to trail. But where were they going, what was their purpose? The enemy were not heading into the centre, they were hiding, lying in wait.

The monk expected to find that the tracks headed north of the village, aiming to cut them off somewhere ahead. But that wasn't it at all. The trail led to a field, just to the east of the village, sheltered by trees.

Eustace moved through them carefully, a small, curved dagger removed from his belt. He knelt, spying through the thick mess of bushes and shrubs. There were two men on guard, just two lousy men guarding a whole herd of horses. Eustace almost chuckled at their stupidity, their arrogance. The main group had left, headed back towards the village. The monk stayed though, moving out from the trees, ducking between the tethered horses.

One guard was down quick enough, the curve of the dagger ripping through his jugular and splintering his jaw. The second had attempted to speak to his comrade and turned when he didn't reply. In the dead man's place he saw Eustace standing with his long-hafted axe. Eustace wasn't a particularly frightening man, but here he stood, crimson spurts up his face and spattered in his long, grey hair. The soldier's dead friend was lying close by with the sun behind, causing Eustace to become an ominous sight.

The enemy didn't even draw his weapon, he couldn't

speak for fright. Depending on what type of man you are, fright does an array of things. It can make a man go mad, berserk in fact, all rational thought leaping from their mind and making him a dangerous foe. It can make a man feel calm run through them, like a warm sun that follows a thunderstorm. Or it can do what it did to this man, make him stain his pants and glue his joints and muscles firmly into place. The soldier tried to speak as Eustace's axe found him, but the sound crept out as a squeal quieter than a field mouse.

Eustace removed the saddles from the horses and cut their tethers, slapping them on their backs, urging them to run. Then he moved away through the trees, following Guy and his group towards their destination.

It was a simple thing to know their plan once he saw where they were, the rows of trampled flowers gave away their position. So Eustace moved around the perimeter, keeping to the thicker parts of the garden. He came across a small wooden house in one of the thickets and heard voices from the inside. His axe was drawn and the door was opened. However, he did not find the soldiers he was expecting, instead, he found an old woman and a young man.

"Don't hurt us," pleaded the man.

"Who are you?" asked Eustace. It was more of a demand than a question.

"We're Sir William's housekeepers, he owns this place."

"These vile men," interrupted the old woman. "They think they rule the world, they reckon they can do as they please with no consequences."

Eustace smiled. "I am here to show them consequences."

It didn't take long for Eustace to get the keys to the

house. The young man showed him the master key and Eustace was about to leave until his nose twitched at a familiar scent. "Which barrel is the lantern oil?" he'd asked.

The young man helped him move some crates before they found the torso-sized barrel. It had a small cork at the bottom, this could be removed to allow a thin line of oil to release. The oil would flow into a different container, which would then go into a lamp.

He moved it from the small store and locked the doors behind him for good measure. They didn't object to that, there's no doubt they felt safer in there than out.

Eustace continued down the edge of the garden, the barrel of lantern oil in his arms. At first he moved stealthily to the house, peeking through windows and looking for patrols, but there were none. There weren't ever going to be patrols with a trap or it would be sprung too early. So Eustace walked confidently into the house, removing the cork from the bottom of the barrel and allowed a thin stream of oil to splash out onto the floor. It amused Eustace how loud the soldiers were despite them attempting to hide. A cough here, a stamp there, the clatter of armour touching armour. His own boots made less noise as he walked through with pace.

The oil lightly splashed through the kitchen and into the hall, soaking rugs, dusty drapes and old floorboards. The house was one spark away from igniting without the oil never mind with the lashing Eustace gave it.

It didn't take long for the barrel to be completely empty, but he felt as though he'd given the property a thorough soaking. Lastly, he removed the master key from his pocket and walked to each door, locking every one he came to. As he'd walked through the house with the oil, he'd taken notice of the muffles and creaks that came from each room. He made quick work of it. He walked past four rooms. *Thrust, turn, click*. Four times, over and over. Loud enough to raise questions, but too fast for them to do anything about it.

Eustace reached the kitchen, the room where he'd started. Shame, he thought to himself, it is a wonderful house. Then he struck the flint in his hand, holding it close to the oil.

Initially, there wasn't much to see; a thin line of fire, streaming through the house. Then the flames latched on to the fabric and wood, seeming to feed on it and grow like maggots in a corpse. It didn't take long until the flames were half the height of the doors, heat pulsing at him.

Eustace smiled and turned. He could hear a lot of clattering now, shouts too, fear lining their tones. As he walked around the side of the house, he could hear windows smashing and saw smoke beginning to billow. As the monk reached the front, he saw Hood and the outlaws. They were already stopped, looking up at the house. "Looks like you've had some fun for yourself, monk," said Hood, joining Eustace as he walked. The outlaws said nothing, they just turned with their leader and followed.

"This was not for fun," said the monk. "Although, I can't say it didn't bring me any joy."

Chapter 17

Ten years earlier

After leaving Fitzwalter at the battle of Rochester, Hood rode his horse north, attempting to follow trails and routes that he'd travelled on when he was younger. Familiarity bred comfortableness and that's all he wanted now. The first few days of being alone were exciting, but then the hunger set in. His provisions were low and hunting wasn't something that he was adept to.

The night before had been stormy and lashed down with rain, he was far from a familiar place and nothing but a warm bed and a blazing fire called his name. He pushed on though, for there was a fire still crackling within him, lit by the need to live. Now thoughts of glory and fame were a whisper in his mind, all that mattered was survival. The irony was that Hood's saddled bag contained enough money to allow him to eat for two months, but he was so lost he hadn't seen any signs of civilisation for a week.

The young man had tied his horse at the edge of a damp forest and removed his bow. Once again, like every day before, he went searching the forest for game. The King's game nonetheless, but that mattered nothing to Hood. It comes eventually to everyone, when hunger overrides a person's thoughts. Self-preservation kicks in and suddenly nothing else matters.

He lay in wait, soft rain pattering down through the trees, slowly soaking through to his skin. Then he saw it. A small movement of brown through the trees, practically camouflaged into the floor and bark. Hood notched an arrow to his bow and pulled back, then shot. The arrow flew with speed, hurtling towards the target. But just as fast as Hood had seen it, it'd disappeared. The arrow had struck an empty place where the deer had once been.

Hood stood there, where the arrow had struck. It was embedded into the tree, brown and white fur pinned to the arrowhead. The bowman felt like snapping the arrow, but he feared the outburst would use his remaining strength. Pain entered his stomach, twisting pain that was only brought with crippling hunger.

"Did no one ever teach you how to hunt, boy?" came a voice, cutting through the rain.

Hood looked up, his eyes falling on a powerfully built man with blonde hair. The hair was cut short and a neat stubble lined his middle-aged face. "You scared off my deer," said Hood, an edge of anger in his voice.

The man laughed, his voice deep and warm. "I did not. You took too long with your shot and you were too far away. If you didn't look like you were about to keel over, I'd say you could follow those tracks to it."

Hood looked lamely down to the floor and off in the direction where the deer had bolted.

The newcomer furrowed his brow. "No one taught you how to track an animal either did they?" Hood said nothing and the man looked at him with pity. "Come with me," he said finally. "We'll get you some food and warmth."

The two walked back through the forest and collected Hood's horse. From there, they walked a mile east until they came to a shelter under a shelf of rocks surrounded by trees. The man knelt by the remnants of a campfire and began to light it back up. Then he turned, unrolled his own pack and chucked Hood an apple. "I've got my own meat here, I'll cook us some up and get your belly full."

Hood was grateful for the kindness. He had no doubt that he wouldn't last more than a few more nights by himself. Only now could he admit that, now that he was safe and warm. "What are you doing out here?" asked Hood.

"Ah, it's bad luck to ask a road brother his business," replied the man, skewering the meat over the fire.

Hood smiled at that. *A road brother.* He liked it. His business was no one's but his own, for all anyone knew, his past had never happened. A clean slate. "What's your name?" asked the young bowman.

"It's Peter and yours, boy?" he asked, a warm smile on his face.

"Hood," he said, his hand outstretched.

Peter shook it and nodded. "It's good to meet you."

They sat peacefully, all that could be heard was the rain pattering outside the shelter and Hood's teeth ripping at the flesh of the apple until it reached the core. Peter handed him a skewer of meat, Hood didn't know what it was, but the smell made his mouth overly salivate. It was precious liquid his body decided he could spare. "You're a canny shot with that bow, Hood. How about tomorrow I teach you how to put it to good use in this forest?"

Hood nodded gratefully, his mouth too full of food to speak his words.

Peter laughed and patted the younger man on the back. "You'll want to sleep after that. There are some blankets in that pile there, just help yourself when you're done. I've got some business in the forest to attend to."

Peter was right, once Hood's stomach was full, the warm fire began to relax his body. The shelter around him put his mind at ease and the kindness of Peter had helped him rest easy. His heavy eyes shut and soon the bowman was sleeping deeply.

Birds were singing loudly and the constant sound of rain on leaves and ground had stopped. Hood woke with a start, the events of the previous day slowly returning to him. A long, deep sleep did that to an exhausted mind. It brought confusion and made anything previous to it seem like a blurry haze.

Hood's hand instinctively moved to his right, feeling for his bow and long knife. They were not there. That's when he sat up, his eyes urgently shifting around the scene, taking it in. The campfire was smouldering, his horse gone.

The bowman rose furiously, a burst of energy flowing through him. He saw Peter, the man seemed bigger today, his hair more blonde in the morning sunlight and his eyes brighter. Hood strode towards him, his hand snaking out and grabbing Peter's tunic. "Where the hell are my weapons? My horse?!"

Peter laughed and lifted his hand, his friendly face softening. "Calm, lad," he reached for the pack on his back and unravelled it on the floor. "I've oiled your bow and cleaned the grime from your blade. A rusted knife is good to no one."

"And my horse?" asked Hood, his grip loosening itself from Peter, his tone calming.

"Fed and watered it down at the stream. It was just as tired as you were."

"I'm sorry," said Hood, collecting his bow and knife.

"I've heard bad stories about men on the road. I was caught off guard."

"Don't worry about it. Trust is earned, can't expect a thing like that to come overnight. Now, string that bow and I'll show you how to catch some breakfast."

The two men went out that morning and Peter began to teach Hood everything he knew about hunting in the forest. Weeks went by and the two remained together, Peter teaching him to track, cook, find shelter, hide from foresters. Surviving was no longer the lesson, thriving was.

One morning they caught a score of rabbits and went to a nearby market to trade them. The coin they got wasn't much, but it was enough to spend the day in the nearest tavern. Peter went and sat at a table by the window while Hood went to the barkeep and ordered ale. The barkeep was young, not much older than Hood, his face chivalrous and his eyes bright. He was tall, much taller than Hood and his shoulders were broad. "What would you like?" he asked politely.

"Jug of ale and two tankards, please," said Hood.

The young barkeep nodded and got to it, but then he stopped, his gaze hardening as it fell on Peter sitting by the window.

"Is there a problem?" asked Hood.

The barkeep shook his head and continued with the task, handing Hood the jug and tankards.

Hood and Peter continued to drink all day, jug after jug of ale sloshing down their throats until they decided to head back to their camp at the edge of the village. As they walked, Peter lay his huge arm across Hood's shoulders and smiled. "You know, boy, you're like a son to me. These past two months have been some of the greatest."

Hood smiled and patted his hand on the big man's back. The bowman was thankful he'd met Peter, without him, he could not have survived, or thrived, even.

Hood woke, his head ached and his eyes were blurry. The birds' tweets were just sharp notes piercing the brain. The young man tried to sit up but nausea swam over him. No snoring, he realised, his comrade must be awake. "Peter," he said, his eyes closed. "Peter, shut those damned birds up."

No reply, the man must be off getting breakfast, he thought. But time went on and no breakfast came. Hood roused himself and stood, opening his eyes to look upon the scene around him. His horse was gone, all his packs, his weapons, his spare clothes, even the blankets. "What the hell," said Hood, his voice low, almost a whisper. Robbery was his first thought, but robbers would not take their smelly old blankets. Even if one desperate man wanted their flea-ridden sheets, there were no tracks to suggest this. There was only one set of tracks – Peter's and his horse.

Hood followed them, his pace quickening and his emotions bubbling. Could he have been betrayed? The thought found itself breeding, squirming in his mind like a disease. He shouldn't jump to conclusions, but his gut told him otherwise.

Finally, after four hours of tracking, he saw his horse, the saddlebags still on its back, but no Peter. The marks on the floor around him indicated a struggle of some kind. Hood grabbed his bow from the horse and strung it, his quiver over his back. The bowman followed the marks on the ground through dotted trees until, finally, he came across Peter. His legs and arms were tied tightly, his face bloody and his nose broken. "Hood!" he shouted with need. "You must help me."

Hood looked between Peter and his captor; it was the barkeep, he was opposite Peter, perched calmly on an old tree stump. Hood's bow was pulled and the arrow aimed at the new enemy. "Now, now," said the barkeep, a sword at his side. "Stop and think a moment. Really think and look at this scene. Try and work out who is the enemy."

Hood's bow was still pulled, he was looking between the two, attempting to grab hold of his frenzied thoughts.

"Shoot him!" screamed Peter.

Hood turned the bow at Peter. "Shut your mouth," he said coldly. "You, explain yourself," he said, shifting back to the barkeep.

The tall man stood from his tree stump and unsheathed his sword, digging the blade into the ground. "This man," he said, pointing at Peter, "comes into the tavern every few months with a new person. Be it an old man, a young lad such as yourself, or a rich man's daughter. He comes in and robs them blind."

"And you've come here to what? Make him pay for his crimes?"

The barkeep laughed then. "I came to bloody take his stash."

"And what if I kill you?" asked Hood.

"You won't, for I've done you justice. I've caught the fox in the hen house."

Hood lowered his bow and sat opposite Peter, the barkeep watched on in silence. At first, Peter would not admit to his deeds, but then the barkeep found his stash and Peter began to spill the truth. At first, the captive gave an act of regret, but as time went on it turned into rage. "Let me go dammit!" roared Peter as the sun began to fall. "Get up off your pitiful arse and let me loose. You think you're more important than gold, Hood? Nothing is. Now untie me so I don't have to see your face again."

The words hit Hood hard. Something snapped in him. The bowman was tired of the world chewing him up and spitting him out. He was tired of letting other people's actions impact his fate. In that moment, he decided he would be the bearer of his own torch. Strength and success grow from being cold, hard and focused.

Hood swept up an arrow from the ground and dug it into Peter's gut, twisting it, mangling his intestines. Peter's voice was no longer friendly, his eyes were warm no more. He sang curses to the heavens, screams that could form their own ballads to perverted ears.

That day stretched longer than any Hood could remember. He'd tasted his very first bite of betrayal, of trickery, of evil. Depending on how you deal with those encounters, they can latch onto you, as they may have done with him.

Hood had turned away once Peter had quietened and saw the barkeep still sat, the loot beside him split into two piles. "I don't care about the coin," Hood had said.

"You will do," he replied. "Once the morning comes, you'll be thankful for it."

"What's your name, barkeep?"

"It's John," he said proudly, a smile on his face. Not overly warm like Peter's, but not cold either. The face wasn't hiding anything. It was a smile a man could trust.

"You should go, John, no doubt someone will have heard his cries and they'll come."

John shook his head. "A person should not be alone during a time of hurt, it can cause scarring on the soul."

Hood's head was lowered a while, his hazel eyes on the floor. "Why would he turn on me like that? We were friends, we were road brothers."

"He probably did like you," said John. "Just liked whatever coin you had on you better." Hood said nothing, his blood covered face unable to read. "You should get yourself a dog," John said, louder now.

"What?" said Hood, lifting his head.

"I had me a dog once, it loved me more than anything else, even if it were starving it'd rather me eat. Their trust is something that's pure, it's total. But it's something you must not betray. And the people who would do that are the people you need to be wary of." John pointed to the corpse of Peter with his crimson sword. "He's the type of man to do that."

"And you would not, not even for gold?"

John shook his head. "I would not."

Chapter 18

They say man thrives where angels would die of ecstasy and pigs would die of disgust. But not the Sheriff, he thrives where most men fall – on the cusp of death, when he can taste it on the tip of his tongue.

The Sheriff sucked in a deep breath and coughed until he couldn't breathe. Then the sound came to him, the crackling of wood and the pop of flames. The last thing he remembered was it getting hot and the air becoming heavy, Guy and the men throttling the door in hopes of it breaking. Darkness had come after that. At times, unconsciousness was a blessing, taking you away from the pain that was promised. Sometimes though, it can hold onto you with a more permanent, undesired grip.

Soldiers ran to the Sheriff as they realised he was conscious. Three helped him to his feet and the Sheriff battered them away like flies. "Get your damn hands off me. What the hell went on in there?" asked the Sheriff, looking around the scene. Around twenty-five of his men were in the garden they'd entered through. A small group were huddled around a figure on the floor.

The Sheriff could feel a deep heat at his back, prickling on his neck. He turned and saw the once grand house was now being torn apart by vicious flames. He realised no one had responded to him and anger rose. His eyes pulled away from the ruined home and back to the men before him. The Sheriff walked towards the huddle of men, pushing through without care. The man's thin-lipped mouth widened as he saw the ruined figure of Guy sprawled on the ground. Part of his face was burned badly, his long, dark hair was singed down to the scalp and his eyes were tightly shut. "Is he dead?" asked the Sheriff. No one answered, the soldiers stepped back and stared glumly. Irritation had well and truly crawled under the Sheriff's skin. He pulled his sword now and held it to one of the soldier's throats, the point digging into his flesh. "I said, is he fucking dead?" veins popped from his temples as he roared it.

"No, I don't think so," managed the soldier, before the blade was removed.

"Well get up off your arses and carry him to an inn, if he dies, then you all die. Understand me?" The Sheriff didn't need an answer, his cold, dark eyes let them know they didn't have any options.

The Sheriff walked at the head of his men. He needed water, his head was banging and his thin body aching. But he wouldn't show it, not to the hungry dogs. They only follow until they see your naked neck, vulnerable and bare.

They came to the inn on the other side of the village, William and two soldiers lying dead outside of it. The Sheriff smiled and spat at the body. His phlegm was thick and black, the bitter taste lingering. "Take him upstairs and you lot rest down here. Get the innkeeper to cook you some food, no ale though, I need your minds sharp," said the Sheriff, throwing a pouch of heavy coins at the nearest soldier. Their expressions showed surprise at the Sheriff's act. The truth was, the Sheriff had noticed only five were dead from the inferno and he had twenty-five men left, the rest had deserted. Desertion. The word was acid to the Sheriff's skin and if or when he found them, the deserters would regret being born.

Guy's ruined body was carried up the inn stairs and laid on the bed, the Sherriff asked for the door to be shut and a jug of water left. As the lock on the door clicked and privacy was secured, the Sheriff sat down heavily on the nearest seat. The weight of his years was not going unnoticed on this conquest. It had been too long since he'd marched miles or even rode his horse for more than a hunt. The adrenaline, at first, had fuelled him, but now he was tired. Bone tired. All he needed was a good rest, he told himself, a good rest and he'd be ready to tackle the wretched outlaws.

His eyes rested on Guy. There was a man that truly had a reason to hate them, to want vengeance. His daughter dead and his wife as good as, now he looked like a shrivelled corpse. Those outlaws had taken everything from Guy and the Sheriff envied what drive he must feel.

He pondered his own reasons. The obvious was that he'd be stripped of his title if the outlaws were not caught. The King's advisors would question his ability to sheriff the area and then no doubt strip him of rank. Word was spreading about Hood, it had already reached the King and the Sheriff had promised him squashed. But the outlaw was more slippery than he first appeared. The Sheriff thought about his sister Athella then. In the beginning, when he'd seen her taken, a fear gripped him, his last remaining immediate family. He was, of course, a distant relative to the King himself, but that counted for nothing except his title, and that would soon be gone. Then the loss of Athella had started to lie at the back of his mind, did he miss her? Did he want her back? The answer was unclear, all that was certain was his pride had been dented and he needed it repaired. Once his pride was intact, everything else should fall back into place.

The Sheriff opened his eyes slowly. The room was darker and the distant sound of a cockerel had no doubt roused him. He felt energised, his muscles leaden no more and his mind less foggy. His gaze fell to Guy. The burnt man's eyes were open, narrowly staring at the Sheriff. "I'm going to go after Hood," said the Sheriff, quietly.

"No," croaked Guy. "You must wait for me."

"Wait? The man has humiliated me. If I am to wait then he will escape. I've a mind for tracking, I can find where his group is headed."

"You will die," said Guy, softly.

"I'd rather die," said the Sheriff, "than live life disgraced."

Guy shook his burnt head. "Don't make me carrying you out of there be for nothing."

The Sheriff was taken aback, he was not aware this was how Guy had sustained his injuries. He laughed then, cruel and low. "You are a foolish man, Guy of Gisborne. You're weak and this is why your life is in tatters, this is why your wife and daughter are gone." The Sheriff got up then and headed to the door. He looked back at Guy, his eyes were wide and they were burning with hatred. "You should have let me burn, because I would have let you roast."

The heartless man set out instantly, he'd told his soldiers remaining at the inn to ready themselves and follow his tracks the next day. The Sheriff wanted to do this part alone, to track Hood and his gang independently. Partly to prove to himself he was as good as anyone else, as good as Guy. But he'd never admit that.

His pack was full and his sword was sharpened. He felt invigorated after his rest in Guy's room and he felt more driven as he saw the hatred in Guy's eyes for him, the regret of not letting him die. The tracks were easy enough to follow at first; they had horses with them and the big man Gilbert left an unruly mess as he moved.

As the day went on and the Sheriff travelled through fields and small streams, following every sign he could, the sun began to set. The ageing man knew he should stop and set up camp before it became completely dark, but he couldn't help himself, he felt close and didn't want to stop, he knew the outlaws certainly wouldn't.

All light was gone now, and the Sheriff travelled on long into the night, his relentlessness carrying him on for hours after he should have stopped. The man finally let his pack fall from his shoulders, looking to set up camp. Then a faint glimmer in the distance caught his eye, not half a mile away. A fire. His black heart beat faster and new energy ran through his body. Could it be the outlaws, could he have finally caught up with them? He started towards it and began thinking of the many ways he could sneak in the camp and drive his dagger into their leader. The Sheriff could already taste the glory. That was until he saw what truly sat around the fire; it was only three figures and they weren't outlaws at all. They wore the Sheriff's colours, fire gleaming off their ash-blackened faces. They were deserters.

They couldn't see him at first, for the firelight did not reach him. He could hear them talking, laughing, making plans for the near future. The Sheriff felt calm as he walked amongst them and sat at their fire. The soldiers, however, did not. Their conversation ceased and their bodies stiffened. Everything seemed to freeze except the Sheriff. He sat, poked at the fire and removed a long knife from his belt, digging it into the dry soil beside him.

"Your fire needs more fuel," said the Sheriff, casually.

The soldier closest to him reached for his sword, his hand wrapping around the hilt.

"I wouldn't do that, boy. A sword is not the weapon of choice in these confines. I'd have my dagger in your neck before you even drew it," the Sheriff's voice was confident. The idea these men could take the Sheriff in moments didn't even occur to them, for the very presence of him cowed them, castrated them with his mere presence.

"We're sorry, Sheriff, you've got to—" began one of the soldiers.

He was interrupted by the other, the one with his hand on the sword. "Shut up, Tom, don't—"

It was the Sheriff's turn to interrupt. "But all this has taken place to fulfil the scriptures of the prophets. Then all the disciples left him and fled," he quoted. There was silence, just the sound of the fire crackling. Their eyes on the Sheriff. "Jesus forgave them," he continued, his finger tapping lightly on his dagger hilt. "I, however, am not a forgiving man." The dagger slipped from its soil sheath and glimmered in the air, passing through the campfire and into one of the deserter's foreheads. The Sheriff was pleased with himself at that, it took force to break into a skull and pierce the brain. However, he couldn't focus on his skilful feat too long, for the soldier to his right was upon him, still trying to pull that sword of his.

The Sheriff grappled him, the soldier's sword hardly grazing the ground never mind his flesh. "I told you," said the Sheriff, his voice strained as he used all his weight to push the soldier's face into the fire. "That weapon is useless at this range."

The soldier didn't reply, instead, his screams began to echo out as the skin bubbled and blistered on his face. The Sheriff was not a heavy man, nor was he strong, but when it comes to death, he found a strength that no others occupied. The soldier's screams died and his body went limp. The smell of burning hair and shit was strong in the air.

The Sheriff fell back onto the cool grass, sweat rolling down his head. His heart beat like a smith's hammer, but a tiredness swept over him. He didn't need to watch out for the third soldier, the Sheriff could tell on sight that the man was a coward. He'd heard his boots begin to flee as he grappled the second man. The Sheriff began to laugh. Nothing reveals a man the way a battle does, it separates the cowards and the courageous. A coward can hide in plain sight behind a veil of courage, but when the blood starts to pour and they need to take a stand, that's when the curtain is opened.

He stood and took what food and water they had, slipping them into his own pack. He was going to spend the night there, staring at the battle he'd won, but the smell was starting to bother him. He made his own fire, not too out the way, but in a shelter where his light could not be seen. The Sheriff slept well, the comfort of blood on his hands easing his dreams.

He awoke slowly, just before the sun had started to rise. He was hungry for Hood, the deserters' deaths had awoken the beast that lay resting. The Sheriff had forgotten what going it alone had felt like, almost always he had men to do his dirty work, men like Guy, who would just about fulfil any task while he sat on his arse growing old. The taste of Guy's second-hand victories had grown stale, now he had his teeth firmly sunk into the concept of his own victory. He recognised it was more dangerous, his life being at risk in every moment, but that was part of the appeal.

The tracks were followed continuously and he was impressing himself more and more with each mile he roamed. To his delight, he found himself tracking almost completely fresh prints. He moved carefully now and in the distance, he saw two horses tied loosely to a tree. The Sheriff smiled, the wrinkles on his ugly face stretched wide. The sun had only been raised an hour and the chances that the outlaws still slept were high.

He moved carefully to a patch of trees near the horses and saw there was a clearing beyond. The Sheriff crept, his mouth dry and his hand clammy around the hilt of his sword. Then he saw it, the group of sleeping outlaws. There was John, huddled close to the far tree sleeping soundly, the old man sleeping back to back with Scarlett and then Gilbert, whose face was pointed at the sky. Then the strangest thing happened, a choice that seemed to define him. Closest to him he saw Athella, her soft, young face sleeping, an angelic look to it. Equally close was Hood, his form lounging against a tree and the ridiculous hat tipping off his head and down to his chin. Now he was faced with a choice. He could wake his sister, sneak her away quietly and hope he would once again catch up to the group. Or he could end it all and kill Hood right now. The Sheriff found himself treading towards Hood, each step moving him closer to the bandit and further away from his sister.

The vengeful man paused to take in the moment, his sword raised high above Hood. "Rot in hell, you bastard," he said, a whisper from his lips. The sword was driven down and plunged into the sleeping man's body, ripping into the flesh and bone. As he did so, the hat fell from the outlaw's face, revealing a man that was not Hood. Instead there was a face of death, the eyes bulbous and blood filled, the skin waxy and pale.

The Sheriff's heart dropped as he realised his mistake. He felt a rope loop around his neck and then tighten, his feet began to rise from the ground and the sound of an aching tree branch could be heard.

His dark eyes watched with agony as Hood strolled into view, a great smile on his face, his teeth bared. "I did you a favour, Sheriff," he said, his voice bright and irritating. "That soldier was a deserter of yours. My man Gilbert snapped his neck, just as he's trying to do with your own."

The Sheriff could hear Gilbert's deep laughter from behind him. The sound was childish, disturbing even. The giant was the only person he knew strong enough to levy him over a tree branch with a rope.

Now the surprise of the situation was over with, the panic had come. He could feel his face purpling and his sight begin to blur. Death was once again slowly creeping into his pulsing veins and the Sheriff found a strange peace settling over him.

Chapter 19

The smell of the burning house was thick, putrid even. Burned flesh outlined it and Hood didn't need to be told the Sheriff and his men were inside. The group of outlaws walked away, moving back through the town, the villagers staying well clear this time. Scarlett was shocked that they were about to walk into a trap. Usually his companion, old man Stutley, could smell a lure a mile off, but not this time. "So how did you know? How did you trap them?" Scarlett had asked Eustace, the bearded young man berated him and the monk tried to explain in as much detail as he could.

Old man Stutley had wrapped his arm around Eustace's broad shoulder, a smile on his face. "You're turning out to be a useful bloke after all."

The whole group seemed to warm to him suddenly and Hood enjoyed seeing it. The bowman had long known Eustace was a loyal man, a man of his word. If he weren't, Hood would have slit his throat and disposed of him long ago. John, however, watched him with a baleful glare. John grimaced at each word that came from the monk's mouth, and when he spoke to Hood in private, John would anxiously sit, almost disturbed.

The group collected their two horses, still packed with what loot they could carry, and led them out of the village. There was no rush. From what they heard, the Sheriff and his men would have their hands full, if not charred.

Hood had watched the group as they headed north.

Gilbert was talking non-stop to Eustace, once he'd seen the other men had decided to trust him, his own mind was made up. Far back, Hood could see Athella and John walking; her body language was relaxed and easy-going. John was laughing, their conversation inaudible. She had appeared untroubled as she had been told the story of her brother, the Sheriff, potentially being burnt alive. It was as if the information freed her in some way. The woman had come out of her shell the past few days, seeming to enjoy her time with them, forgetting that she was a captive. Hood himself even forgot sometimes.

It was two hours until sundown and the outlaws decided to make camp. Eustace moved off, wanting time to meditate on his own. Hood was familiar with the act, he'd seen it as he travelled some of the eastern countries with his father as a child. To him, it was like praying, except it wasn't to a god. It was an act to search for inner peace, contemplation beyond conversation. Some of the men he'd met believed their souls were part of the world and in order to find inner peace, they'd need to become one with it through meditation.

The act was an odd one to see, a contradictory one to Eustace's actions. The monk seemed a man of honour, but some of his more sinister deeds spoke of anything but the love and compassion he'd seen coupled with the meditating men of the east. One man's definition of good and bad differed from another's, the lines blurred and wavered. The monk's, it seemed, was misted beyond recognition.

There was a river nearby the camp, not a ten-minute walk. Hood decided to go down to it scrub the dirt from his body, the smell of smoke and ale falling from his skin. Gilbert wanted to join him, insisted in fact. The giant loved water as a fly loves dung.

Hood had removed his clothes and entered the cold water slowly, attempting to acclimatise his body. Gilbert, on the other hand, leapt in head first, submerging himself completely. The water ran up to Hood's shoulders and just past Gilbert's waist. The bowman dipped his head, scrubbing the water into his long, dark hair. He watched Gilbert swim and splash with a fondness, his hands dipping into the water as he saw fish swim by, a great smile on his face. "Why do you love water so much, Gilbert?" asked Hood.

"Feels nice on my skin, fresh in my mouth," replied the giant, his eyes wide.

Hood frowned. "Don't drink the water, Gilbert, you'll get sick."

"I know, but I can't help it."

Hood shook his head and climbed from the river. "You can help it, the only thing stopping you from doing anything you want is yourself. That's what makes us different from dogs or pigs or cows, it's that we can decide whether we want to act on a thought or an impulse."

Gilbert nodded, impersonating an expression of understanding. The big man lowered himself further into the water, allowing it to flow past his face.

"What do you think of Athella?" asked Hood. He wanted a different perspective, a one he could not guess.

"She's pretty," said Gilbert, a look of guilt plastered his face then, remembering his attack on her. "I'm sorry I tried to take her, Hood, I didn't mean to make you mad."

Hood waved his hand dismissively. "Forget about it,

Gil, I know you're sorry."

"I know she's John's now, I ain't gonna touch her. Not even talk to her."

Hood's eyes narrowed then. "What do you mean she's John's?"

"Well, I saw him and her kissing. Twice now I've seen it and he's always smiling with her."

Hood was shocked, he knew they were close, but he didn't think she was interested in him like that. John would usually talk to him about such things, but the man had been distant of late, cold even. "Come on, Gilbert, get dressed, it's going to be dark soon."

Gilbert stepped from the river, grabbing his clothes and pulling them on, soaking them in the process. "Did I say something wrong, Hood?"

"No, Gilbert."

"You're not lying?"

"No, my friend," said Hood walking from the river. "I would not lie to you."

Chapter 20

Gilbert and Hood headed to the camp, from a field over they could see the fire burning brightly. Eustace was sitting next to Scarlett and Stutley, chatting between themselves, John and Athella at the other end, quiet words between them. Hood felt something as he saw it, something he couldn't identify. The bowman shook it off and continued. As he'd said to Gilbert, he was the one who decides if he acts on a thought or impulse. Get rid of it, crumple it, burn it, do what it takes, anything to stop it from taking hold of the reins on your mind.

Hood sat at the camp and meat began to be roasted on the open flames. The smell would usually rouse his appetite, but not tonight. Gilbert sat with him for a while but soon moved to Stutley, listening to the old man's stories. He always seemed to tell the same ones, but Gilbert never tired of them.

John rose from his seat, leaving Athella, and came to place himself next to the bowman. John was bigger and wider, dwarfing the smaller man, creating a shadow over him. "You're quiet tonight," said John, staring into the flames.

Hood shrugged. "Just have nothing to say this evening."

John laughed then, the sound warm and familiar. "Of all the years I've known you, Hood, you've never had nothing to say. Remember what you said to me? You told me that a man will never be heard, never be remembered if he's got nothing to say."

"I've learned that a lot can be said without words. Words are more often than not used to mask what a person really wants to say."

"There you are," smiled John. "Using those words of yours again."

Hood grinned and shook his head. The two men sat for a while in silence, just the murmur of Stutley's voice could be heard. Then John rustled at his side, unclipping something. "Here," the bigger man said, handing him a fine leather scabbard. "I stole this from the Sheriff's house, hanging on his wall like some ornament. But I tell you, Hood, this blade should not sit idle. The weight is perfect, the steel is strong and sharp, it could be used for years to come and not dull. I've not seen a blade finer."

Hood held it in his hands, the gleaming silver hilt was inlaid with blue jewels that glittered in the firelight. The bowman unsheathed it and felt the weight of the short sword. "It's perfect," said Hood, his voice soft, his hazel eyes sparkling.

"It's yours, brother, I thought of you as soon as I saw it."

Hood looked at him in shock. "No, this thing is worth more than most of the loot we've taken. I can't accept it."

John laughed again. "Look at it, Hood, it's too short for me, I like my longsword. Besides, who'd suit a sword as fine as that other than you?"

Hood nodded, staring at the blade, his serious expression curving into a smile. "Fine. But only because it's a token of friendship, nothing more."

"Aye, nothing more."

"Aye," said Hood, agreeing. "It is a fine blade though, I'll probably even be able to best you with this."

"If the Sheriff cuts my arms from me, then aye, perhaps you're right."

The sun rose and bathed the camp in light. Hood's eyes flicked open and he clapped his hands for his companions to wake. "For God's sake, Hood," muttered Scarlett, rubbing dirt from his thick beard. "Why always up so bloody early?"

"The earlier we wake, the less speed we need to travel with," replied Hood, packing his things.

"What does speed matter?" said John. "You said yourself that they'll be more than occupied with their burns from the fire."

"I don't like to depend too much on another man's perception of events," said the bowman, turning to Eustace. "No offence, monk, but I trust no man's eye more than my own."

"None taken," said Eustace, his voice calm and deep. The monk had stood ready, almost before Hood. He looked well-kept, his hair tightly brushed back into a knot and his great axe on his back.

Gilbert was never very fond of waking early, but he'd learned from many previous lessons that lying in would only mean he'd get the piss-pot over his head. The giant grumbled and shoved stale bread in his mouth while the group slowly made their way further north.

They walked at a leisurely pace, stopping once or twice to eat. The day was mild and the sky was littered with puffs of cloud. Hood walked ahead with Eustace, discussing tales from the monk's past and places they'd both visited. "Wine in France," Eustace had said, "leaves a taste as if the gods have made love in your mouth."

Hood shot him a look of confusion. "I can't tell if that's a good or a bad thing."

Eustace smiled. "There are far worse things to taste in life than that."

"I hear the monks are famed for making that wine, did you partake in winemaking?"

"I am a different type of monk, bowman."

"Ah, yes, the infamous dark monk," said Hood mocking. "Tell me the truth, this whole dark magic thing, it's a load of bollocks, isn't it? To scare the masses, to give yourself a reputation."

Eustace's grey eyes rested heavily on Hood. The bowman thought he might have to jam his dagger into the man's gut for a moment. But then the glance softened, moving back over the land before them. "In the future, Hood, you need to be careful who and what you choose to disrespect."

Now it was Hood's turn to feel irritation. "Sometimes a man cannot choose how he feels about someone or something."

"That's true, my friend, but you of all people should know that you have a choice to act on thoughts. Every man does, it's what separates the wolves from the sheep."

His insight intrigued Hood, it was as if he'd been listening to himself and Gilbert speak only the previous night. "Tell me then, tell me of this power you have."

"It's not a power, Hood, it's a gift. I'll tell all when we reach my ship, when we reach safety and gold."

Hood laughed. "Not much of a seer then are you, for I crave something other than gold and safety."

"Respect? Fame? Your name etched in history? You'll get that, Hood, you'll get all that, but remember, there'll always be a price to pay."

"Aye, well, to be remembered through time is priceless," said the bowman happily.

"There are many things that are priceless, Hood, but that's not one of them. Our resting soul cares not for what reputation we hold with the living."

That was enough for Hood. Spend too long in conversation with a monk, he thought, and it always comes back to philosophy and judgment. Their views against yours, a tiring concept that seems never-ending.

The bowman took a horse and rode ahead, telling them to follow his tracks and that he would set up camp ahead where he'd catch the supper.

Hood rode for two hours upon the horse, setting up camp in a thicket of trees looking out onto a plain of grass. The campfire was built but not lit and Hood set out for a hunt. He strode into the nearby forest, his bow in hand and a quiver on his back. The forest was peaceful and soothing, thoughts of John and Athella rolling from his mind. Even his irritation at the monk eased up. Who wouldn't want their name spoken on the lips of every man? Who wouldn't want to outplay the King's men and the King himself? The monk spoke in riddles at times. We're born to live, thought Hood, born to thrive and survive in the world we've got. Do what we can to stand out amongst the rest, take what we need, kill who we have to. The frustration built more as he thought of the words he'd wished he'd spoken. Then the feeling flew from him and his arrow was loosed from his bow.

There was barely a sound as the stag dropped. The majestic beast collapsed with death heavily, thudding onto the ground. A King's stag in the King's forest.

Hood smiled at that. "This is my forest," he whispered quietly. "This is my world."

Chapter 21

It was almost sundown as the group trailed into the camp Hood had set for them. John could be seen leading the way, Gilbert trailing at the back, his huge feet dragging. "Is that deer I smell?" shouted the giant, his sullen mood lifting.

"The King's very own," replied Hood. The carcass hung from a tree deeper in the woods where Hood had stripped it of meat. "We're eating well tonight, brothers."

"And what about me?" said Athella, her voice light, touching Hood with surprise.

"You are the lady of the camp," said Hood. "This means you get the finest cut."

Gilbert and John frowned at that, both for different reasons.

Athella smiled and sat beside Hood looking through her selection of food. The group went on to eat, each person filling their stomach with juicy, tender meat. It was the best meal they'd eaten in weeks, the best John had eaten in months. Often you'll find that when a person stuffs themselves with as much food as possible, it takes a great deal of energy to digest. This means soon after, sleep will whisper seductively in one's ear.

The crackle of fire is a loud noise, a noise that you'd think would keep people awake. Not in the forest it won't, it acts as a blanket to the mind. It lets you know you're warm, it keeps you from the deadly silence of the night.

Hood pushed himself to his feet, he wasn't tired. He

had watched the group fill themselves until they drifted off. Make sure your men ate their fill first, for hunger is one of the many things to turn an ally into an enemy. Especially this bunch, as loyal as Gilbert was, hunger and priests were the two things that turned him into a bloodthirsty animal.

The bowman walked out of the trees and away from the fire, watching the moon in the sky. It wasn't a clear moon, it was a faded glow behind illuminated cloud. Something about staring at the moon makes a person think deeply, deeper than one cares to delve. He felt a hand on his shoulder then, light and graceful, a perfumed smell followed it. It could only be Athella, for the only smell his brothers would bring is piss, smoke and sweat. "How can a lady who travels on the road who spends her time with a band of unwashed men still bring the scent of a rose with her wherever she walks?"

Athella smiled and the cloud moved from the moon, highlighting her delicate features with white light. "That is a secret no woman can tell."

Hood grinned. "Are you not tired? We will be rising early in the morning."

"A little, but sleep doesn't come easy on the hard ground when you've been used to a bed."

"It gets easier."

They stood in silence after that and she sat herself in the long, soft grass, grabbing Hood's hand and pulling him down next to her. "You don't seem like the cutthroat the Sheriff spoke about, you know."

"The Sheriff," said Hood, "is not my biggest fan."

"Was not, you mean," she lowered her dark eyes to the ground, something was present there, perhaps it was sadness, Hood couldn't tell.

The bowman, by all accounts, knew he should say

something pleasant, *'I'm sorry for your loss?'* No, it didn't sound right, it wasn't sincere.

She spoke again so he didn't have to. "You know, you don't come across as quite what the people of Nottingham describe you as either."

This was more like it, thought Hood, the opinions of the masses, the verbal historians. "What do they have to say?"

"They say you're a hero, a man who cannot be captured or killed, a man who cows the rich and powerful and fights for those who cannot."

Hood couldn't help but chuckle. "They've got quite the imagination."

"Is this not the man you want to be?" she said, her voice suddenly serious.

He looked at her face, he hadn't met a woman who stirred him like that in years. His eyes were on her lips, he couldn't help it. "At times, certain people make me feel like I want to be that man." He shivered at that. The ridiculous things a man will say in the presence of a pretty woman.

But it worked, her eyes fluttered and her head moved in towards his. John, the Sheriff, Guy of Gisborne, all thoughts had left his head as he moved in on Athella. Then he heard something, it was footsteps moving quickly, running in fact. The figure moved by them and into the thicket of trees where their camp lay.

The moment was interrupted and the two ran back to the camp. As they came closer they could hear commotion, an unfamiliar voice, whining and pleading. On entry they could see Eustace had a hold on their new guest. It was a dark-haired young man who looked thirsty and tired, his chest heaving with exertion. The monk had his arm twisted into a lock and his captive squealed with pain the more he struggled.

"We have a visitor," said old Stutley, his voice sickly with threat.

"A visitor," repeated Gilbert, his wide-set eyes were pinned on the man, the muscles in his body twinging with excitement.

The last man that caught Hood's eye was John, he sat there, his handsome face pained as he watched Athella and himself enter from the darkness beyond. Hood knew this was not the time to deal with such a matter, now it was time for the fun to begin.

Scarlett perked up now, tiredness leaving the burly man. "Look, Hood, he's got the Sheriff's colours on."

"Gilbert," said Hood, removing the hat from his head and pulling his dark hair back. "Hold onto our new friend. Make him feel welcome."

Gilbert moved slowly towards the man Eustace held and took him from the monk. His huge arms wrapped around the newcomer's torso and Gilbert stood behind him.

Hood sat casually at the other end of the fire, his outlaws watched as the interrogation began. "First thing's first, your name?" asked Hood.

"Beven," said the man, uncomfortable in Gilbert's grip.

"Beven, a piss-weak name to match the man that beholds it," said Hood, Beven lowered his eyes, worry plastered on his face. "My brothers and I do not take well to cowards. Killing a coward is easy. However, killing a man you respect is harder. Please, Beven, you need to make this hard for us, it's part of the game."

The outlaws chuckled in unison, they knew what was coming.

"I'm not with the Sheriff, we left him, me and my

comrades had enough."

"So the Sheriff's alive?" said Hood, leaving any trace of disappointment from his tone. He wanted to look at Athella, to gauge her reaction, but he could not.

"Aye, he got out there alive. Guy saved him, he's pretty burnt up though, I've seen men die from less."

"Interesting," said Hood untroubled. "Guy of Gisborne is many things, but he isn't a man who will die easy. How far away is the Sheriff?"

"Not far behind, five miles maybe? I don't know. He attacked me and the others at our camp by himself, killed them I think."

"Now, I know the man's a bit deranged, but why would he attack his own men?"

"We deserted, you see, like I said we…"

"Ah," interrupted Hood, clapping his hands and rising from the ground. "Now we have a problem. You were almost on your way, Beven, on your way with a pack full of food and water. But you see, my brothers and I," he stretched his arm, his hand falling on each of his dirt covered outlaws, "we're men of honour. And despite who you're deserting, I'm afraid we cannot let such a shameful act pass unnoticed."

The outlaws laughed and Gilbert began to breathe heavily with excitement, his huge chest pushing Beven back and forth. Beven started to shake uncontrollably and his leggings were sagging with wet piss. The outlaws' laughs became louder and more feral as Gilbert threw Beven in disgust, the man half landing in the flames of the campfire and struggling to stand.

"Come on," said Hood, helping Beven to his feet. The bowman brushed his hands down his captive's clothes and across his shoulders, removing the dirt. "Now, you get one chance, Beven, one chance. Are you listening?" Hood lightly touched Beven's cheek before handing him his bow, an arrow along with it. "You hit me with my own bow and you're a free man. My brothers will cause you no harm, that's a promise."

Beven held the bow loosely and Hood began to walk within the trees, placing himself in a clearing where the bow could be shot. Hood's back was against a tree and he stood straight. "Shoot, Beven!" the bowman shouted.

Beven pulled back the bow and took aim, the outlaws silent around him. When the arrow was loosed, it flew by Hood, not even coming near.

"Too much hesitation," shouted Hood, beginning to walk back. "Hesitation is the enemy of every warrior, Beven."

Beven began to panic as the bowman moved towards him and the outlaws edged closer. Beven took his chance, he leapt for a stray arrow from the floor, he fixed it to the bow and didn't even bother to aim. The arrow was shot towards Hood before the outlaws could stop it.

Hood didn't move, he continued to walk, for the bowman truly believed he could not be struck by his own bow. Arrogance can get a man killed, in fact, it's probably their biggest murderer. Today, arrogance did not kill Hood, instead there was a noise, loud and sharp, metal on metal. The arrow had struck the handle of the sword John had given him, glancing from it and embedding itself into the ground.

Beven's head dropped and he truly knew his fate.

The men rarely saw Hood angry, he became even more ruthless than usual when the emotion surfaced. On this night, however, to everyone's surprise he was not angry. He had looked down at the jewelled sword at his side with adoration and patted John on the back as he entered his circle of brothers. "Gilbert," said Hood, his voice was soft and quiet, this was when the men knew death would follow. "Break his neck."

Gilbert chuckled with glee and moved towards the pinned captive. "I'll crush this worm's neck with one hand," he bellowed.

"Don't mess around, Gilbert, just do it like you normally do and crush it with both hands till they meet," said Scarlett, maybe he'd said it because he knew the spirit of competition would come forth. The men argued a bit with this, bets were placed, and as predicted by most, Beven's filthy neck could be snapped with the strong clench of Gilbert's right hand.

The snap was loud and hollow, echoing through the forest. Beven's eyes were blood red and half popping from his skull. The monk had watched on in silence, as had Athella, she looked at Hood with an unrecognisable stare. As if she had higher expectations of the outlaw.

"Now, my brothers, now that the entertainment is over, I have a plan. It starts with stripping poor Beven here from his soiled clothes and slipping him into some finer ones," said Hood, he turned to Scarlett. "Since you lost the bet, young Scarlett, and because you're so fond of arse, you can have the pleasure of carrying that out."

Beven was stripped and re-clothed, then placed against a tree around the campfire, his head bowed and Hood's hat tipped over his deathly expression. Now they lay in wait, Hood watched them from the trees. All of them feigning sleep, it looked real enough, thought Hood, half of them probably were sleeping. He knew one that would not be – Athella. She lay there, her eyes closed and her head on a bunched up blanket next to

John. The woman played with his mind. Hood was many things, arrogant, a cheat, a thief, a killer but loyalty was a notion that lay close to his heart. He did not hold it in value to redeem himself in any way, or to hold on to any good that was left within him. Yet, he felt it was important, no matter who the person is. Without loyalty, a person has nothing to offer to anyone. Athella had made him compromise this notion. John was his friend, his brother, and he was willing to compromise that for her. Hood knew in his heart that John would not do that to him and he loathed himself for it.

Then the bowman saw it, a silhouette creeping into the camp from the grass beyond the trees. Hood had his eyes on the Sheriff. The older man stood there for a moment, his sword in his hand, staring down at the sleeping form of Athella. Hood thought for a second he would try and wake her, stripping away everything he thought he knew about him. But no, a tree cannot change the fruit it grows and the Sheriff moved across the camp quietly towards the corpse of Beven.

The bowman watched from the trees with awe, the scene was surreal, as if he was witnessing his own death. Of course, he knew, he would never die at the hand of such a man. The King perhaps, but not this serpent.

The Sheriff raised his sword, as if it were a holy act and whispered something inaudible. The sword dropped and started to viciously plunge in and out of Beven's body. Hood watched as old man Stutley approached him from behind with a ready noose that was draped over a nearby branch. Gilbert held onto the other end, ready to pull every ounce of his weight down onto it.

Now it was time, the hat fell from Beven's face and

Hood signalled. The loop of rope was slung over the Sheriff's head and around his neck, and that's when Gilbert began to pull. The tree branch ached and moaned as the Sheriff's weight spread over it.

Hood stepped out and his brothers stood, his smile was wide and bright. "I did you a favour, Sheriff," he said. "That soldier was a deserter of yours. My man Gilbert snapped his neck, just as he's trying to do with your own."

Gilbert began to laugh uncontrollably as he watched the Sheriff dangle in the air.

Hood looked the Sheriff in the eyes; the hanging man stared at him with hate. The bowman took great satisfaction from it. Then the eyes rolled back, the Sheriff's face purpling, the veins in his neck bulging. Hood turned to Athella, an expression could be seen on her face. It wasn't fear, nor was it panic. It galled Hood that he couldn't identify these things easily. He'd seen it before, many times before. A memory flashed into his head from when he was in a whorehouse on the outskirts of Stafford. His lady was riding away atop of him, doing a marvellous job until the door swung open and her young son stood there, staring at his mother while her tits were bouncing up and down. It was the look on the mother's face as her boy witnessed his first lesson in the art of lovemaking. The whore's features had twisted into uncomfortableness. That was it, Athella was uncomfortable! Hood praised himself inwardly and chuckled at the memory. He turned back to stare at the Sheriff, the man was limp, his face a mix of red, blue and purple. Then the branch snapped, the sound wasn't overly different from a neck.

The Sheriff fell to the dirt floor like a sack of grain. Hood strolled to the body and lay his hands on his neck. "Well, it's still intact and the bastard's still alive." Hood removed the dagger, from his belt and held it to the Sheriff's neck.

"Wait!" said Athella, the words bursting from her mouth.

Hood turned his head towards her, the dagger ceasing to move. The rest of the outlaws turned their eyes on her too, the most surprised was John, the man was perplexed. "Tell me why, Athella? Why do you wish to spare this wicked man's life?" asked Hood.

"I do not. I wish to take it myself," she replied, opening her hand, gesturing for the dagger.

Hood nodded, handing her the blade. There was something about the way she snatched it from him and the pause that came after. Her dark eyes did not venture down to the Sheriff; instead, they stayed on Hood. Locked, unblinking. The muscles in her arm bunched, the way they did before the limb was going to strike. Confusion swept over Hood for only a moment. Then clarity hit him; this was her brother, her blood. Despite the man being a cruel bastard, they had still come from the same line, the same womb. Hood had forgotten she was even a captive. In those moments he was ashamed of his foolishness, were she a man, she would have still been bound in chains.

A scream interrupted the moment, it was a noise for battle, for blood. It came from the darkness beyond the camp and Guy of Gisborne emerged, his sword plunging into the nearest outlaw, his face plastered with rage. Scarlett roared with pain as the sword entered the side of his torso, then pulled his own. Before Hood knew it, dozens of soldiers had entered the camp, their weapons drawing and unleashing themselves upon the outlaws.

Hood pulled his shortsword, the blade light and graceful. At this moment Athella was far from his mind, and he from hers. He tried to move towards Scarlett, but the bowman found himself on the defence, batting away several enemy attacks.

Eustace had taken action, his axe pulled from his back and into his grip, he was swinging it back and forth, blood and screams of guards following. In the heat of the action, Athella was frozen, the dagger still in her hand. A soldier grabbed her shoulder and instinctively she swung the blade, embedding it into his neck. The soldier stepped back, gasping as his blood drenched her.

Gilbert had long since disarmed a soldier and took his weapon. The giant had grabbed the handle, tearing it from his enemy then used it against him. Men tended to stay clear of Gilbert, but this time they tried to swarm him like crows on a corpse. Swords swiping at his back, men jumping from all angles to drag him to the ground.

"Retreat!" ordered John. Hood could not see the man, but his voice was clear and strong. He looked at the scene around him, no matter how many soldiers were downed, more came from the darkness. Guy was in the centre of it, the man's skin was burnt and half his hair was singed to the scalp. The wounds glistened and were far from healed. A man determined is a man unstoppable, thought Hood. Scarlett fought fiercely, though Hood knew the young man was done for. The wound in his side poured with blood, his face was pale and dark rings surrounded his eyes.

"Retreat!" there was the voice again, further away this time. Stutley was not budging, he'd fought his way to Scarlett's side. The old man would not leave his friend, the two were inseparable and Stutley would rather die by his side than see Scarlett die alone.

The rules were simple, thought Hood, as he sliced his sword down an opponent's chest. We do what we can to survive, we don't stick around when the odds aren't in our favour. He looked to Gilbert, the giant had four men pinning him, struggling with every morsel of strength to keep him down. "Someone finish him!" shouted one of them.

Gilbert's wide eyes were on Hood, like a man's dog begging for help, begging him not to leave. Hood took another step back towards the wooded area behind him, on the verge of running. The bowman killed the last man before him and lifted his arm, hurling his shortsword through the fire-lit camp into the back of one of the men who held Gilbert.

The soldier let go of the giant's arm and Gilbert pulled the Hood's sword from his back. Within moments the men who pinned him were tossed away and Gilbert sprinted through the overwhelmed camp, knocking men from their feet as he ran with Hood into the dark trees beyond.

The two ran and ran, they didn't know if anyone was following, they didn't look back to find out. As Hood knew, from many instances before, the runner has the advantage, the chaser has to follow. There's more concentration in that, they need to listen, look, be careful of ambush. In the blackness of night, while the mood is hidden by the trees, losing someone is the easiest task one can be set.

Eventually Hood came to a stop, the slim man bent over, his hands on his knees, his heart pounding. He cocked his head back to look for Gilbert, but the man was no longer there. Hood wanted to shout, call for

John, Gil or Eustace, see if any of them were still alive to hear. However, he knew it would be ridiculous to start bellowing names in the middle of a black wood while you're being pursued. "For Christ's sake," muttered Hood, realising he was alone.

Chapter 22

Guy of Gisborne had lain in bed, his burns layering his body with crimson pain. He was prepared to lie there and squirm, let the clean sheets stick to his open wounds while he tried to rest. That was until the Sheriff had visited him and knocked him out of his pitiful daze.

The sheer impudence of the Sheriff. Guy had saved his life, he'd pulled the snake from the flames and the Sheriff had no kind words, only sneers at Guy's expense. "Should have let you burn, should I?" murmured Guy, attempting to move his body.

As predicted, the bedding stuck to his wounds and pain seared as he peeled them away. He sat on the edge of his bed reeling in pain. Pain is focus for some men, suffering can give birth to power. For other men, it can deplete them, their bodies give up as their minds lose the will to live. Guy, however, was fuelled by such things. It galled him that he had the ability to save an evil man like the Sheriff and not the angels that were his daughter and wife. Stop, he said to himself, the thought of them only pained him more.

It'd taken him a few hours, but he was clean and dressed in new clothes, his fire scorched leather vest donned. Guy buckled his sword to his side and stepped in front of the mirror. His stomach flipped and his heart dropped with shock as he saw himself. The man was unrecognisable. His long, thick hair half scorched away to the scalp, one side of his face red and weeping. It was a miracle his eyes were untouched by the flames. Guy turned away swiftly and wrapped his oozing hands with a clean bandage so he could wield a sword more comfortably if he had to.

Guy had gone down the stairs of the inn, half the men were eating, gambling, doing whatever they liked while the Sheriff was off on his own death wish. "Men!" he called to them, his voice deep and resonating.

The soldiers looked up at the man they thought to be almost dead. Their eyes were wide and their ears were primed for listening. "With the Sheriff away, I'm in charge. You'll gather your supplies and follow me, together we will take down those wretched outlaws. You'll aid me so I can have my revenge on whichever men have wronged us!" The soldiers had an idea that he wasn't just talking about Hood and his brothers; Guy had the Sheriff in mind. This didn't bother the soldiers. However, what was in it for them? Guy answered their silent question. "If we bring them down, if you help me get what I want," continued Guy, "I'll triple your wages this month and any soldier you can muster from this sorry village."

The soldiers were roused by this, they cheered, nodding and agreeing amongst themselves.

"You like that?!" shouted Guy.

"Aye!" chorused the men.

"Well get a fucking move on, we're leaving imminently!"

The soldiers readied themselves for Guy, more were gathered from the local patrol to join them after word got out that they were after the famed Hood. The soldiers wanted blood and bounty, they cared not of the man who supposedly fought against their oppression.

They took three hours to gather the horses that were

dispersed around the village, but they would need them if they were going to catch the outlaws in time, they already had a day on them. So Guy and his men were riding, riding hard. A band of them, just over forty, galloped through grass and cow shit at an impressive pace, led by a man who was almost burnt pretty badly.

For Guy, the tracks of Hood and his outlaws were simple, the Sheriff had made them even more so. As the day went by, Guy thought he would collapse and topple face first from his horse, his wounds were angry and raw, demanding attention. He ignored it, pushed the feeling from his mind.

They gathered momentum as time went by, their pace quickening as the sun began to set. The soldiers were struggling behind Guy, they were tired, used to too much rest and standing around, but they carried on, for gold spoke their name.

Guy could see by how fresh the prints were compared to the outlaws' that the Sheriff was making good time, remarkably good for a useless man such as himself. The Sheriff had drive, a different breed to Guy's, but it was drive nonetheless. The cruel man was foolish, thought Guy, he did not need to exhaust himself, travelling constantly. This only meant when he faced Hood he would get slaughtered like a lamb, his mind absent of any cunning.

Once the sun had set, Guy ordered them from the horses. They were left to graze in a field, sleep if they needed. The men envied them, but they knew Guy would not sleep now, not after how far they'd come.

Guy came to a fresh camp, two of the Sheriff's soldiers lay there dead. The men who were with him looked on in distaste, they assumed Hood and his men did the deed. However, Guy could see by the marks on the ground that the Sheriff had been here and the altercation took place between the soldiers and him. He kept that to himself, for it was likely the soldiers would leave on hearing it.

Guy moved on swiftly, the marks were an hour old at most. It didn't take long for him to find the trail to the outlaws' camp. He was about a hundred feet away when they spotted the glow of fire within a patch of trees. His men hushed and readied their weapons. Guy was filled with anticipation as he slowly stepped towards the camp, and when he was sure it was them, he ran, the men joining him.

Guy screamed with fury as he entered the clearing, his sword cleaving into the first outlaw he saw, it was Scarlett, he drew his own sword and swung back. The soldiers entered behind him, filling the space with clashes of steel and screams of death. Guy carried on, his sword battling against Scarlett's, the man's strength was failing as his wound stained his side with deep red blood.

"Retreat!" he heard one of the outlaws call and Guy's eyes quickly searched the scene. He couldn't see through the throng of soldiers fighting, but he cursed as he knew at least one had escaped. The old outlaw showed himself then, it was Stutley, Guy recalled. Stutley had two daggers, his wrinkled face spattered with blood. He fought with ferocity at Scarlett's side, guarding his flanks from oncoming enemy.

He heard the call of retreat again and this time, within moments, the camp was absent of any fighting except that of Scarlett and Stutley.

A kind of silence enveloped the camp. All other outlaws were gone, only Stutley and Scarlett stood side by side, circling with weapons clutched in their grips.

They were surrounded and the soldiers stood watching, ready to pounce with their blades. Scarlett's laboured breathing could be heard above the crackle of the dying fire.

Guy stepped forward through the soldiers. "I am not like him," he said, pointing to the Sheriff's body on the floor. "Lay down your weapons and we'll take you prisoner."

Scarlett laughed, pain etched onto his face. "I'm a dead man already, this wound will kill me in an hour if not a little more." The broad-shouldered, bearded man turned to his old friend. "You, Stutley, you can lay down if you want."

"Nah," said the older man, shaking his head. "I'd rather die than lay down for the likes of this lot." Stutley spat at Guy, a white mess splattered on his leather-clad breast.

Guy nodded. "I'm not a man partial to slaughter, so I'll make this quick." The half burned man gestured to his soldiers to fall back into the trees and clear the dead from the camp. His sword rose and he waited for Scarlett and Stutley to come forward.

The two outlaws took no time to question it and dove at Guy, their blades falling close to his body. Guy moved around, swinging his sword towards Scarlett's unguarded side. Stutley was there, his daggers stopping the blade and pushing it back.

Guy span on his heel, twisting backwards around the two and scoring his blade across Scarlett's back. The injured man fell to his knees with a groan. Stutley stepped in front of him, guarding while Guy stood back. A face of defeat was plastered on Stutley and he took one last run at Guy, using every bit of skill with his daggers he had. They flashed close to Guy's face and even closer to his neck. A lesser man would have been killed, but Guy of Gisborne was not a lesser man. His blade found Stutley's torso, entering through the bottom of the rib cage and into the heart. The dying man dropped his daggers to the floor and fell forward against Guy, his mouth close to his ear. Only dying breath could be heard and then he spoke. "Finish him quick," he said, his voice quiet and weak. "He's a good lad, better than the rest of us." Stutley fell to the ground, dead within moments.

Cheers went up from the trees where the soldiers watched on in awe. A man ran out, stumbling and half bent over. It was the Sheriff, he'd woken as he'd been moved into cover. The man was grasping a small knife in his hand, heading for Scarlett. Guy knew what the Sheriff's intention was, put out an eye maybe, run the blade up his spine. Anything to draw out the suffering for his own pleasure.

Guy stepped forward and blocked the Sheriff's way. "We're doing this quick," said Guy, quietly. "Don't make me stop you."

The Sheriff's hand went up, attempting to jab his blade into his neck. Guy caught his wrist and head-butted the Sheriff, the surrounding soldiers watched in silence as he crumpled to the ground unconscious.

Guy picked up the dagger and turned to Scarlett, he'd begun to cough up blood now and his green eyes fell on him. "You won't get Hood, Guy," Scarlett spat, a pained smile on his face. "No one can."

"We will see," said Guy, slicing the dagger across the dying man's throat. Blood poured from the open wound and the outlaw was dead in seconds. Guy turned back to the men after pulling his gaze from the figure of Scarlett. "We camp here until dawn, wake me when the

Sheriff comes around." Guy settled himself against a tree, away from the pools of blood around the camp. Sleep came easy that night. Not just because he was exhausted, but because he was in control. The Sheriff had been tamed and two of the outlaws killed. The outlaws had caused him and many other people much pain and misery over the years and to down two of them in one night gave him satisfaction beyond belief.

Chapter 23

It's not wise to assume a man who wanders is lost. However, Hood was lost. The bowman was adrift in the dark of the woods, without his bow, without his sword and without food or water. What bothered him most, though, was that he was without his brothers.

Hood had to use every bit of strength to turn from Scarlett and leave him to his fate, but to stay would have meant death. If the bowman were to die, he would not allow it to be in some nameless forest at the hand of a peasant soldier. So he had run, and in a bid to save his friend Gilbert, tossed his sword into a man's back.

When he had first met his group they were pawns to him. Disposable and only there to help his own advancement. They served him a purpose and would be dispatched, he'd decided, as soon as their loyalty faltered. Slowly, the passing of time had forged them. They were brothers and to harm one was to harm all.

As his eyes had fallen on the surrounded form of Scarlett, mortally wounded, he knew he would not have just lost one brother, but two. For old man Stutley knew better than any of them how important the bond between friends was. With age comes an ability to recognise how significant an iron forged friendship is and how meaningless life can be without one.

For some time Hood's arrogance had led him to believe that his brothers were the ones who needed to learn from him, but as life went by, he found there were many things he needed to learn from them.

Hood had wandered for most of the black night until the sun started to rise. The pale morning sky illuminated the path before him and led him from the mess of trees and shrubbery he'd been stumbling in all night.

He was bone tired and his eyes felt gritty. In the distance, he saw hovels spaced out far from each other with goats and such fenced close by, thin streams of smoke coming from their chimneys.

Hood walked by the first and saw an old man out the front, tipping the waste from his bucket. "Is there somewhere I can get a drink close by?" the bowman asked.

"You're in luck," smiled the old man. "Keep walking north of here for about five miles and there will be a tavern. It's small and only got the locals in. Some friendlier than others, mind."

"Thanks, I'll keep that in mind," replied Hood, starting to walk off. He turned back to him, as if forgetting something. "Have you seen anyone walk by recently?"

"No one who I don't recognise. You looking for someone?"

"Yes," said Hood. "I suppose I am." The bowman carried on, heading north for the tavern. The aim was of course to find his lost companions, but without sustenance he wouldn't get far.

The sun had risen fully by the time he reached the tavern. The building wasn't big and it had no name. Hood could only tell what it was by the people sitting out the front, tankards in their hands. There were more hovels closer together in this part, all surrounding the tavern and a well close by. "Oi," said a deep voice as Hood approached the thick door.

Hood turned, it was a big man, sitting with four others with two jugs of ale on the table. "Yes?" he said plainly, turning towards them. Hood was tired, any courtesy he possessed had disappeared along with his friends.

"You can't go in there, it ain't for outsiders," said the biggest of them, his hair was cut close to his scalp and his brow was heavy.

"Do any of you own this place?" asked Hood.

"Well, no, we don't but…"

"Then your words mean nothing," said Hood, shaking his head with irritation. The bowman walked through the door and shut it behind him. The room was warm and there were a few people sitting, eating with their faces close to their plate. They stopped and moved their eyes up to Hood, silence filling the room.

"No outsiders," said the man serving ale. He was tall and looked down at Hood, his eyes were hard and dark.

Hood removed his hat and closed his eyes tightly. "I've got money, a pouch of bloody coins right here," he said, tapping his side. "I'll eat, drink and leave."

"I said no outsiders!"

"Listen, you pig's arse," said Hood, loud enough for the customers to hear. "You'll serve me, cook me food and allow me to sit with this group of inbreeds to eat!"

"And what if I don't?" said the barkeep, his resolve stiffening.

"You heard of Hood?" he asked.

"Aye, I have."

"Good, so you've heard of what I do to men. I'll take their eyes, their limbs and spill their guts for little more than a glare. I'll burn their homes, kill their sons, my brothers will have their daughters and I always get what I fucking want in the end."

The barkeep had softened his look now and unfolded his arms.

Hood dropped his head and put his hands on the counter. "I've killed for far less than to have the pleasure of paying for my own breakfast. Now, get me food, get me ale and don't bother me while I eat."

The man nodded and moved off into the back, the sizzle of meat and eggs erupting from the hole in the door. Hood took himself a seat in the corner and a jug of ale with a clay cup was brought to him. The bowman took his time eating, savouring every bite and washing it down with the fresh ale before him.

The full stomach and no sleep had made him drowsy, but to sleep now would be foolish. He'd find himself dead or in the hands of Guy. Hood rose from his seat and walked to the barkeep. When he saw Hood approach, the man was on edge, fearing the worst. Hood dipped his fingers into his pouch and handed him a silver coin.

"I'm sorry, but I don't have change for this much," the worry in his voice warmed Hood. The power his name had; his reputation preceded itself in these smaller villages.

"Keep it, I'll be on my way," Hood turned and stopped by the open fire to warm his hands before leaving. "Oh, barkeep, have you by any chance seen any other strangers walking through here?"

The door swung open then and the big man who had been sitting outside came storming in. "Ah," said Hood, still staring down at the fire. "Full of liquid courage now, are we?"

The big man ignored him and his four friends came in behind. "Did you serve this wretch, Ted?" he asked the barkeep.

"Yes," he said. "That man's Hood, now I've got my rules, but they aren't worth my life."

The big man laughed as he looked at Hood. "This little fairy ain't Hood. Just because we've had royal soldiers passing through every pissing village asking where he is, don't mean this is him."

"What?" said Hood. "How many groups?" The bowman knew word would be spreading. After all, the Sheriff was distant family to the King, as was Athella. Family of the King being kidnapped wasn't going to go unnoticed or unpunished.

"Shut up, worm," said the big man, swiping his hand back towards Hood's face.

Hood moved and caught the arm, bringing it down over his knee. The arm snapped and bone emerged from the skin. The man screamed and his friends came for the bowman. Hood grabbed a poker from next to the fire and skewered it into an enemy's eye. The man dropped with no sound, dead on impact. He pulled his weapon from the enemy's skull and pointed it towards them. The group were stuck in place while the big one was still wailing about his arm.

"You tell whichever soldiers you see that I've been here. Tell them to follow Hood and when they find me, they'll find their death." Hood walked for the door and the men parted as he came close. The sunlight made his eyes narrow as he stepped from the building. "Death always seems to follow me, wherever I bloody go," he said under his breath. Hood set off once more. He knew he was off track and he'd heard the people in the tavern talk of the coast. It was to the east, so he would head there and search for the bay in which Eustace spoke of. Trying to find prints would prove fruitless, he'd lost them long ago and would require much backtracking. So he walked on, fixing his hat back on his head and cleaning the bloody fire poker on the grass. A man was leading his horse through a field close by and Hood shouted for him to stop. "You there," he said, sticking the poker in the ground next to him. "I'll buy that horse from you for this gold piece," his fingers dipped into his pocket to retrieve the coin.

The man was old and shorter than Hood, his eyes almost white. "Well, I appreciate the offer, young man, but this is my horse, he's not for sale."

"One gold piece and I spare your life, or I kill you and take it anyway, it's your choice."

The old man grumbled his disagreement and led the horse to the bowman, opening his hand for the coin.

"Wise choice," said Hood, hopping onto the horse's bare back. He'd ridden without a saddle a few times and it wasn't his first choice, but he'd have to make do.

As he rode further out of the village, he saw the man he'd seen earlier, who told him about the tavern that morning. He was walking with a dog and a few goats, humming quietly to himself. The man smiled and waved. "Does lovely food, doesn't it?"

"To die for!" shouted Hood, waving his poker in the air.

Chapter 24

"I can see the sea!" shouted Athella, excitement in her voice. No one replied and she looked around at the group. "Are you not all happy? After all this?"

A sullen Gilbert walked behind, Hood's sword in his hand. John was beside Athella, a grim look on his face and Eustace strode ahead, tired and depleted.

The tall monk turned to face Athella. "I think we're all feeling the loss, Athella."

"We can't do anything about their deaths, they knew the risks of being outlaws, you all do!" she snapped.

"He's not dead," roared Gilbert, his face dark. "Hood's not dead!"

Athella felt a sudden fear rush through her as the giant almost lost control.

"Calm, Gilbert," said John, softly. "He'll find us, he always has a plan."

"Well, we're at the bloody sea now! Can't we wait here for him, Eustace? Can't your ship wait?"

"We shall see," said the monk, continuing to walk. Hood's bow and quiver of arrows were slung over his shoulders next to his back. He didn't believe Hood was dead just yet and the chances were good that he'd be on their tail. But so were other men, who would get to them first was the question.

"Where will your ship be?" asked John.

"A mile or two from here, we'll walk along the cliff edge until there's a route down to the bay.

The group continued on their path swiftly, Eustace quickening the pace. Behind them, the land was uneven and enemy troops could be on the crest of any hill. For Eustace, the night Stutley and Scarlett had been killed was a sad one. He didn't know them overly well, but he saw their bond, he saw the bond between them all. It hurt them that their own were killed and hurt them even more that their leader was absent. In truth, John would be a great addition to his crew, however Gilbert, he needed to be controlled and there was only one man that could do that – Hood. Without the bowman to guide him, he would be unpredictable and no doubt fight amongst his crew.

"There she is!" said Eustace, stopping with a great smile upon his face.

"I ain't ever seen a boat like that before," said an awestruck Gilbert.

"You've got quite the crew, don't you?" said John, looking down on them. The men from where they stood looked like ants. Some were sitting and some were moving around the deck or shore, shifting crates or gambling.

"Ho, Master!" bellowed Eustace at the top of his lungs.

The tiny faces on the ship turned to him, their bodies stock still. Then a roar came up from them, loud and ferocious.

"Your crew are happy to see you," said John, a smile on his face. "How did you know they'd be here?"

"This bay is a safe place for us, we've stopped here many times in the past to regroup."

Gilbert did not cheer up at the prospect of meeting the crew, his head was down and he still gripped onto Hood's sword tightly.

The group walked across the beach until they reached the ship, Eustace was leading the way, far in front and eager to see his crew. Most of them had come down onto the beach and an old man stood at the front of them. The old man's back was straight and his face was one of serenity. Eustace powered into him and gripped him in a great hug, slapping him on the back. The rest of the crew surrounded the monk, greeting him excitedly. Eustace went to each man, calling them by their name and giving them words.

The old man stepped towards John, Athella and Gilbert. "Did these people aid you, Eustace?"

Eustace stepped back from his men and beside Master. "These people rescued me." He neglected to tell him that Athella was, in fact, a captive, although, there by choice it seemed now.

"We didn't rescue him," said Gilbert, his face emotionless. "Hood rescued him, we just killed people."

"Well, I thank you all for playing a part, all of the crew do," said Master. "Where is this Hood?"

"We lost him not long ago," said Eustace. "We shall wait a short while though, he's a resourceful man."

The crews' attention was caught by something, their heads all shifting to the distance. Master looked past them too, his eyes narrowing. "Is this your Hood?"

Eustace turned and saw many horses lining the cliff top in the distance, staring down at them. "No, they are not our friends."

"Why the hell is there so many?" gasped John.

"It was only a matter of time before the royal notice reached every town and city within a hundred miles. A King's man calls and his soldiers come," said Athella, her face unreadable.

"Are you enjoying this?" shouted John, pushing her shoulder. "You want to go with them? You can. You knew that a long time ago."

Athella said nothing, her face was one of shock.

"Despite what she wants, I think it's time to board," said Master. The old man turned towards the ship and the crew parted for him to climb the rope ladders first.

"We can't leave," said Gilbert, his eyes not veering from the continuous line of soldiers on the cliff.

John went to him and lay a hand on his shoulder. "What would Hood want you to do? Would he want you to wait here and die for him, or leave on this boat, giving us a chance to find him again?"

Gilbert dipped his head and pulled himself towards the ship. "I'd be able to take them," he said muttering under his breath. "Hood will expect me to be with you lot though won't he, so I best get on this damned ship." The giant turned and pushed through the crew, making a man fall as he did so. The crew almost came at him at that point, but Eustace stopped them and led Gilbert up the ladder.

Everyone else made their way on the boat swiftly by climbing ropes or the main ladder. It didn't take long for the ship to get pushed out into the water. Oars were extended and the sails were being readied.

Eustace was in his element once more, everyone could see it and the crew revelled at the sight. Master stood back, smiling, enjoying seeing the man back at work. "Why aren't they moving for us?" asked Gilbert, almost disappointed watching as the troops lining the cliffs watched from their places.

"There would be no point," replied John. "They know they're too late, by the time they get to the beach we'd be too far out."

Eustace came and stepped alongside them, the monk's eyes narrowing. "They're moving now, but to where?"

The horsemen began to gallop off, some circling around the back of the line with speed. The dust from a hundred horses began to billow into the air, clouding the blue sky behind. "What the bloody hell are they going after?" said John, watching with confusion.

"Look, over there!" pointed Eustace, his finger moving as the ship bobbed up and down. Not far down the cliff line there was a single rider, a stream of dust coming up from behind him. The soldiers raced after the rider, the odd arrow narrowly missing him. All the men on the ship were thinking it, but no one would say it. Except Gilbert, it burst from his mouth before anything could be confirmed.

"That's Hood, he's here. We must wait!" ordered the giant.

"I'm afraid we cannot," said Eustace. "If it even is Hood, if he came down to the beach and we waited, those horsemen would have the boat in moments."

"He ain't coming down on the beach," said John, his hand running over his dark hair. "That man's got another idea in mind."

The lone horseman was riding fast, his head down heading for an overhang on the high cliff. "Make for the cliff!" ordered Eustace, swinging the wheel with all his might. The ship jerked and began to angle towards the towering cliff.

Master stood next to Eustace, watching him make his movements and orders. "There are rocks there, Eustace, hidden by unpredictable waves. The ship could be smashed to pieces and many could die."

"Could, Master, but they will not. Not while I'm at the wheel of this ship. Not while this crew's lives are in my hands."

"There is a fine line between confidence and arrogance, Eustace, do not let one blur with the other, especially not when stakes are this high."

"Honour," muttered Eustace, powering the ship through the choppy waves. "You taught me that honour is a quality that stands above the rest. If one lives their life with honour, people can learn from it, evil people, good people and even great people. A person with no honour lives in spite. A person with no honour…"

"Is not a person," finished off Master. "They are simply an animal."

"Yes, you see?" asked Eustace.

Master nodded his old head and moved back down to the deck, keeping the oarsmen in time. Whichever crew were free had their eyes up at the cliff, but the lone horseman had moved out of sight. All that could be seen were the milling enemy soldiers heading down the mass of land to the edge of the precipice.

A dark shadow moved over the whole boat as the ship moved in. The crash of the waves against the rock became more intimate, as if they'd moved into a hollow. All men were thinking the same, if whoever it was above them jumped, it'd be a miracle they didn't get their body smashed against the jutting rocks. "He should've jumped by now," said Gilbert, his eyes up at the extending cliff above.

Then they saw it. A figure from above the ship appeared. Whoever it was had leapt, it was no dive, the act had been urgent. Arrows flew past the man and into the water below. When they hit the waves there wasn't a great splash, the sea just carried on as normal, ignoring the body that had been flung into it. Deckhands ran to the side of the ship where he'd entered the water, John, Gilbert and Athella craned their necks over the side, searching for the body. There was no sign. John's eyes were wild searching, he'd allowed the possibility of Hood to enter his mind, and for that he was now being tortured by hope.

A face appeared in the water, their mouth was open gasping for breath. It was Hood, his dark hair was stuck to his head and his eyes were wide with life. A rope was hauled over the side for him and he held onto it tightly while the men dragged him aboard. Hood fell over the deck and collapsed on the boards, his eyes shut and his chest heaving for air. Sea spray from the rough waters below splashed over the side and onto his face.

"Give the man space," Eustace had ordered, still standing at the wheel looking down at them.

Gilbert knelt down beside him, his huge hand patting Hood's shoulder. The movement of his hand was light and fast, as if it were urgency and gentleness combined. "I told them it was you, Hood, I told them, but they didn't listen, they thought you was gone."

"Ehm, we didn't think he was gone, Gilbert," said John, kneeling next to Hood. "We just weren't sure when he was going to get back to us."

Hood opened his eyes and propped himself up onto his elbows. He nodded towards Athella who was standing at his feet looking down at him. The sunlight shone on her, creating an angelic glow. She smiled at him, though to Hood, it did not seem sincere. "That bitch was going to stab me with my own knife. Stutley and Scarlett died because of her."

Athella stood back, her glare turning into a scowl. "How dare you," she started.

"You tried to what?" said Gilbert, the dark mask covering his face once more as he began to rise."

John put his arm out in front of Gilbert and spoke softly. "Hood needs some rest. We all do. Once we're all in our right minds and our tempers are even then we'll discuss this."

Gilbert turned his huge body to John, his chest pushed out. John was big, bigger than most of Eustace's crew, but Gilbert was something else. "Hood's the one who's in charge here, John, not you. We do what he says, so if he wants me to pick that skinny cow up and throw her overboard, then that's what I'll do. If he wants me to rip off her arm and eat it raw, then that's what I'll do."

John was ready to fight, Gilbert's words had worked their way into him.

"Now, now, children, calm yourselves," said Hood, rising onto his feet. "We've only just escaped death from those bastards up there, let us live a little before slaying each other." The young bowman turned to Gilbert. "Remember this, my friend, this is Eustace's ship, I'm not in charge here. That means whatever he says, we do."

Gilbert nodded, the fury flowing from him. "Sorry, John, didn't mean to get nasty."

John sighed and his handsome face began to smile. "Show Hood what you saved for him."

Gilbert moved his hands to his side with excitement, unbuckling the jewelled sword that John had given the bowman as a gift. "Been keeping it safe for you."

"Ah!" said Hood. "The sword that saved both of us. I thank you, my friend. But where is my bow?"

"Eustace has it," said John, looking up at the tall, grey man at the wheel. Eustace had powered against the waves and the ship was moving back out into the calmer waters. With that came arrows from above.

None of them hit, most glanced off the deck.

Hood looked up as they were sailing away, the horses lined the edges of the cliff, looking down on them. One man looked over for longer than any others, Hood thought he may jump himself. It was Guy, Hood could feel his stare. Guy had been the first to see him when he rode towards the cliff, he had thundered after him, a hunger for death in his eyes.

Hood raised his hand and gave a wave to the horsemen watching on, most turned at that, he'd hoped the Sheriff had seen it. Guy, however, did not turn, as the ship sailed out further and further Guy had remained until he was a speck on the horizon. Hood swore he could still feel the man's wrath as he stood at the front of the ship, staring out. "He's never going to stop," the bowman said to himself.

"The sea is known to make people go mad," said Eustace from behind. "But not after half a day. What's on your mind, Hood?"

"Ask any man in Nottingham and they'll confirm to you how mad I am. Where are we off to anyway?"

Eustace smiled. "We're off to see a French prince and earn some gold."

Chapter 25

One year later

Time and experience are the two things that mould perspective. Sometimes no time is needed at all and one profound experience can twist a man's perspective in moments. Often though, many small experiences over the course of a considerable amount of time does it.

Hood had made a substantial fortune under Eustace. He owned property in the lush hills of France, with servants and gardeners to tend to his land and a mass of treasure hidden under his home. Home. A word that lacked any solid meaning to the bowman. For a man who's spent most of his life on the hard floor of forests, the word home is foreign.

The bowman had heard from travellers and English pirates that the name Hood carried a meaning to the people back in England. It gave power to the common person and took it away from the privileged, for Hood was the one man to strike them where it hurts and prosper while doing so. He and his brothers had taken the King's kin, Athella, and slain her sister. He'd outrun Guy of Gisborne and the Sheriff, storming their homes and leaving them to burn in another. Hood had sat with the men who had told him these stories from across the sea, they had been in awe of the bowman, constantly wishing to hear more tales of his time in England. Hood had been able to tell many, for every man he met told him a new one he had not heard. They were all heroic, spun with honour and duty, saving men and women from the vileness of raping lords or the death of the gallows. Hood did nothing to correct them. If he were to let them know the truth of the deeds that were carried out, he had no doubt that they'd either run or turn their knives on him.

Hood had finally found the fame he'd been searching for all these years, the commoners of England had made him invincible now. Even if death found him in this foreign country or on one of Eustace's sea battles, his name would live on further than a king's.

The thought of dying had often occurred to him in recent days, he wondered if he'd be fulfilled now, if he'd be able to die with contentment in his heart. The bowman thought back to the first night they'd beached in France.

Fires on the sand had been lit and meat had been cooked. Ale and wine were removed from the belly of the ship and consumed in large quantities. Hood drank with happiness and ate until his belly was full, he was finally away from Guy and the Sheriff, no more would he have to sleep with one eye open. The thought was a fine one.

Eustace had come beside him, sitting down heavily in the sand. "Do you think you will like it here with us, Hood?"

"I think if Gilbert settles in and John gets plenty of loot, then my life will be made easy."

Eustace looked over at the huge form of Gilbert, drinking merrily with his crew. They knew a fighter when they saw one and with that came respect. Gilbert just needed a family to feel at ease and with the crew he had one. The older man's eyes turned to John then, he was sitting with Athella, they were close and facing the sea, her head on his shoulder. "I believe," said Eustace,

"Gilbert will be fine, I don't have any concerns as long as you're here for him. As for John, I don't believe his heart desires loot any longer."

Hood laughed, the sound full of humour. "The day that man's heart is not satisfied by loot is the day it ceases to beat."

"On the contrary, Hood, the day a man's heart is hooked by love is the day it no longer can be filled by anything else."

"If you say so, monk," smiled Hood, sipping on his cup of wine.

"Do you remember that village where I burned the house, where the Sheriff and Guy of Gisborne waited for you in the shadows?"

"How could I forget?"

"I met a woman there, before I'd found the house. It was in a whorehouse..."

"A whorehouse?" chuckled Hood. "I never took you for the sort."

"Yes, well a woman I met there, she was beautiful beyond imagination and her mind was quick like a whip. The words that came from her mouth were full of thought and intelligence. I'd thought I'd stumbled upon a priceless diamond in the steaming pile of dung."

"You devious bastard, you could have told us and all the lads could have stopped by!" said Hood, his voice light and playful.

"Alas, she did not work there; instead, she owned the establishment. It was foolish of me to even expect a woman of that calibre to work in such a place. She went on to tell me how her father was an important man, who went to fight in the Crusades with the old king. Her hair was red like a fox's and her eyes were green like sparkling emeralds."

Hood's mouth was straight now, no longer a smile, his eyes were glazed and Eustace could see the thoughts churning in his head.

Eustace continued. "She'd seen us enter the village, or heard, I'm not sure. She'd told me her name was Marian and she knew you, Hood. She asked me to tell you not to be a stranger." The monk's face was blank, he was looking into Hood's eyes, reading his next move.

Hood dropped his head slowly. "Why didn't you tell me?" his voice was calm, quiet even.

"I just did."

"Then," said Hood, his voice raised. "Why did you not tell me then?"

"I've never met a woman like that, Hood, and I know the chances are that she had your heart in her hand. If I were to tell you then, or when we were in England, you would not be with us, you would go back to her and you would be caught. Perhaps not right away, but you would be, Guy would be upon you. You saved my life, Hood, it's only fair I save yours."

Now Hood sat a year later, Marian haunting his thoughts. He was atop a hill where they were camped a mile away from a town they were assigned to raid the next day. Hood could see down into a mass of trees that Eustace and his men were sitting within. They sat in a large spiralling circle with Master in the middle leading their chant. Small candles were lit so it would not give away their position, but Hood could make them out. The monk's order prayed to some deity that was supposed to give them strength and luck; they told Hood that it allowed Master to see speckles of the future.

Hood was not convinced, but if it worked for them,

then they could do as they please. Gilbert sat next to him, he had his knees bent, watching over them with a wary eye. Gilbert's hate for priests crossed over slightly to every other man of faith from time to time. He largely forgot that his new friends were worshippers, but on nights like this it made him uncomfortable.

Three months earlier Eustace had married Athella and John, their lives being bound by the order in which the monk belonged. For a while they thought nothing of it, but now they joined in on the chants, they sat in the spiral with their eyes shut and their hands joined humming to unknown words.

"We shouldn't be sat alone up here, Hood," said Gilbert.

"Why shouldn't we?"

"Could be assassins, King John's sent over two already for you, why wouldn't he send a third?"

"If a third was sent, you know what would happen to them, Gilbert."

"I'm not sure I do, but I know I'd enjoy watching, whatever it was," replied the giant with a sadistic grin.

The first of the assassins that were sent almost got him; they'd asked to join Eustace's crew and was a welcome addition. For a while he joined in with the rest of them, pitching in with work, gambling, fighting when he needed to. His name was Thomas, his hair was short and his face ordinary. Hood had actually come to quite like the man. It wasn't until they were sailing down the coast of France and edging towards Spanish waters that he was set upon by Thomas. Their ship was attacked during the night by a Spanish vessel, all of the crew were roused and called to deck. Thomas had donned his leather plate and gotten a lace snagged on one of the support beams, apparently knotting it tightly with his own hands. He called for Hood as he was about to go on deck and the bowman came to his aid. When all the men were above fighting, Thomas took his chance, a thin dagger emerged from his side and he thrust it towards Hood's stomach. The bowman instinctively backed away, allowing it to slice the skin. Hood didn't let confusion overwhelm him, he left the questions of the mind for later. If a man stops and thinks in a situation such as that, then he'd find his guts on the floor.

Hood had pulled his own sword and they danced below deck for a while, but there's only so long a man with a knife can last on open ground against a skilled swordsman. Hood decided to disarm him instead of killing him right away. Once the Spanish vessel had been vanquished, Hood had brought Thomas to the top of the deck and gave an exhibition of his bow game. This time he allowed Thomas to climb to the crow's nest and shoot down at Hood, who stood on the edge of the bowsprit, water sloshing beneath him and his arms extended, welcoming the arrow.

The crew had watched with joy as Thomas's arrow had flown by Hood, the water swallowing it whole. Thomas had panicked then and launched himself from the crow's nest and into the water. Hood's bow was dropped to the deck, one of the men captured it and handed it back to the bowman. He thought about shooting his assassin, but they were miles from the coast and the waters were riddled with sharks. It would be too kind to finish him off as he swam.

The second assassin had been less clandestine, less cunning altogether. They were in a tavern in a city controlled by their ally prince in France and a beautiful woman was hanging off every word Hood had said, laughing at his jokes and buying him jugs of ale. Hood knew from the moment she disclosed she was not a whore that she would be an assassin, for he'd never met a woman so forward that did not have a price. In this case, the price was his life and a second after she'd closed the bedroom door behind them, he knew she'd have her dagger ready. As the lock clicked, she turned and saw his bowstring was pulled, an arrow pointed to her chest from the other side of the room. She gave up the act and ran at him with desperate rage. She fell with an arrow in her chest before her third step was taken.

Hood was touched by the lengths England was taking to have his life. The next time though, and there would be a next time, he would be more than ready.

The chants were done now and the candles were out. The crew would be sleeping where they prayed and Hood and Gilbert finally went down to join them. Two men were set to patrol that night, Hood would have preferred four, but he would not make such a request in front of any of the men.

Hood lay down near Gilbert, amongst the many sleeping bodies of the crew. Master came over to him, kneeling down beside the bowman. His dark eyes were friendly, full of compassion. It was hard to believe they belonged to the same man when he was on the battlefield, Hood had not seen a finer swordsman. Except maybe one, but Hood did not want to think his name. "You're ready for battle tomorrow, Hood?"

"Ready as I'll ever be. Hope you had a chant in there for me?"

Master smiled. "Always for you, Hood."

Chapter 26

Hood climbed up the side of the stone house and onto the sloped roof, from here he could see almost everything in the town square. There were around fifty of Eustace's men, all expertly trained in combat. Not the type of combat one would see in a duel, but the type of combat that required something a bit more deadly. They'd use their surroundings, anything they could find at all. Take the ornately decorated gate in Hood's line of sight for example. A beautiful piece of ironwork, patterns twisting in the centre and large spikes lined the edges. The spikes were blunt, slightly rounded at the edges, but with enough force, they could crush a man's skull. That's what he'd seen one of the crew do. The man had lost his sword, disarmed by a soldier with more skill, and kicked to the floor. The crewman grabbed a handful of fine gravel and tossed it into the enemy's face. The soldier clawed at his eyes with one hand and waved his sword with the other. With that, the crewman was up, and in one swift motion, the soldier's skull was being pounded off the now crimson-stained gate. These men were true fighters, vicious bastards to the core.

Hood fired arrow after arrow from the rooftop. The bowman was on form today, never missing a shot he took. Even when the few armoured guards came, Hood's arrows found their way through the eye-slits in the helmet, or the gap between the torso and groin plate.

A cheer went up from Eustace's men as they

gathered in the town square and the last of the soldiers ran off through nearby alleys. The crew were split into parties of ten to sniff them out and each group given a trumpet to blow if the enemy began to regroup.

Hood saw Gilbert from the rooftop, he was lathered in blood, his face thick with it. Eustace did not permit rape during assaults, if a man wanted to rut then he needed to find a whorehouse. But the bowman knew Gilbert better than anyone, better than the giant knew himself. Once Gilbert started fighting, his bloodlust would fuel his appetite for something more carnal. So he'd seen Gilbert slip down one of the alleys, presumably looking for fleeing enemies, but Hood knew his true target.

In assaults, Athella had stood behind the men or on top of a building, firing arrows and killing where she could. She had initially wanted to learn to fight with the sword, but it had proven too heavy for her frame, the weight of it dragging her slight body wherever she swung it. To John's relief, she no longer wanted to learn the sword and instead wished to know how to shoot a bow. Hood was sceptical at the idea of teaching the Sheriff's sister how to use a weapon that could kill from a distance. The bowman did not trust her, he didn't know whether this was because she was slowly taking John from him, or because he believed she wanted to kill him. Either way, he taught her what she needed to know, the rest could only be learned by practising when she found the time. However, the best lessons were learned on the battlefield, when pressure is mounting and live targets are moving to kill you or your allies.

Now the battle was over, John moved to her, laughing with the relief that follows a fight when you know your loved ones are safe. He didn't seem to check on Hood anymore, rather, he just expected him to be alive. Everyone did for that matter, Hood was a man marked as unkillable. In fact, he'd heard rumours that enemy forces were promised riches or a place in the royal guard if they delivered his head.

"You're getting slow," said Hood as he walked to Eustace. The monk's axe was covered in blood and a shallow cut was on his side.

The monk scowled. "There were three of them and you could have at least taken one."

Hood smiled and patted his hand on Eustace's back. "I just wanted to see you move that axe a bit, it's encouraging for a man to see his leader in action."

Eustace gave a wry smile back. "You have no leader, Hood, everyone knows that."

"I wasn't talking about me."

"You two," said Master, the old man's sword was sheathed and tiny specks of blood covered his robe. "Come with me, I need assistance."

Hood and Eustace followed Master through the narrow streets, a soldier darted in front of them and arced his sword down at Master. The old man swerved back and drew his own sword with a backhanded swipe, angling it up and into the man's neck.

"Where are we going?" asked Hood, stepping over the dead man.

"A place these barbarians deem holy, where vileness and devilry are spread through the streets," replied Master.

"In other words wherever we're paid to," said Hood, sarcasm in his voice. Hood didn't mind doing as the prince bid them. He paid generously and the skirmishes served as a well-needed distraction for Hood. Distraction from what though, Hood did not know. All he knew was that when he sat, when they had no purpose, no orders or no mission, most of the crew turned bitter or angry, souring the mood. Self-reflection can do that to a man whose soul is unsettled.

The three men came to a building with heavy oak doors lined with bronze casting. The doors were ajar and a heavy perfume filtered out into the street. The smell was sour and musty, like herbs being burned.

When they entered, their weapons were drawn and an arrow was notched in Hood's bow ready for any further resistance. The room before them was long and the ceilings were high, painted with scenes of blood and sacrifice.

At the end of the room there was a raised platform, velvet cushions and garish fabrics piled to create a seat of sorts. A smoking pipe that was raised from the floor sat before the heap material. Something seemed to move within the cushions and blankets, then a croaky voice emerged. "You seek to kill me?"

Hood's eyes narrowed and he saw a face, small and wrinkled like one of the many fabrics. The old woman's body blended perfectly into the cloth.

"We seek to end your evil," said Master, his voice even.

"How righteous you are. You kill an old woman because someone has told you I'm evil. Not only that, but I believe you're paid. Tell me, would you have killed me if your pocket was not being lined with gold?"

"I can put an arrow through her now, Master, just say the word," said Hood.

The old woman cackled, the laugh haunting. Her dark eyes moved past Master and onto Hood. "Ah finally, the lost boy with the bow decides to speak. You know, you've doomed these men, you've doomed your crew. Iron Mask seeks blood, he seeks vengeance. He was not done with you and you knew he was not."

Hood's face twisted with confusion trying to sew together her words.

The old woman laughed once more, this time it was guttural, echoing through the hall. "Even as we speak, he's close to your friend, the vile giant, the one that took his kin. Of course, he plans to kill him and it was your actions, bowman, that led to that."

For once in his life, Hood was left speechless. The man wanted to lift his bow and shoot his arrow into her rotten heart, but his arms would not move.

The old woman went to speak again, inhaling before expelling her words. However, she didn't manage to get them out. Eustace had raised his axe above his head and catapulted it through the air at the old woman. The axe blade lodged itself deeply into her chest, crushing through the bone and organs until the edge clove through her back.

Not even a sigh came from her mouth as she fell back into the pillows. Her black eyes were open and her long, greasy hair fell over her face. Eustace walked to her and heaved his axe from her body. As he did so, the old woman came to life, jolting forward at the monk, a long, sharp hiss erupting from her. Eustace stepped back suddenly, shock plastered on his face. The crone fell back once more as Hood's arrow drove into her forehead, forcing her to the floor.

Eustace and Hood looked to one another, Master was stood staring at her, his face unreadable. "She said someone's slaying my friend," said Hood, his voice cold.

"She is a mad woman, listen not to what she says," replied Eustace, but the bowman had already left, the door open behind him.

Chapter 27

Hood ran back through the alley in which they came, hopping over the dead soldier that lay where Master had slain him. The bowman moved quickly back to the town square, pushing past screaming civilians and part of his own crew. Hood knew only two people that could be considered giant and the prospect of any of them dying galled him deeply.

Hood heard screaming and a familiar laugh from one of the avenues, the deep, childlike laughter that could only come from one man. Hood ran towards the sound. "Gilbert!" he shouted.

Gilbert stepped from a doorway down the narrow street, the dopey smile falling from his blood-covered face. "Hood, I ain't doing nothing wrong," he said, his breeches hastily pulled up. "There was a soldier in there and I killed him. We've gotta kill all the soldiers, it's what Eustace told us. You said yourself we do what he says."

A young woman tried to run from the doorway then, but Gilbert's huge hand stopped her, throwing her back into the home.

Hood had no time for it, relief had flowed through him now that he had seen his friend alive and well. The relief, however, was short-lived, for if Gilbert was fine, John may not have been. He thought then of the old woman's words *'the one that took his kin'* John had taken Athella from the Sheriff and when it comes to vengeance, the Sheriff knows no bounds.

"Gilbert, for God's sake leave the woman alone,"

said Hood. Eustace did not permit the rape of women during raids and Hood would usually do all he could to stop Gilbert from following such atrocious instincts. But right now the bowman felt he had no time, he'd turned from Gilbert and began to run once more into the direction of the town square.

Hood finally reached the square and most of the crew that had been sent out were back now, some were sitting around quietly, some were chatting amongst themselves others were even laughing. The bowman saw Athella at the far end, sitting with one of the crewmen, pointing to the roof in which she placed herself during the battle. "Where's John?" Hood asked, the urgency of his eyes weren't missed by the woman.

"He went into that tavern over there," she said, pointing across the square. "Why, what's wrong?"

"And no one went with him?"

"Why would we? There's no one left to kill."

"You damn fool!" he hissed, turning from her and running towards the tavern doors. Before he could reach them, the doors were booted open, and John emerged with two casks of ale under his arms.

"Drinks are on me, you bastards!" roared John. The crewmen gave a hearty cheer and moved towards the tavern, collecting tankards and bowls.

Hood stared at him in disbelief, words failing to escape him.

"What's wrong with you, my friend? You look like you've seen a ghost," said John, concern in his tone.

Hood sat down on a nearby wall, he began to feel the dripping sweat on his head and his heart pounding in his chest. "I feel like I have, John."

Gilbert watched as Hood ran away down the alley.

Gilbert hadn't lied to Hood, there was a soldier in the woman's home, only he was dead now and just his wife remained. The giant ducked back through the door frame and saw the woman trying to scramble from the window at the other side of the room. "Oh no you don't," said Gilbert, taking two vast steps towards her and pulling her back.

She fell and yelped as her head bounced from the windowsill. She spoke words to him in a foreign tongue, words of pleading and mercy. Gilbert took no notice though, even if they were English, the sound would have been drowned out by all of his other senses.

Gilbert bore down on her, on all fours staring at her face. His hot, rancid breath made it difficult for her to breathe and saliva strung out of his open mouth. The spit touched her face and she flinched with revulsion. The giant's concentration broke and he roared with fury as a blunt knife was jabbed into his calf. He let go on the woman and turned to see her husband crawling away, blood leaking from his body.

Gilbert shifted after him and dragged him back. The soldier tried to bite him but that only made Gilbert angrier. The giant shoved his fingers into the top of his mouth and then stuffed whatever fingers he could fit against the bottom set of teeth. "Bite me, will you? You'll not be biting anything again." Gilbert pulled as hard as he could, ripping the jaw away from the skull. The man was making a sound he'd never heard before. The closest thing to it he could think of was when he was riding a horse back in England, they'd stole it from one of the manors in Nottingham. The horse was too small for Gilbert, its joints already being crushed by his weight. The horse had lost its footing when they were crossing a shallow river and fell. The leg buckled and snapped, bone jutting from the skin and impaling the horse's body. The sight wasn't pretty and Stutley almost immediately released it from its pain.

Gilbert looked down at the man before him, the skin on his cheeks was torn to his ears. He was a mess. "No one's gonna save *you* from the pain, are they?" he said with a smile on his flat face.

The giant turned back to his original conquest – the woman. She was quivering in the corner now, her head tucked tightly to her chest. The dying man's screams had suddenly stopped and he heard the scrape of metal on bone. "What fool has spared him of the pain that was promised to him?" Gilbert slowly turned and saw a man standing above the soldier, a bloody sword in his hand. The man was smaller than Gilbert, though still bigger than the average. He wore a fine black tunic underneath chainmail painted the same colour, his boots and leggings were finely made and by all accounts he looked like a noble.

Apart from one thing, one detail that had made Gilbert take a second look. His whole face was covered by an iron mask, leather straps were fastened around his head where patchy black hair tufted through. Iron Mask made the first move, swinging his sword at the giant. Gilbert was unarmed, his weapon in the corner of the room, propped against a far wall. Iron Mask's sword sliced into Gilbert's leg and he screamed with fury, grabbing the next sword thrust with both hands, trying to force it from the enemy.

His huge hands bled and the floor was becoming slick with crimson. The sword was close to Gilbert's gut, penetrating the grip on his hands slowly. Then in one instant, Iron Mask had let go of the handle, spinning in a fluid motion around the back of Gilbert, the pool of blood on the floor supplying the means to do so. The assailant had removed two daggers from his belt as he moved, slicing them across Gilbert's Achilles heels.

Gilbert cried out with pain and tipped forward, his weight tearing the tendons further. The sight was like a great tree being felled, slowly plunging onto the sword he held in his grip. Iron Mask moved alongside the body of Gilbert and kicked him onto his side, the protruding blade not allowing any further movement.

"Who…?" said Gilbert, the words struggling to come from his mouth.

His enemy unbuckled the straps on his mask ceremoniously, pulling it off slowly.

Gilbert's eyes widened with astonishment and in that moment knew his fate. Iron Mask went on to pry Gilbert's mouth open with his knife and remove the tongue. Gilbert had seen this done before. It's a messy business removing a tongue, the blood loss can prove fatal and the pain is immense; he'd often giggled uncontrollably as Hood carried the act out in the past but the irony did not hold to him. By the time Iron Mask had finished, Gilbert had blacked out. The man had much strength in him and would most likely survive a little longer than a normal man would with his injuries.

Iron Mask rose, leaving his sword embedded in the dying giant. He fastened his mask back onto his face and stepped over Gilbert towards the woman in the corner. His leather gloved hand was held out in front of her and she looked up. He was weaponless it appeared and he'd just killed the man that intended to cause her harm, yet she still would not grab his hand. Iron Mask sighed and turned, making his way back to the door through which he'd entered. He stopped in the doorway and looked back at Gilbert, taking in the gruesome image, attempting to feel some form of retribution. Iron Mask left the house unsatisfied. "Perhaps another one will do it?" he thought.

Chapter 28

Hood had sat in the square enjoying a cup of the ale John had looted from the tavern. His nerves had receded and he'd felt almost foolish for taking the old woman's word as gospel. Why should he believe an old crone on her deathbed? Why would she warn him if she meant to cause pain?

The sun was beginning to set and Hood walked to the barrel of ale that had been split from the top. The bowman dipped his cup into it, bringing it back up with the sour liquid. The taste made his stomach churn, but the strong ale relaxed him, it's what was needed after a battle. For some men it worked the opposite way, the ale would cast a darkness on their mind and suddenly remorse would bubble to the surface, creating a sombre mood. Master was that type of man. The old man lived by discipline, he was known for having an impenetrable lock on his emotions. Alcohol unhinged him, Hood had never seen it, but Eustace had and it wasn't a pretty sight.

Hood saw Eustace and Master walking from the alley that he emerged from earlier. The bowman filled another cup for Eustace and walked over to him, offering it to the monk. "You two took your time, did that old woman spring back to life?" said the bowman, a smile on his face.

"Hood, you must come with me, bring John too," said Eustace, his voice soft and serious.

Hood said nothing, the smile vanished from his face and he went to collect John.

Master and Eustace stood in the doorway, their weapons drawn as John and Hood entered the house.

"Christ," said John, his voice a whisper.

Hood was quiet as he knelt down next to the great body of Gilbert. The giant's breathing was shallow and shuddering. Blood was still trailing from his mouth and his stomach wound was plugged by the sword that caused it.

Gilbert's dark eyes opened and tears began to form as he saw the small figure of Hood beside him. He tried to speak, but the sound just came out as a pained muffle.

Hood reached out and placed his hand on the side of Gilbert's head. "Don't speak, Gilbert, you don't trouble yourself with that," his voice was calm and his eyes did not leave the giant's own. "I'm sorry, Gil, but I've got to remove that sword. If I don't, you're going to be in an awful lot of pain for much longer than you'll care for."

Gilbert nodded and slowly curled his huge arm around Hood's crouching legs, pulling his head in close to the bowman. Hood held his hand tightly and stroked the back of Gilbert's head. He turned his eyes back to John and gave him a nod.

John bent down and grasped the handle of the sword, wrenching it from Gilbert's torso. The giant groaned with pain and squeezed Hood's grip.

"It's alright, Gil, there's no more pain now," said Hood, his tone hushed.

Blood began to pump from the wound onto the floor below and within moments Gilbert had taken his last breath. Hood dropped his head and the grip on his hand became loose. "Someone's gonna pay for this," he said, standing suddenly. "He may have been a bastard, but that was my big bastard." The bowman saw a woman in the corner, she hadn't moved since they'd entered. It was the same woman Gilbert had pushed back into the home from the street earlier. Hood rushed to her grabbing her by the clothing at her chest and jerking her up. "Who did this? Describe them to me or I promise you, you'll die a worse death than the one he was going to give you."

Eustace ran in and stood next to Hood, softly placing his hand on the bowman's chest. The monk knew not to force a man in circumstances surrounding death, during such times the mind is irrational and simple scenarios can turn ugly very fast. "She does not speak English, Hood, but she has spoken to me already, she's described the man responsible."

Hood let the weeping woman drop to the floor and turned to John, who still held the sword that had killed Gilbert in his hand. "Look at that sword. That, my friends, is an English sword. Not just any English sword, but a finely made one, fit for a man bred for fighting. Another thing to consider," said the bowman, stepping over the body of Gilbert and taking the sword from John's grip, "who would leave such a fine sword stuck in the body of a man who was destined to die from the wound anyway?"

"A man who wanted to inflict pain upon Gilbert," said John, his face still staring down at the mess.

"Exactly," said the bowman. "This isn't just an assassin. This is a man adamant to cause pain, a man absolutely determined for some form of revenge."

"Well who could it be?" said John. "How many rich Englishmen have we wronged over the past few years?"

"That's a figure only God himself will know," the bowman paused and looked down at Gilbert. "And Gil, he'll know now that he walks with angels."

"Aye," said John, his eyebrow raised curiously. "Angels."

Hood swung back to Eustace. "Luckily, this fine woman has given Eustace his description and we'll be able to identify him in moments."

Eustace shook his head solemnly. "I'm afraid not, Hood. It was as the old woman said, she described a man with a mask made from metal, strapped to his face. He wore black and carried knives on his belt. That was all she saw before she turned away from him, too scared to watch."

"Too scared my arse," said John. "We can get it out of her, whatever she's hiding."

Eustace's face darkened at that and Hood saw reason.

"I've had just about enough of blood and death for one day, John. But you're right, the woman would tell us something, except it probably wouldn't be the truth, and even if it was, how would we know it? The torture would be folly."

Eustace nodded in agreement. "I'll fetch some men to bring a cart to carry Gilbert's body. We need to leave here before nightfall. We've done what we needed to and now it's time to go, reinforcements will be on their way and it won't pay to be stuck in this town when that happens."

Men such as Hood don't like to show their emotions. They think it's a sign of weakness, that it'll hold them back or open them up to more pain. When it comes to a fight, they're right. Allow yourself to feel fear during a battle then your opponent will see it, they'll sense it and leech onto every bit. Arrogance or anger can be equally as deadly. With arrogance, you'll underestimate your opponent and your performance will falter eventually, a chink in the armour will reveal itself. Anger's a different creature altogether. Anger can make a man too eager, lunge for a gap that was open for the sole purpose of creating a lure.

Perhaps that's why the others have died and Hood and John have not. Gilbert was a man of fury, Scarlett was a man of passion, eagerness enveloping him. Stutley was careful, better than most, but the emotion he felt for Scarlett overwhelmed his judgement. Now they were dead.

Hood and John had taken the body of Gilbert away from the crewmen after they'd left the town. They dug the grave themselves, it was wide enough for a bull and a foot deeper than a normal man would need. Once he was lowered in they called for the crew, many of them had pleasant words for the giant.

When they'd first arrived aboard the ship, everyone, including Gilbert, had been apprehensive. The man wasn't known for being overly friendly and his temper was as brittle as a leaf in autumn. But he was warmly welcomed and in the end, even Master had grown to find flecks of likeability in the brute.

Hood had lowered his dead friend's longsword on to him as the others had gathered. He didn't say any words, he didn't need to, for the giant would know the feelings that lay in Hood's heart. The bowman turned away and headed back down to their camp while the crew threw handfuls of dirt down onto Gilbert.

John came and walked alongside him. "He'd be happy with that, he liked having a fuss made over him."

"True," said the bowman. "Strange though isn't it."

"What's strange?"

"Two weeks ago we lost Piers, those sodding barbarians speared him through the throat. He'd been with this crew for four years and he was thrown in a ditch with a copper on his tongue. Completely forgotten about."

"That's because Piers was a sod," replied John.

"And Gilbert wasn't? He must have killed a parish full of holy men, raped more women than I have hairs on my head. And I know he's killed children, some not old enough to hold a bloody spoon."

"Aye," said John, his voice even. "A rotten bastard really."

Hood chuckled. "True enough. But I had a soft spot for him, as did many. Let's leave it at that shall we."

John nodded towards the far end of the camp at Athella, shooting her bow at a target. "Now there's a woman who was not fond of him. Hated his bloody guts."

Hood frowned. "If she wasn't your wife…"

"You'd what?" said John, stopping him in his tracks.

"I didn't say I'd do anything. But I'll say this, she hated Gilbert, she hated Stutley and Scarlett and she hates me."

John's face loosened. "No, she liked Stutley." He walked off then towards his wife and began remarking on her form.

Hood looked on, his eyes burning holes in her back. Eustace came alongside him and handed him a cup of the ale that had been rolled from the town. "Why don't you like her?" asked the monk.

"I don't trust her."

"Why not?"

"Just got that feeling and usually I'm a good judge of character."

"A good judge?" asked Eustace.

"Yes, like whether they're good or bad, honest or dishonest. That sort of thing."

"You realise that statement's contradictory to the company you keep and the things we do for money."

"Ah, you lot may be a bunch of dirty mercenaries, but I wouldn't be with you if I didn't think I had a good judge on you. Do you trust her?" queried the bowman.

"She's done nothing to earn it, yet nothing to break it either. But I agree with you, I find her cold and from the day you took her—"

"We," interrupted the bowman.

"No, I had no part in it. But from then I've found her… odd? Marrying her captive, fighting against her flesh and blood. Giving up a life of fortune for a life of fighting. I can't understand it. However, just because I can't understand it, does not mean it's wrong."

Hood downed his ale in one, turning away from the sight of John and Athella. "Where to next?"

Eustace smiled. "Our target is a major influencer that schemes against the man who pays us. We're to dispatch him, then our next trip is back to England. I may have a higher bidder for our services there."

Chapter 29

Count Renaud sat in his chamber looking out from his balcony onto the small village surrounding him. His castle was not large, but it was heavily guarded, the walls around the village were manned by armoured archers and spearmen. Count Renaud had come from nothing, his father was a blacksmith and his mother dead – he didn't stand a chance at wealth. But determination held its ground and soon Renaud found his way closer to the top than many people were comfortable with. The man had a silver tongue and a mind for finances. Investments here and there along with friends in all the right places, Renaud eventually found his treasury swelling beyond capacity.

That's when he realised a silver tongue wasn't needed to earn power, just a full purse. A man who hated you could be turned with the right price. They always had a price. That's what Renaud had thought before he met the French prince that wanted him dead.

The count sat on his stone balcony, a pear in one hand and a small knife in the other, slicing pieces away and placing them in his mouth. "You would never want to hurt me, would you?" he said to his dog. The small animal sat next to him watching with adoration as Renaud fed him a pear slice.

The rich man stood and walked back inside his room. The walls were finely decorated with paintings from Italy and rugs from Spain. Fine French furniture lined the room and Renaud caught his own reflection in a mirror. The man was once handsome and women longed for his company. Now he was middle-aged, closing in on sixty and his looks had almost completely faded. His stomach and face had become bloated from fine food and wine, his back and knees were sore towards the end of the day and his injured shoulder ached in winter. However, Renaud's arrogance led him to believe that all women still wanted him. His advances were never shunned because they knew what type of man he was. Anyone denting his vanity would pay with their blood. Obviously not by his own hand, he'd pay an urchin.

Renaud smiled at himself in the mirror and twisted the end of his grey moustache before helping himself to a sweet pastry and walking back out onto his balcony. As he sat, his sword handle dug into his side, where the fat had recently begun to protrude. He looked down and frowned, adjusting the belt slightly.

When Renaud was younger he was a fine swordsman. He had won high stakes tournaments all over France as he was building his fortune. Of course, he hadn't used the blade in years, but Renaud still believed he could best mostly anyone.

He'd put more guards on duty today and the walls surrounding the small castle had their gates barred. The people that inhabited the inside of the walls were concerned, but Renaud's men were not known for their understanding, which meant there was little complaining. Renaud narrowed his eyes and saw movement in the treeline before his walls. That's when he realised the intelligence he'd received was sound. Two nights previous when the unpleasant man with the metal mask had approached the castle and requested an audience with him, he'd been sceptical. When Renaud had asked the man what he wanted in return for the information, he'd said he wanted nothing, aside from to be present when they came.

The man was tall and had an air of danger about him. His French was broken, but Renaud had men who spoke English that could translate. Renaud didn't ask why he wore a metal mask. A man who wears such a thing is hiding their face for a reason, to ask would be pointless. The count would far rather wear a mask than show a hideous face. Nevertheless, Renaud thought it harmless to entertain the idea. If he was telling the truth, then it was to both of their benefit, if not, then Renaud had no doubt that he'd be able to defend himself in his own walls against the rogue.

A smile spread across his face as the supposed enemy emerged from the trees, bows in their hands and swords on their backs. They would have stood a chance if Renaud was not warned, but not now, not now his own men were prepared. A horn sounded and Renaud's archers formed a neat line across the wall, fire-pits by their side. Swordsmen were waiting below at the steps just in case they managed to breach. Renaud chuckled at the thought, a handful of men, maybe close to fifty planned to overrun him. It was preposterous.

The metal-faced man that wanted to wait for them would have little chance of confrontation with the enemy, for they would not get a chance to come near the castle. The masked man looked like a swordsman, he had walked with grace and his weapon looked new but finely picked. Probably hadn't seen much action, Renaud had thought, a man looking to wet his blade.

The count had heard of this man 'Eustace', who was supposedly at his gates. He'd heard the pirate had joined forces with an outlaw from England, who killed rich men and robbed any he could find. A man masterful at his craft. It was no wonder he'd locked arms with the foulest pirate in Europe.

Renaud was still mystified why the French prince had hired men to kill him though. He'd never insulted him, he'd never wronged him financially or otherwise. He supposed that it simply came down to eliminating men that threatened to become too powerful. Renaud was flattered in a way.

He'd heard his door click open and the masked guest walked in silently, his large boots barely making a noise. "Only the finest fighters walk like cats," said Renaud, a smile on his face. The man said nothing in return, he probably didn't understand a word he was saying, decided Renaud. The count turned back and watched as arrows were exchanged between the two parties below. "Well, this will come to nothing thanks to your information… Errr, what was your name?" Renaud asked in his best English.

The metal faced man didn't reply, he stood silently, his sword sheathed and his grey eyes looking out beyond the balcony.

Renaud's face twisted slightly and he shook his head. "Rude man," he muttered in French.

Clashes of metal could be heard from below and Renaud ran to the balcony to look down. Two men were fighting three of his soldiers, except, they all wore Renaud's colours. "Traitors!" he hissed. Then he saw more fighting on the inside of the walls at the gate. A small group of men in his colours were lifting the bar and were surrounded by dead men, presumably his own. Renaud turned to the silent man behind him "You engineered this!" shouted the count, unsheathing his sword and running at metal face.

The man sidestepped Renaud and used his weight to

throw him across the room. Just as the count bounced off a wall and dropped his sword, two men burst through his door, blood on their blades and death on their minds.

The masked man moved with sickening speed and unleashed his sword. Renaud had never seen any man use a blade like that. Within moments the two intruders were dead and their killer loomed over them, checking their faces.

Then Renaud heard metal on stone and he turned to the balcony to see two grappling hooks stuck in place. Renaud ran towards them, picking up his sword and planning to cut the rope from the hooks, but metal face grabbed him, hoisting him back. "Let them come," he said, his voice muffled, his eyes focused.

Chapter 30

Friendship breeds pain, Hood had once heard a man say. He didn't believe it. Friendship was the only thing that had kept him afloat all these years. However, as the bowman sat on his own, the moonlight on his back and his eyes staring at the grave of Gilbert, he finally realised what the man had meant.

Everything else didn't seem to matter, he felt a hollow pain in his chest as he thought of Gilbert, Scarlett and Stutley. The men were his brothers. They thought that Hood was their leader, that they needed him. The truth was that Hood needed them more. He needed them so he could be the man they wanted him to be, the leader they needed him to be. They were his crutches and they didn't even know it.

Hood finished the contents of the dark bottle and threw it into the distance. The bowman reached his hand out and uncorked another, taking a long swig. Hood's bow was in front of him, next to his jewelled sword from John, the moonlight bouncing from its handle. "Who knew," he thought, "that my weapons could not guard me from pain."

Hood woke slowly, a sharp pain in his side. He removed his hat from over his face and saw John silhouetted by the sun. "Toe me again and you'll lose that foot of yours," said Hood, grumbling to his feet. He swayed and John steadied his arm.

"Red wine last night? You're not usually one for it," said John.

"How'd you know?" asked Hood looking for the evidence that he thought he'd thrown.

John smiled and pointed to his teeth. "Your famous smile is black."

"Dammit," said Hood, rubbing his jerkin frantically on his teeth. "These are my pride and joy."

John laughed. "Come on, Hood, saddle your horse, we've got a fair bit of riding to do."

For three days the group rode. Hood ate mechanically and mostly kept to himself when they camped. No one approached him, for they knew Hood could be ruthless at times during a dark mood. Well, they thought he could, for his reputation preceded him.

On the third night, Master came to sit with him, they were not five miles away from their target and Hood had once again sat away from the group. "Do you mind me sitting here with you?" asked the old man. His English was good, he wasn't from France, not even from Europe it seemed. The Far East, if Hood had to guess.

"Of course I don't," said Hood, sitting himself up.

"You know, they're scared of you. They respect you, but they are scared. Even John is sometimes weary when your mood is dark."

"Respect earned through fear is nothing special. They do what I say not because they love me, but because they don't want to die."

"But you would not kill them, Hood," said Master, his kind eyes looking at the bowman's face.

"I would have, at one point. A man could not tell me no and hold on to his life. Now, well, I believe life is less fickle than that."

"And what has changed you?"

"I'm unsure, Master, I'm unsure if I'm even changed

at all. Perhaps I've just lost too much while trying to pursue something that doesn't really matter."

"Time," said Master, propping his old hand on Hood's shoulder. "No man can stop time from doing its work. People believe that they always remain the same on the inside, that they are one way forever and will never change. But look around you, time is unstoppable. It changes everything, nothing remains the same. The young get older by the second, roses bud, flower and wilt, the sun is constantly moving, the earth shifting. Are we so arrogant to think that time does not change who we are on the inside?"

"Time," said Hood. "The unsuspecting assailant." The bowman sighed once more. "My aspirations are in question, my whole life is," said Hood.

"And keep questioning," smiled Master. "It is the only way we grow."

Hood nodded and lay back. "Eustace said we may go to England after we complete tomorrow's objective."

"We might and you do not have to stay with us while we are there. You can depart if you want."

"I'm part of the crew, I would not desert Eustace and yourself."

"You value friendship and loyalty above all else, Hood, even, it seems above your own happiness." Master rose then, twisting his back and stretching the muscles. "Join us tomorrow if you wish, or do not, it is up to you. From then, you must decide what you want."

The morning came and Hood was brought breakfast by John. Fried fish caught in a river nearby, John always did know how to fry a good fish. "So," said John, smiling. "We have a plan on how to get into that castle.

Athella and some of the lads were out scouting and came across a merchant heading towards the town we're heading for and hit big."

Hood sighed. "Surely we've got bigger targets than a bloody merchant's loot."

"Oh no, we didn't rob him, we paid him actually. Here this, so he was on his way to the castle town we're about to sack and he's got a few new uniforms in his wagon that were on their way there."

"And what makes you think he won't just turn us in for more coin?"

"Nah," replied John. "He won't do that."

"Why not?"

"They killed him," said John, simply.

"I thought you said we paid him?"

"Well, they did, but then they thought the same as you just said, that he could just turn us over for a bigger sum."

Hood took a bite of his fish and swallowed. "Couldn't we have just tied him up until we finished with the castle?"

John's eyebrows rose in surprise. "What the hell's happened with you, Hood? Don't let the lads hear you talking like that," he laughed.

Chapter 31

The plan was simple. Hood and John, along with three other crewmen were to hide in the back of the dead merchant's covered wagon. They would ride into the town beyond the small castle's walls and then make their way to the target, dispatching him efficiently. Nothing ever runs smoothly and there's no doubt that guards would be drawn to the count being attacked or killed. This meant that the rest of the crew would need to provide a distraction, they would take men down at the walls so the main force would be pulled towards them. Once enough guards had been killed, the crew would then enter the walls and finish off the job. The prince that had commissioned this job advised that not only would they be paid, but they could take as much loot from the count's home as they wished.

"It's too easy," said Hood, as he was slipping into the count's colours. "I say we wait another day, two days perhaps."

"I know you have a nose for trouble," replied John, strapping on a sword. "But this isn't one of those times. Just because it's easy doesn't mean it's questionable. Sometimes life's just like that."

"Life is never like that."

John and Hood lay down in the back of the wagon, two more of the crew joining them. Master sat at the front of the wagon, his short sword hidden in the back. Eustace was at first sceptical about having Master place himself at the forefront of the plan, but he was old and didn't register as a threat to the common soldier. Many merchants were not from these lands and Master didn't look local, only benefiting the deceit.

The rest of the crew stayed back, planning to travel to a nearby forest later in the afternoon once the plan was in place.

The wagon had made its way past the gates with no problem. The guard on duty had nodded them through hastily, along with other merchants and farmers. Count Renaud was a man of business, it wasn't uncommon to have distant traders entering his castle market day in and day out.

Master found a quiet place between buildings and pulled off the cover of the wagon. The men grabbed their weapons slowly and narrowed their eyes at the sun. "Bloody hot under there," said John, huffing in cool air, his handsome face red and puffy.

Hood leapt from the wagon and brushed himself down. "Many guards on duty?"

"Quite a few," nodded Master. "Most lining the walls, preparing their weapons and such."

The men looked at one another and then their eyes rested on Hood. "Preparing their weapons?" said the bowman, satirically. "Preparing for what, I wonder?"

"Damn it," said John, sighing and rubbing the back of his head.

Master stepped forward. "Relax, my friends. There's no question that they're aware of something. But us? I think not. Why would they allow us to come this far and not cut us down as you lay hidden and I was unarmed?"

"Perhaps a hunter spotted our group and reported back," suggested Hood.

"Exactly. That is the most likely answer, although, there could be many others."

"Right," said Hood, gathering the men. "The plan is as follows. John and I head towards the gates, blending with the guards there, waiting for our force to emerge. You two," he said, gesturing towards the other two crewmen. "You wait near the entrance of the castle and when the sun hits noon, we shall execute the plan. Master, you stand close to the gate and when John and I begin the attack, you take down any that you can."

The men disbanded and headed to their stations hastily. It wasn't long until the sun hit noon, but while on their way Hood and John saw the doors of the gate being closed and a wooden bar being locked in place. "We stay back for now," said Hood. "We don't want to be given orders in French and not be able to follow them." The two of them stayed back, watching from a closed off alley while Master looked at the wares around the market.

The atmosphere was tense, Hood could feel the fear radiating off the folk within the walls. The soldiers seemed on edge, but they still stood firm to their stations. A pang of guilt struck him as he sympathised with the men and women around them that worried for their loved ones. "Not now, Hood," he thought to himself. He bolted away the feeling and stored it somewhere dark and forgotten. Such thoughts in this scenario could get everyone killed.

The bowman looked up at the castle and saw a balcony high up. A grey-haired man was sitting on it, eating and looking out over the walls. The bowman wondered if the grappling hooks left at the wagon would reach. He also wondered if he should end it all now with his bow, whether he could hit the target from where he stood.

John noticed him and read his mind. "Reckon you

could get him?" said John. "It could save a lot of blood."

"Not with my short bow I can't, too high up. If I tried and missed then we'd have the whole place on us."

They heard a horn then and the soldiers started to shuffle into their places, solidifying their positions. "It's time," said Hood, a grin appearing on his face, his white teeth baring once more.

"There's that smile," said John, moving off towards the gate.

Hood couldn't help it, the feeling of exhilaration running through his veins was upon him. A situation of such danger, where one's life hangs in a delicate balance makes every breath taste finer than the last. Previous thoughts of confusion and guilt had whittled away like soap in a stream. Now his blood was hot, racing around his body, urging his muscles and mind for a fight.

John and Hood placed themselves below the gate, Hood's bow and quiver on his back and his jewelled sword in his hand. They were standing amongst lightly armed soldiers, around fifteen of them crowding the barred gate and a further thirty swordsmen spread out across the bottom of the walls. The bowmen above them were perched, facing the forest beyond where the crew would now begin to make themselves seen.

Hood looked up at the sun; it was almost time to execute the plan. He could hear arrows being shot above them, out towards his crew. Equally, he could hear the arrows coming back, plunging into some of Renaud's soldiers and tipping them from the walls. Hood saw a man with an arrow in his chest fall into the small mass of men near him. The soldier moaned with agony and was dragged off by one of his comrades, blood leaking from his wound.

Master was closer to them now and Hood looked up at the sun. It was noon, the time had come. The soldiers nearby said something to Master, Hood couldn't understand it, but it didn't sound pleasant. It was an order of some sort, an order that Master did not follow. The soldier was mad now, speaking through gritted teeth he moved towards Master, his hand reaching out to push him in the chest. Master reacted with speed, his robe opening up and a curved short sword sweeping out and cutting the hand from the man's arm. The soldier dropped his sword and grabbed onto his stump, squealing like a pig.

The other soldiers on the ground took notice now, they turned their backs to Hood and John, moving in on the old man. Master used his sword like an extension of himself. When a swordsman grows old and they want to maintain their skill, raw power no longer can factor into it. They use the blade as a surgical instrument, not attempting to make a spectacle. The key was to go for the quick kills, open the artery in their leg so they bled out within moments. Or slice their brow so blood blinds them into being clumsy and helpless. However, before he needed to stretch his skills beyond his ability, Hood and John were upon them. The two outlaws had killed five of them before they realised they were being attacked from behind. Before long, the soldiers that were left were scattered, regrouping themselves further along the wall with the other waiting swordsmen.

"Get this gate open with me, John," said Hood, running to one side of the bar and heaving it up.

John grabbed the other and hefted it. The heavy chunk of wood dropped to the floor and the two men flung the gates open. The crew from the forest saw this and armed themselves with wooden shields, sprinting from the trees, roaring with battle cries. Some of the crew stayed within the shelter, firing arrows at the archers that found themselves distracted by the mass running at them.

Hood and John sprinted from the gate as their reinforcements reached them, battling what was left of the count's men. The two men reached the wagon they arrived in and removed two grappling hooks with long, thick ropes wrapped around the spine of the tool.

Hood and John walked through the deserted marketplace and stood below the balcony where they saw Renaud sitting earlier. The entrance of the castle was unguarded, dead soldiers at the doors. "Could be a free passage through the castle to his room with our lads making their way to him?" said John, daunted by the climb above them.

"The count's door could be locked from the inside, there could be a mass of men waiting in the halls. Best we follow the plan," smiled Hood. "Besides, this way is far more fun, don't you think?" The bowman twirled the grappling hook expertly in his hand and let it go, the hook flying up towards the balcony. His aim was perfect.

John moved to the bowman's rope and handed him his own hook. "You take mine, I don't have the eye for it."

The bowman flung the second and the hook found its way to the balcony's edge. The two men began to climb, shuffling themselves up the rope as quickly as they could. The movement burned the slender bowman's shoulders, but John's massive build only aided him in the act.

When a man uses a grappling hook to enter a building or swing to a ship, the key is to save your strength until the end, making sure you're over the edge within mere moments, your weapon ready for anything. If not, then a blade may find itself lodged in one's chest as soon as you finish the climb.

Hood and John hopped over the edge of the balcony sprightly, not allowing the fatigue to be realised by their bodies. What they saw then could not have been predicted, no matter how many times they planned. The door to the count's room was open, the crewmen from the wagon were dead. Count Renaud stood there, a sword in his hand and his fat belly wobbling like a soap bubble. Close to him was a tall man, his face covered with a sheet of metal, grates where his mouth and nose were and small holes for his eyes. "Iron Mask," said Hood, his voice quiet, surprise evident.

Hood's instinct was to make sense of the situation, calculate how it could have come to this, what actions were set in motion by someone else. He would need time for such a calculation. Now he needed to focus on murdering this bastard.

John began to walk forward, his huge sword in his hand. He swung it from side to side, letting himself feel the weight. Iron Mask did not budge, but Renaud ran for John, screaming with his sword held high. John blocked a blow from the fat man and launched him to one side, all while his eyes were still on Iron Mask. Renaud fell into the corner of the room, smashing into a wooden cabinet and crumpling to the floor.

John was not a man to shy away from a sword fight, in fact, he encouraged sport with a blade. John made the first move that was blocked with ease then backed away, twirling his huge sword in deceiving motions. John sprang again, this time faster, his sword attempting more complex movements. Iron Mask met the attack, his own weapon blurring into action.

The clash of metal on metal was loud, deafening even. Hood saw the expression of John change steadily. He'd started with a smirk, aware that few men came close to his level of swordplay, then it shifted to concentration, allowing no emotion to penetrate his mind. Now he was in trouble, for he'd moved past the point where he'd usually finish a man and concern was etched onto his face.

Hood knew it was time to intervene. Although he would have no use for the bow on his back, for the two combatants moved with speed that went beyond the bowman's eye.

As Hood drew his jewelled sword, he saw a figure appear in the doorway that leapt into the midst of the fighting. It was Eustace, his axe entering into the clash of weapons. The room was big and mostly clear, but the fighting men used it well. Every spare inch was stepped into, calculated into their battle. Hood had never seen anything like it, by all accounts Iron Mask should be dead. Eustace and John had seemed unbeatable, invincible even. But now they faced a foe that was matching them both at once, if not coming out on top. John was bleeding from a shallow wound on his upper arm and Eustace very nearly had his chest ripped open. John would have been dead if it wasn't for Eustace joining the fight, and if Hood had joined in, he knew he too would have been slain.

A horn sounded from below the castle, close to the walls. Hood and John had no idea what it meant, but Eustace did. The monk saw an opening and booted

Iron Mask in the stomach. The man flew from them, stumbling backwards out of the count's door and into the hall beyond. Eustace slammed the door and clicked the lock shut.

"Oh no," said John, huffing. "I don't run from a fight, we're finishing him."

"Don't be a fool, John," warned the bowman. "The man fights like he's possessed! You must know when you're beat."

John was about to argue, but Eustace interrupted. "We must go back down the balcony. That noise we heard, it means there are reinforcements. Renaud must have caught wind and sent word earlier."

The bowman looked over the balcony and saw that at least a hundred soldiers had entered the walls, moving towards the castle entrance. What was left of the crew gathered at one side, fighting off the enemy and moving their backs towards a stairway on the wall.

Banging could be heard on the other side of the door, loud and vicious. Iron Mask was working his way through.

"Come on," said Hood, hopping back onto the rope of the grappling hook. "It won't be long before these get noticed."

Eustace and John joined him, making their way down to the bottom of the ropes and dropping lightly onto the ground below. Hood removed his bow, firing arrows into two oncoming soldiers. They dropped silently, no others were close yet.

They could see in the distance a mass of soldiers gathering near the walls, the crew backing up to the top of them. Each one would be slowly climbing down the outside of the wall to safety while the others fought. The problem with this was that there were less and less crewmen to defend as more escaped.

"Was Master amongst them?" asked Eustace, a hint of panic in the usually calm man's voice.

"Aye," said John. "I believe he was."

"Then he will be the one who dies, for he will not leave any behind. I must help him." Eustace pushed through the two outlaws and started to walk towards the group.

"It's fruitless, Eustace!" warned Hood. "He would not want you to die this way."

"Fruitless?" said Eustace, turning with a look of disgust on his face. "If you believe dying while trying to save your friend is fruitless, then I have you pegged as the wrong man." The monk turned back, his axe drawn walking towards the mass of soldiers.

Chapter 32

As Eustace came closer, he could see Master clearly at the stairway of the wall. It was sheltered on one side so arrows could not reach him. This meant he and another two crewmen could fit on the stairs, blocking the passage while the others made an exit. Master used his position well, this meant only three of the enemy at a time could face him and being on the higher ground, he had the advantage.

Eustace wondered if Master could make it out alive. He doubted it. As skilled as the old man was, his stamina would soon run low making him open to injury, followed closely by death.

None of the soldiers had spotted the silver-haired monk yet, so he needed to choose his position wisely. There was a smith's workshop not twenty foot from where the soldiers were. If Eustace stood in the doorway, then he could use a similar technique to Master and draw them towards him, fighting them one at a time. The only flaw was that if the soldiers used their heads, they could just take Eustace with an arrow before they came to him. He had to depend on the soldiers' lust for blood, for their need to kill something with a blade.

Eustace moved to his position and cleared his throat. "Cowards!" he exclaimed. "You cannot kill an old man, how could you ever expect to kill me?" The words were chosen carefully to fire the soldiers' anger, to humiliate them. Men acted irrationally when fuelled by such emotions.

The soldiers ran at Eustace, parting from the main force facing the rest of the crew. Eustace clove through the first, then the second and third. By the time he was onto the fourth, the fighting had slowed, bodies needed to be dragged from the doorway for a new man to face the monk. With each man he executed, it only made the next want him more.

The opponents seemed never-ending and a seed of doubt was planted into Eustace's mind. Soon the men would calm, realising they could not face him. They would find a backdoor into the workshop, surrounding him and slowly take him down. As the next man came to face him, the soldier had stopped, peering past Eustace, taking in the environment. They were sick of death and now the soldier was forced to think of another route. It was happening. The beginning of the end.

An arrow slammed into the enemy's neck that stood in front of Eustace, startling him. The arrow came from above and confusion swept over the faces of the men before him. The soldiers then looked up towards the roof of the building, confusion was swapped for panic and their eyes widened. Arrow after arrow began to plough into the enemy, each shot as deadly as the next. Eustace knew only one man capable of that mastery – Hood.

A roar was heard from the back of the herd of men and Eustace could see the top of John's sword cleaving through the flesh of the soldiers, blood rising into the air as the sword took another life.

The numbers of the enemy started to dwindle. Between Master on the stairway, Hood, Eustace and John, the ferocity of the attack had brought them swiftly down to around forty men. When people are in groups, it's as if their minds sync together, forming a hive of thoughts and feelings. So the moment when two men faltered as they neared the doorway of Eustace, turning their backs to him and running, so did the rest of them. Fear spread like wildfire, turning the most hardened warriors they faced into fleeing lambs.

The crewmen cheered and Hood hopped down from the roof and onto the ground below. Eustace came to him, a smile on his face and his arm outstretched, grabbing Hood's arm and pulling it into a warrior's grip. "I knew I did not misjudge you, Hood."

Hood gave a smile and nodded. "We must leave now over the walls with the crew. The soldiers may have been broken, but they will regroup and come for us at any moment. The fear will disperse as soon as it arrived."

Eustace didn't need telling twice and the two ran for the stairway, hurrying behind Master and the crew. Each climbing down the outer wall as quickly as they could, fleeing for the safety of the forest beyond.

Chapter 33

The crew had reached the forest swiftly and retreated into their temporary camp that lay a couple of miles deep into the trees. The crewmen were bloody and tired, Hood had watched their excitement of the battle fade away slowly as they walked through the forest, spaced out amongst the trees.

When they reached the camp, the crewmen who had stayed there greeted them happily at first but soon realised the losses. Almost half of the crew's force was gone, lying dead in some count's castle for a prince half of them had never met.

Hood lay down, a darkness settling upon his mind. This happened sometimes after such a defeat, the only cure seemed to be time and sleep. So the bowman closed his eyes and shut off the noise around him. His mind started to drift instantly, warmth shrouding it and his lids becoming heavy.

"Hood," came a voice. "Hood!"

The bowman opened his eyes to see Athella standing above him, anger on her face. "Where is my husband?" she asked. She'd been waiting in the camp while the men had attacked, John had said he'd prefer her to wait there.

Hood's mind reeled with dizziness, coming back to reality. "We retreated and we all came back, he's around here somewhere."

"No he's bloody not!" said Athella, something close to panic in her tone.

Hood didn't say anything, his mind caught up and he

relived the situation back at the castle. "Eustace!" he shouted, jumping to his feet.

The monk ran to him. "What is wrong?"

"John, we left John!"

The monk stood for a moment and his mind too relived the retreat. He swore in a foreign language. "We must go back."

"Just us two," said the bowman. "They'll spot us and just overrun us if there's any more."

The two made their way back through the trees they had retreated into. Hood's mood was no longer dark. Panic had set in, almost uncontrollable. His pace was fast, quickening every time he thought of his friend in trouble. "Remain calm, Hood," said Eustace from behind him. "We have to think with our heads when we get there, we have to have our wits about us. It could be even now the soldiers are tracking through the forest, coming towards us this instant."

Hood said nothing, the bowman refusing to slow his pace. They reached the treeline and could see the castle gate from where they were. The walls were empty and the gate was unmanned. Hood was about to walk out when Eustace grabbed him by the shoulder. "Hood, there is something I must say."

"Make it quick, monk, for our friend needs help."

"That man, Iron Mask, his swordwork it's—"

"I know," said Hood, cutting him off. "He's better than anyone I've ever seen."

"It's just that," said the monk, his face serious. "I have only fought one man with that style, with that skill. It's unmistakable, Hood, that's Guy of Gisborne."

"Don't be ridiculous, Eustace, he's long gone. He's a dog of the Sheriff's and always will be." Hood went to walk from the treeline and Eustace pulled him back.

"Think about it for one second. Do you know anyone who can track across country day and night, anyone other than Guy? This Iron Mask has known our every move, hunting down the crew. Not just any of the crew either. First there was Gilbert, now… well, he was here."

Hood's face began to drop. "The words of the old hag we killed, she said he seeks vengeance. That the *giant* was going to be killed, the one who killed his kin. Gilbert has killed many men's family."

"But did he kill any of Guy's?"

"Yes," said Hood simply, recalling the night Gilbert had come to him on the ship while crossing the Channel, the night they escaped. The giant had been guilt-ridden, not because he'd figured out he'd killed Guy's daughter, but because he believed that action had caused Guy to try and kill them all.

"And the mask. Guy of Gisborne's face was burned to a crisp, his scalp weeping sores. This, I believe is the reason for his mask. He's here for us and he won't stop until he's got us all."

The reality of the situation dawned on Hood. It was all a trap, a setup. Was Guy in league with the prince? With Renaud? Or someone else. All would show itself in time. The only thing Hood knew for certain was that he needed to get John.

They saw movement at the top of the gate then. Two men were carrying something large and threw it over the top of the gate. It was a torso, dangling from hooks with chains suspending it. Men at either side of the castle walls showed themselves, skewering what looked like arms to spears. Finally, a man came from the centre of the gate through the doors. It was Iron

Mask, a huge, unmistakable sword in his hand.

"That's John's weapon," said Hood, the words a whisper.

Iron Mask dug it into the ground blade first and removed a head from the bloodstained sack at his side. The head was pushed onto the pommel of John's sword, looking out at Eustace and Hood.

More men came to the walls and stood, their weapons not raised, just peering out into the trees where Eustace and Hood were standing.

Hood lost control, he shoved through the trees and onto the grass verge beyond, showing himself to the men at the castle before him, showing himself to Iron Mask. Eustace thought he may run for him, but Hood stopped, just outside the range that the archers could reach. "Guy of Gisborne," he shouted, at the top of his voice.

Iron Mask moved a step forward, as if to register the remark.

"You will regret the day you sought to hurt my brothers and me. You will regret coming against me, for every man who faces me falls!" Hood turned away as if to stop himself running towards the walls. Suddenly, he turned back, as if the words needed to escape him. "I promise you, Guy, you will die by my hand and you will never quench your thirst for vengeance!" The bowman turned back, walking into the forest behind and towards the camp once again, fury overcoming him.

Part of him wanted to run at Guy, to take him down with a single arrow or sword wound, just before the soldiers got to him. But he'd seen too many people die from such rash actions. The key was to be calculated, to attempt to use one's brain when anger is trying to force them to do something stupid.

The thing that bothered Hood about the confrontation most was that Iron Mask did not even attempt to come at him, he could have had the soldiers leave their position, sending them forth. Instead, Iron Mask had stood, taunting him, enjoying the game and savouring the taste of Hood's anguish.

Chapter 34

It wasn't hard for Iron Mask to pay a guard for uniforms, then force a merchant that was on route to Renaud's castle to take them. Outlaws were predictable, they were drawn to anything that could bring them the most measly piece of profit. The easiest part was getting to Renaud himself, a man like him was obsessed with self-preservation. Even the idea that a group of men might be coming to kill him would cause him to listen to anyone. Of course, Renaud had no idea that Iron Mask had essentially handed his killers uniforms. It was the only way he could get close, Renaud would not have let him within the castle without the information and the outlaws would not have reached him without the uniforms.

The plan was perfect, thought Iron Mask. He would kill John and perhaps Hood if he got the chance. Then the world would be one step closer to being right again.

As Iron Mask was battling in Renaud's room, the dark monk Eustace had landed a boot at his chest, sending him out of the door, then locking shut. But this had worked in his favour. He had walked down the stairs of the castle, past two soldiers that were heading to the locked door. Iron Mask had stood at a distance, watching Hood shoot from the top of the smith's workshop, while Eustace battled below him. He enjoyed watching the monk use his weapon; the man had talent and killed without hatred.

However, he watched John swing his sword viciously, cutting men up like a butcher. The man annoyed him, he was arrogant and thought himself a god with his sword. Iron Mask had longed to humble him for a final time.

Renaud's soldiers did as he expected them to. They ran. As they fled, he watched as Hood and Eustace joined their crew, swiftly making their exit, not allowing themselves to be gripped by slaughter.

John, however, as predicted had gotten caught up in the bloodshed. He followed the running soldiers, cutting them down where he could. Renaud's men were weak and gravitated to anyone that radiated power.

They formed a line behind Iron Mask, positioning him at the centre. John had cut down a man and looked up to see who his next target was. The idiot was met by surprise when he saw Iron Mask and a squad of armed men.

John looked about him, realising his comrades were gone. Iron Mask stepped forward, his sword in his gloved hand. "Do not piss yourself, John, you need only beat me and you can go."

John cocked his head at the English accent and the mention of his name. "Who are you?" asked the outlaw.

"Search your mind and you will know," said Iron Mask, leaping in with his weapon.

John raised his own sword, blocking the attack and sweeping his blade for Iron Mask's legs. The move was blocked once more and the pace of the swords quickened. John was better than he was in Renaud's room, there was open space, more men to see him perform. A vain fool would feed off such things. Although, despite his increased skill, he was no match for Iron Mask.

The two weapons clanged once more and the force brought both their sword arms backwards. John took the opportunity to throw a punch at his enemy, John's massive fist slamming off Iron Mask's face. The move had little impact and John's hand came out worse in the exchange. Iron Mask flung his head forward as John tried to raise his sword, cracking the metal mask off the bridge of John's nose.

Blood began to pour instantly and John stumbled backwards. Iron Mask raised his leg and booted John in the stomach, enough force to make him drop to his knees.

John was in a daze, the head-butt almost taking him to an unconscious place. Iron Mask batted his blade off John's own, making his sword fly from the outlaw's grip and across the ground.

John looked up, his thick dark, hair was plastered to his head with blood and his features were handsome no more. "Who…are…you?" he managed.

Iron Mask raised one hand to the back of his head, unbuckling the straps and removing the mask.

John's eyes widened and his mouth was about to open. Before he could speak what he wished, Iron Mask's sword had cut through John's neck, the outlaw's head toppling to the ground. Iron Mask searched for a feeling, a satisfaction of some kind. He couldn't find it, he felt nothing. No relief, no triumph. *It will come,* he thought.

From there he went on to sever John's body into cuts. First his arms, then he cut through the top of the thick thighs. The job was messy and Iron Mask knew a sword was not the right tool for the job. Despite this, he completed his task and sent some soldiers for chains and hooks.

Renaud ran to him, his grey hair a mess and his face bruised. The man's tight-fitting clothes were ripped and his belly protruded through fabric. "Renaud conquers again," said the tubby man with a smile.

Guy picked up John's sword and placed his head in a nearby sack. "Gather up the body and help the men hang it from the gate."

Renaud was shocked, this man telling him what to do in his own castle. "Pardon?"

Iron Mask stopped and turned, his cold eyes staring into Renaud's, no words were needed, for Renaud knew what would become of him if he didn't obey. Renaud turned away from his glare and began helping his soldiers heft the large, bloody torso.

Iron Mask had waited at the gate, looking out into the trees, waiting for a sign of movement. Then he saw it, no more than two men rustling like idiots. "No one ever thinks," he said to himself. Iron mask signalled for Renaud's soldiers to make their move and toss the torso from the wall, followed by the arms to be mounted and displayed like wings at the edges.

Finally, Iron Mask walked from the gate, digging John's huge sword into the ground and thrusting his severed head onto the pommel.

Hood had shown himself then; Iron Mask didn't expect an attack. The man was wily like a fox, more slippery than most people and his mind was sharp, controlled to an extent. He could have been a fine man in the army, he could have risen to high places. Instead, he chose to be scum, dealing pain and unhappiness to all he encountered.

Hood had shouted, losing his composure, promising him death. Oh, but Iron Mask quivered with pleasure as Hood had finally realised who he was. The outlaw should have known long ago, from the moment he was chased off the cliff in England, that Guy of Gisborne would stop at nothing.

Hood knew now that he would not be able to stop moving, he could no longer rest, for he knew that Guy would be on his trail.

The bowman did the wise thing and left, heading back to calculate the next move. The game between Guy and the outlaws was similar to chess. John, Gilbert, Stutley and Scarlett; their minds were too rash, they only thought about their next move. Hood, however, thought three moves ahead. Guy, on the other hand, thought four.

Guy turned and walked back in through the gates, heading towards the castle. None of the soldiers stopped him as he entered the kitchens to fill his travelling pack. He picked between an assortment of dried meat, fruit and black bread. These would last him at least two weeks if he rationed them correctly. Guy then walked down to the count's treasury where no guards stood. He filled his purse with silver and gold coins before returning to the surface, exiting the castle doors.

"Have you stolen from me, metal face?" asked Renaud, plodding along angrily next to Guy, a score of soldiers following him.

He said nothing in reply and walked to the nearest well, filling his water skins. Guy then turned to one of the soldiers with Renaud. "Fetch me a horse," he said simply in the French tongue. The soldier had nodded and was about to move off.

"Do not get him a horse!" raged Renaud. "Kill him!"

The soldiers looked between one another and then back at Guy. They'd seen him fight, they'd stood behind him ready to battle. They respected Guy, they knew if they attacked, many would die before they killed him.

Renaud was outraged, his face almost purple.

Guy pulled back his arm and slammed his fist into the count's face as hard as he could. Renaud dropped without a sound, his fine clothes sinking into the mud below him, his jaw wobbling loose.

The soldiers looked between one another, stunned. "A horse," said Guy. "Fetch it." The soldier ran off, bringing back the finest horse they had in the small settlement. Guy rode from the castle, leaving it in disarray. He didn't care, it didn't touch him one bit. Renaud was a ghastly man who didn't know when he'd won. Guy had warned him of the outlaws coming. If it were not for him, he most certainly would have been dead. The gall of the little French man. Guy had looked back before leaving, watching his soldiers run from the castle with treasure in their hands, packing what belongings they had to leave the count's service. Guy had chuckled to himself. The vast majority of people were all so predictable, loyalties changing at the click of a finger. Your servants become your robbers, your friends become your worst enemies, it's rare to find a feeling or friendship that can't be tainted or is unbreakable. It seemed to Guy that almost everyone had their price.

As he neared the treeline Guy opened the map he'd acquired from Renaud's castle. The patch of forest was long, tracking them would be impossible with a horse. However, he could see that if he rode round it, he could probably beat them out the other side.

Guy gave a hint of a smile then stopped. Such a movement made the mask rub against his face, irritating the burnt skin. Guy scratched underneath with his gloved finger. It didn't bother him too much, for smiling was a rare occurrence.

Chapter 35

Hazel eyes looked up at the figure of a sleeping woman, she lay in her bed, sweat drenching her pale, gaunt face. He wanted to hug her, to climb in the large bed and cling onto her dying body, never letting it go. He feared this was the end and his small hand reached out to touch her clammy arm.

She called out then, a sound of sharp agony leaving her mouth. Servants ran in, dabbing cloths on her head and forcing medicine into her mouth. "Lord!" one of them shouted, pushing the boy out of the way and running towards the large oak door.

Heavy footsteps came and a powerful man appeared in the doorway, his dark beard thick and his eyes friendly. He ran towards the dying woman, kneeling next to her, holding tightly onto her hand. The servant women left and the room went deathly silent.

The man waited next to the woman, speaking quiet words and kissing her gently on the forehead. The hazel-eyed boy didn't know how much time had gone by, it could have been minutes, hours or days, he could not tell. Finally, the man called to him. "Say goodbye to your mother," he said, his voice deep and strong.

The boy went over and her eyes opened, as if sensing her last moments were upon her. Her gaze was blue like a winter morning sky and she looked at the boy with love, tears brimming and falling to her cheeks. Then they closed and she was gone, slipping away to wherever souls went.

The man dropped his head to the body of the dead

mother, hiding his sobs from the young boy beside him. After a while, he lifted his head, drying his face on the dirty bed sheets. "Robin," he said to the small boy, putting his arm around his shoulder. "Grief is a thing that will never end. However, it does change shape. It doesn't feel like it in the moment, but it forms into something less painful, less sharp. At times it will give you a cold chill in the summer sun, it will torment you during dark nights in your bed. But, son, remember, you must never let it conquer you."

The young boy said nothing, his eyes glazed over, looking beyond the man and at his dead mother lying in the bed.

"Son!" he said, shaking him. "Are you listening? Son!"

"Sun!" said Eustace, rousing Hood from the forest floor.

"What?" said the bowman, his eyes adjusting to the light, his mind pulling itself from his dreams.

"The sun is up, we must move."

Hood rose, taking a swig of his water skin and brushing down his dirt covered clothes.

Eustace looked him up and down, noting the lack of care the bowman had for himself. His clothes were stained and his face had been unshaven for days now, a dark stubble growing in. "You need to look after yourself, Hood."

"And why is that, monk?"

"Your appearance is reflecting your state of mind."

"Tell me," said Hood. "What is my state of mind?"

"It's a mess. Now come on, we'll be at a village by sundown where we have friends. There will be an inn and a surgeon to tend to our wounded."

The group walked slowly and they moved at the pace of the wounded. Just over twenty of them remained and half of them weren't able to fight. Three of those who were injured had souring wounds, two would never fight again and another two would die before the week was out.

Eustace was right; it wasn't until sundown when they reached the village. They were given a fine welcome and wine from nearby vineyards had been acquired for them.

Master had moved off to his room within the inn. The old man had been quiet since the disaster at Renaud's castle, in fact, the whole group had.

Hood sat opposite the monk. The man's skin was glowing and his grey, long hair was thick and shiny. No matter what they went through, Eustace never seemed to look worse for any of it. "How the hell did it come to this?" said Hood, pouring himself a goblet of wine from the clay jug in front of him. The wine was red and aged to perfection. Hood nodded with agreement as the liquid touched his lips. "Bloody good wine that."

"You won't find better," said Eustace, pouring his own. "And we were outplayed, Hood, it's as simple as that. Our success blinded us. We could no longer find the chinks in our own armour."

"And what were those chinks?" asked Hood.

"I'm yet to find them. Perhaps it's time to turn our backs on this. We need to know when we're beaten."

Hood snapped, his voice sharp. "There's no turning our backs on a man like Guy, can you not see that by now?"

"Do not lose your temper with me, Hood. I am your ally, your friend. We're here to help one another. We need to put our heads together. The man was a fine tracker, but to find us across the sea? That is something different entirely."

Hood was about to reply when Athella walked in. The woman's pale skin was blotchy from crying, making her face seem older. She walked to the innkeeper and asked for another jug of wine with a goblet to be brought over.

She sat, sliding in next to Eustace, facing Hood. "It saddens me," said Hood, "to see you're in pain over losing him. I want you to know, the grief I feel holds no bounds."

"You know not what it is to feel loss like this, Hood, for you do not know what it is to love."

"I've experienced loss too, Athella. I loved John like a brother."

"You would not have left him behind, you wretch, if you had an ounce of love for the man!" she hissed.

"Do not be so ignorant, you foolish girl, my heart is broken, a break that I fear will not heal," said the bowman, standing, pulling his dagger from his side and tossing it in front of her. "Go on, Athella, you've wanted to do it for so long, you've been looking for an excuse since the day I met you."

"An excuse? You think I need an excuse?"

There was silence as Athella looked down at the dagger waiting in front of her. Eustace grabbed it, sheathing it in his own belt. "Loss, my friends, fires emotion like nothing else. Calm yourselves and drink, for tonight we drink for John."

The tension eased and Hood sat, grabbing his goblet once more.

"Where are we off to next?" asked Athella, swiftly changing the subject.

"We head for the coast, back to the harbour where our boat lies. We'll need to hire a few crewmen to man the ship, then from there we'll head to England. I have some lucrative business to attend to. We'll leave the wounded here and ride west in the morning, following the traders' road."

"Sounds like a well thought plan," grumbled Hood. He grabbed the full jug as it came to the table and swept up his goblet. "If you'll excuse me, I'll be up in my room."

Athella grinned. "Good night," she muttered.

Eustace half rose. "Hood, wait."

But the bowman did not.

Hood walked up the stairs of the inn, the noises below becoming fainter as he moved up each step. He walked down the long hall, doors at either side of him. Only one was slightly open and in there was Master, sitting on his bed, the moon illuminating him. The old man's eyes were shut and his legs were crossed, his back sitting up straight. Hood was going to walk in but decided against it. "Enter, my friend, you wish to talk," came Master's quiet voice.

Hood walked in, placing down his jug and removing his hat. "I'm envious, Master, you seem so peaceful amongst all this death."

"We mainly have no control over what goes on around us, Hood; however, we are in control of our own inner peace."

"Can you teach me?" he asked, feeling pathetic at the desperation in his voice.

Master smiled, opening his eyes. "You will teach yourself. Every action, every choice you make will count towards it. Soon you will find it, I have seen it."

Hood sat, placing himself on a chair at the other end of the room. "You have visions? Like the witch?"

"She saw only darkness, the hatred and evil that was close by. I have glimpses of the many possible futures there could be."

"And what does mine hold?" said the bowman, lifting the goblet to his mouth.

"It's not as simple as that, Hood. We each have choices, those choices can change the course of what happens in each of our lives. Therefore, we each have hundreds, if not thousands of potential futures."

"And am I content in any?"

"Many," said Master. "And in many you are not."

Hood chuckled to himself and rose. "Well, that's as much use as a priest in a whorehouse. Goodnight, Master."

"Goodnight, my friend."

Hood left the room, walking down the hallway to his own. The door clicked as it opened and he moved to the window, pulling a wide backed chair towards it. The bowman didn't bother putting the lantern on, he preferred the darkness when the moon shone brightly. Hood thought on the ramblings of Master. The man was either gifted or had a wild imagination, whichever it was Hood did not care anymore. He looked to the corner of his room and sighed as he saw the light bouncing from the hilt of his sword from John. Turning away, he pulled his hat down over his face, slowly drifting off to sleep.

Chapter 36

Hood woke slowly, his hat had fallen from his face and his bladder was full. The wide back chair had made his bones stiff and he cursed as he saw the moon was still high in the black sky.

The bowman moved to his bed, pulling the cold chamber pot out from underneath it. While relieving himself, he stared out of the window, looking down onto the dirt packed street below. It was dark mostly, but he saw a hooded figure that caught his attention. They moved with caution down the road and came below the window of Hood's room. The figure turned, looking behind them. That's when Hood saw their face. It was Athella, of that he had no doubt. She went onto walk quickly, hurrying herself towards the edge of the village.

Hood's attention was brought back into the room when he realised the chamber pot was no longer beneath him and the floorboards were instead being splashed.

The bowman had prided himself on his instincts, his gut feeling was to follow her because it was John's wife. He felt as though he had a duty to protect her if she was in trouble. However, for the most part, he did not care, the woman despised him and he despised her.

Hood turned to look at the large bed beckoning him, but once more the moonlight struck the hilt of the jewelled sword. He shook his head and reached for it, fastening the blade to his side. On his way out he grabbed his bow and quiver, slinging them over his shoulder.

The air was cool as he stepped outside the silent inn and he could see Athella in the distance, her pace faster than before. Hood started into a slow jog, easing his muscles into a run to catch her. There were hanging lanterns every so often through the village, which helped guide his feet as they moved. But Athella had soon disappeared from the edge of the village, out onto the fields beyond. Hood slowed as he entered the darkness and now, instead of concern, he felt in its place curiosity. The bowman quelled the urge to call out to her and pulled his sword from its scabbard, moving warily into the black of the night.

Hood's eyes adjusted and he could see Athella making her way across the field ahead of him. Hood knew if she looked back then he would be spotted, so he moved towards the edge of a lightly wooded area, following the treeline as she travelled.

A huge cloud moved across the path of the moon, blocking all light. Hood cursed to himself and narrowed his eyes, trying to find the figure of Athella once more. He kept moving with as much stealth as he could until he saw a figure meet another. He was not sure whether the darkness was playing tricks on his eyes. From this distance, she could have been standing next to a tree, or a fence, or nothing at all.

The cloud moved and once more the silver moonlight shone down onto the scene, highlighting the two figures speaking closely. Hood was at a distance, but he had no doubt she was speaking with a man. He was tall and broad shouldered, his back to Hood.

Then final words were spoken and the figure turned. Hood's blood ran cold as he saw the glint from the iron mask on the man's face. He felt a mixture of emotions, the one that fuelled his rage more than any was fear. The bowman realised it now; Guy was better, he always was. Inevitably, he would die by his hands just like the rest of his friends. This is what he feared. Hood was a man who rarely felt fear. Some would say that was a gift, others would say it's a curse. For fear is man's oldest instinct, it's what helped us survive throughout the ages. It's why we get nervous when there's an unnatural silence in a forest, it's why our hearts beat faster when we hear a noise at night. Hood, for whatever reason, was not shaken by these things. One would think that would make him more vulnerable. However, in most cases it had made him more dangerous.

Except now, the unfamiliar emotion made him feel unhinged. He didn't know whether to run or battle, both of the choices seeming like bad ones. Both of the choices he imagined death waiting at the end, one sooner than the other.

Guy had left, he'd turned and walked back into the trees from where he'd come. Athella had started her walk back, her pace slower than before. Hood followed her, his hands clammy and a darkness settling on his mood. He crossed the field and cut in behind her. Now he was close, the sound of the wind against the landscape muting his footsteps. He could smell her, that sweet smell that she always seemed to have, no matter how many days on the road.

"Athella," he whispered.

She didn't turn right away, she'd frozen in place instead, like a rabbit hit by fright. Then he saw her stiff hand reaching for her waist. She moved quickly when her fingers had touched the dagger hilt, but not quickly enough. Hood had his sword ready and slammed the pommel off the side of her head. Athella dropped, the weapon fell from her grip and blood began to trickle from her temple.

Hood had looked down at the body of Athella, wondering whether to end it all now, to plunge his sword into her side and finally rid her from his life. He considered taking her to Eustace and explaining what he'd seen. However, he knew she would spin a lie and Eustace would leave himself no choice other than to consider it. He'd let her go, tell her to never come back. But she would, Hood knew she would. The woman was like Guy, determined and deadly.

He picked up her limp body and draped her over his shoulders, carrying her away from the village. In the distance he could see a storehouse, sitting atop a hill, a fire made outside of the building. As he moved closer, he could see a man sitting in a curved wicker chair, his feet stretched out close to the flames. A dog sat beside him on the ground, curled up tightly taking in the heat.

Hood dropped Athella in the darkness, leaving her in some long, cold grass before he moved into the man's view.

The man was old and his eyes were dark, his body was frail and grey hair lined the side of his head. He said some words in French that Hood could not understand, though his tone was not aggressive, more inquisitive.

"I'm here to watch, to guard," said Hood in English, attempting to convey some sort of understanding.

"Ah," said the old man, a smile on his face. "English?"

"Yes," said Hood, impatience in his tone. The dog lifted its head and growled. There was a time, thought

Hood, when he'd stick an arrow in the old man and cut the dog's throat. Instead, Hood bent his knees and gestured to the dog to come. "Here," he'd said, his tone friendly, yet dominant.

The tired dog rose and the growl disappeared, its tail wagging as it came and sat between Hood's open knees. The bowman stroked the hound and the old man gave a laugh. "He likes you," said the man, a thick accent surrounding his words.

"I'm with Eustace," said Hood. "I've come to relieve you of your watch duty."

"Ah," said the old man, rising from his seat. "Yes, I like Eustace, a kind man. Always has us in his mind." The old man was eager to get away and back to the village, Hood guessed the chair was far less comfortable than it appeared. "You want the dog? For company?"

"No, that's fine," said Hood.

The old man gave a weak whistle and the dog padded off behind him.

Hood was about to move off to grab Athella when the old man came back, shuffling from the darkness. "No fire in there," he said, pointing to the storehouse. "Boom." His arms extended outwards as he said the word and his old eyes opened up far.

The bowman nodded in understanding and the old man moved off. Hood moved back into the darkness once the man had disappeared, pulling Athella's body clear of the long grass and into the clearing before the warehouse. Her breathing was less deep and it wouldn't be long until she started to wake.

In the meantime he walked to the building, pushing open the heavy wooden door. The smell of fermentation and spirits hit him. There were stacks of barrels piled and lined up at one side. At the other was much the same, but in one corner there were a few sealed bottles of dark wine, Hood made his way towards them. The room was dim and illuminated only by the limited moonlight finding its way through the dirty windows. He moved slowly, the floorboards in the centre of the room were creaking under his feet. Hearing wood begin to splinter, he moved off and stepped with caution towards the wine.

There was a hatch in one corner of the room, leading to a cellar below and no doubt used to store empty barrels. Hood had seen vineyard storehouses before in England, he'd even stayed at one for a short time during a particularly cold winter. The wine was like vinegar, but it warmed the insides.

The bowman strode from the building, pulling the cork from the dark bottle he'd acquired and took a deep swig. Athella was groaning now and Hood sat himself in the old man's wicker chair. It was comfortable at first, allowing the muscles on his body to relax.

He sat, watching the woman from across the fire. Hatred began to bubble as he looked at her. She'd ruined his life by killing all he cared for and now it was time for him to ruin hers.

"Ah, you're awake," said Hood, holding an arrow loosely in his bow as he sat.

Athella began to back up and her eyes were wandering wildly into the darkness around her.

"Oh no, you don't get to run," said the bowman, pointing the arrow at her.

"What do you want with me?" she asked. "I've done nothing wrong."

Hood's face darkened and she knew the look, she'd seen it before many times. It was the kind of look he got before all rationality left him. "I'll give you this moment only to tell me the truth, to be real with me this once. If you're not, well, you know what happens."

Athella touched the side of her head where the hair was stuck to her face with blood. "What would you like to know?"

Hood rose, disgust on his face. "Why you bloody did it? Why you led Guy here? Why you didn't just kill us in our sleep?"

She laughed, the sound dry and humourless. "Guy is a good man and you lot are wretched. You roam the lands, killing husbands, letting your men rape wives and slaughter children. You took me from my home." She paused then, a tear in her eye and her voice breaking. "You killed my sister."

Hood's face was emotionless, he could almost understand it. Almost. "You're twisted, you know that? Just like your damned brother, you're sick in the head. Marrying John, you never gave a toss about him, did you?"

She smiled, her eyes looking up at him from over the flames. "He had it coming. As did the rest of you. You see, it's too simple to kill you all in your sleep. You outlaws pull people's lives apart bit by bit, so I shall do the same to yours. Guy wanted revenge and I was here to help him get it."

Hood shook his head in confusion. "You're unhinged, Athella, I can understand revenge, but—"

"But what?" she interrupted in. "Have you ever had your family butchered, been stolen away from your home, your loved ones gone?"

"Yes," said Hood angrily. "You have done it to me, you and that damned metal face. You've taken my brothers." Hood tried to feel fury, but he couldn't. Athella's words had hit him, he understood them.

Through his own torment, he could see how his actions had twisted her, how they had tortured her mind. "In no world are your actions acceptable, but nor are mine." He walked around to her while she lay on the ground and threw his arrow onto the grass beside her, along with his bow. "You have one chance, Athella, one chance to hit me like all the others. If you miss, then know this, I will kill you with my sword and one of us will know revenge."

"Are you mad?" she asked, as he walked away, standing in front of the storehouse.

"I made the first move, I started it all. It's only fair you get the first chance to finish it." The dark-garbed bowman stood straight, his eyes staring at Athella. He was about a hundred paces away from her and a big part of him hoped she would strike him. A different part of him knowing she could not, for his bow had never made a mark on his skin.

Athella held the bow firmly and took aim, the flames of the fire illuminating the figure of Hood. His handsome face was dispassionate and his eyes were resting on her.

She shot the bow and Hood watched the arrow fly towards him, he knew it was going to miss, but only by a hair's breadth. Perhaps the wind would catch it, or God would kindly prod it in his direction.

"Hood," he heard a familiar voice call. It came from behind him to his right, the voice was followed by a blade hissing from its scabbard.

Hood turned instinctively, pulling his own sword free. Then the arrow hit him, plunging high into his chest. The bowman's eyes were wide with shock and he saw Athella run into the darkness. His hand reached up and touched the wound, not believing he'd been hit.

Adrenaline surged through him and an unexpected smile appeared on his face. *Has death finally caught up with me?* he thought, turning to face his enemy.

Chapter 37

Guy sat in the shelter of the woods, waiting for Athella to show herself. In quiet moments such as those he thought about his wife often. She'd always say to him, "Do you not get lonely going out all day doing the Sheriff's bidding?" He'd told her no, for it was a type of solitude for him when he was alone. He could think, reflect and feel his mind at peace in between the petty tasks of the Sheriff. She'd shrugged at that, saying solitude was just a finer word for loneliness. She was wrong though, now he knew true loneliness. The thought of having no one to speak to, no one to connect to, not even if you yearned for it. Now that was true loneliness.

Guy thought back to his final months in England. After he'd watched Hood leap from the side of the cliff and into the water below, he'd decided to attempt to free himself from the anger. He'd ridden back to Nottingham, his face and body horribly burned. Guy had strolled into his house and saw a doctor at his wife's bedside, he told Guy she'd been unresponsive for days and her condition was only getting worse. The doctor went on to tell Guy of eyewitnesses that had informed him about Gilbert exiting his house, leaving his wife and dead child behind in his wake.

Guy didn't want to hear it, he sent the man away and spent the next few nights watching his wife fade away. Not once did she come around, a priest had arrived at one point and told Guy her soul was far away, finding its way to heaven and her body would eventually pass when her soul reached the gates. Did he believe it? He didn't know, in his heart he certainly wanted to, but how could he after all that had happened.

Once his wife had gone, he rose from his place and strode through the streets of Nottingham. Thunder had clapped and lightning lit the sky while rain washed down the alleys and roads. There were only two guards at the Sheriff's gate and one put his arm up in front of him. "Sheriff's not expecting anyone." He was tall and well-built, a look of arrogance on his face.

"Let me through, boy, or you will regret it," said Guy, no anger in his voice.

The soldier stood taller and broadened his shoulders. "Call me boy again and I'll cut you to pieces."

Another soldier stepped in, a man Guy had travelled with while tailing Hood. "You know who that is, Freddie?" he asked the taller soldier.

"Yes, it's the pathetic man who couldn't catch a measly outlaw. A man who's also been dumped from the Sheriff's service."

The second part was news to Guy, but it only made him more determined to enter.

Freddie laughed as he looked down at him. "You think you scare me? I've won eleven duels and I'm not even twenty-two yet. I could best you with an eye shut. Now, walk away, dog, before I start to get mad."

Guy had smiled, the action caused the skin to break on his face. He pulled his sword and held it by his side. "Let me see how good you are."

Freddie unsheathed his own and stepped forward. "It's your death wish." The soldier was excited to cut down Guy of Gisborne. The men, for some reason, had held him in high regard. They talked of his skills as if he were some demon. However, when Freddie looked at a man, he could tell if they were a fighter. Guy, he knew, was not.

Freddie started slowly, testing Guy's movements, sending light attacks and seeing how he worked. Guy battered them away easily but did not attack. Instead, he stood back, his attitude relaxed and his eyes glittering with excitement.

"Good," said Guy, parrying a fierce slash with ease. "You've got talent, but not enough, I'm afraid, to save your life."

Freddie lashed out at him, no more games, he had thought, as he moved quicker and quicker. By now, he would have finished his opponent, except Guy was nowhere near finished. Freddie was pushing his skills, daring a lunge here and a swipe there. Then the soldier saw an opening and pounced for it. He only realised in the last moments of his life that Guy had given him bait which he'd happily taken. Guy's sword cut an arc across the bottom of the soldier's stomach, his bowels falling to the cobbles below him, steaming in the rain.

Freddie squealed and begged for help from his comrades. But they stood, eyes wide and swords sheathed as Guy walked past them and into the Sheriff's house.

The cries of Freddie were muted by the storm as the front door shut behind him. Guy looked around, water dripping from him onto the rugs lining the floor. He heard voices coming from upstairs and Guy followed them. One was unmistakably the Sheriff's and the other he did not recognise. His heavy, wet boots walked down the corridor and stood outside the wretched man's room. Guy stretched his fingers and pulled the handle down slowly, letting the door swing open. Within the room was the Sheriff, his naked, pale body sitting on top of a girl stripped of clothes, his hands gripped tightly on her neck. Another one was in the corner watching, a look of terror on her face. These were not whores, Guy knew, for the Sheriff only wanted what didn't want him. These were girls from the town, barely old enough to be women and without a doubt forced by soldiers from their homes.

Guy walked slowly over and the shuddering girl in the corner ran out behind him, heading down the stairs. The girl below the Sheriff was blue in the face and Guy's shadow fell over her.

The Sheriff let go and turned ready to slap the girl. "I told you to...." his voice trailed off and his eyes fell on the half-burned figure of Guy. The Sheriff peeled away from the girl on his bed and backed away to the corner of his room. "Guy, you're no longer in my service, we do not have to see one another ever again." The sight was pathetic. If the man weren't so evil, Guy would feel sorry for him.

"Don't worry, we will not see each other again." Guy's hand reached out and grabbed the Sheriff by the neck, leading him to his bedpost. The bedpost was of carved wood and the end was a finely crafted apple. "Bite it."

"What?" said the Sheriff, as his head was pushed down and his open mouth bit onto the carving. The apple didn't fit all the way in, it stopped halfway and scraped on his teeth. When the Sheriff was in place, Guy threw his elbow down onto the back of his head. The first time the Sheriff kept on struggling, the second time his jaw snapped loose and the screaming began. The third elbow was the last and the dead body of the Sheriff fell to the floor, twitching desperately.

Since then, he'd decided to travel to France, seeking

out Hood and the outlaws, for it was too late, he realised, to let go of hatred. Letting go wasn't making him feel better, so perhaps when every man responsible is dead, he would feel at peace. The first goal was to find the monk, Eustace. This would not be hard, as the man was famed on this side of the water. It took over a year to finally hatch a plan. He didn't want to be on their tails, he could have done that long ago. Instead, he found out their ideas and their movements. He knew their game inside out and they didn't realise it, but Guy was playing it too.

Athella was the first pawn, the woman was young and confused. She hated her brother and had taken refuge with the outlaws as an act of rebellion. Guy knew these mindsets wore off sooner or later and she would come to see them as they were – outlaws.

Now he waited in the trees once more for Athella to bring him information. As he spoke to her and she told him of their plans to move to the coast, he nodded gratefully, speaking kind words to her. In truth, he was not fond of her. She was sly and cunning, with too much of her brother in her.

When they finished speaking he turned away, as he always did, appearing to head off into the other direction. Guy would edge around though, following her back to where she'd come. Not for her safety, but for his. He didn't know much about Athella, but one thing he did know was that she shared blood with the Sheriff and that blood was not to be trusted.

It came as a surprise to Guy when he'd spotted a figure move from the trees and fall behind Athella. He scolded himself for not being careful enough. Whoever this was had seen their exchange and could ruin his plans. So Guy hung back and watched as he saw the figure knock Athella unconscious. He'd followed behind while they made their way to the storehouse on the peak of a hill, and as the figure had stepped into the firelight of an old man's camp, Guy could see it was Hood.

It hadn't entirely surprised him. In fact, he'd thought Hood would have caught on earlier that Athella was a traitor. Hood had sent the old man and his dog away and went onto retrieve Athella from the darkness. Guy knew he needed to step in at some point. But he wanted to hear their words, their own justifications for their actions. They went on to question each other's sanity and Guy had almost laughed aloud at it. There was no doubt Athella was not entirely balanced. However, when Hood had left his bow at Athella's feet Guy was confused.

Hood didn't seem arrogant when he gave her the chance to shoot, he seemed almost sad. As his knowledge that the arrow would not hit disheartened him. Did this man want to be punished? thought Guy. Impossible, for men such as Hood do not feel guilt, they do not change.

As Guy watched the arrow in flight, he could see it was not going to puncture the standing bowman. Athella was skilled but her confidence was sullied tonight, she had shaken as the bow was pulled and fear had taken her ability.

Guy stepped forward at the last second and into the light. "Hood," he said, pulling his sword.

The young bowman had turned, pulling his own sword clear, causing the arrow to catch him high in the chest. Hood was shocked, his eyes were wide and his fingers touched at the wound where the arrow entered. Guy felt a chill as he saw the bowman's shock turn into something else. Hood had smiled, twisting further to face his new enemy.

Athella had run, sprinting off into the darkness and dropping Hood's bow.

"Finally," said Hood, pulling the arrow from his chest and throwing it across the camp. "You show yourself like a man. No more tricks or traps, or following me like a hound in heat. You've come to end it as you should have done."

Guy circled round and onto the flat ground in front of the storehouse. "You have caused this, Hood, your actions have brought yourself this fate."

Hood laughed, the shadows of the fire bouncing from his face. "The hypocrisy, Guy, your family die and your life falls to pieces, so what do you do? You try and do the same to a man you think is responsible. Your own actions led you to the position you're in, right from the moment you began working with the Sheriff. You think any of this would have happened if you'd chosen an honourable man to work for?"

"If the Sheriff was Jesus himself, I believe you still would have pushed a blade into his grip and forced it upon yourself."

Hood smiled, his white teeth baring in the firelight. "Perhaps," he said, leaping with his sword at Guy.

The swords clashed and Guy was pushed back towards the crackling fire. The masked man stumbled as the fire neared his already burnt skin. Hood laughed. "Wouldn't want you to fry again, would we?"

Guy swung his sword to Hood's right, focusing on the side of his wound. The bowman battered the slashes away as pain lanced through his chest. Hood was never a great swordsman, but he could usually best the average man. However, Guy of Gisborne was no average man with a blade. Soon, he wore Hood down, his attacks becoming faster and faster.

Hood focused his mind and moved with Guy's blade. No more was he thinking about the next move, his head was clear and his body had taken over, its instincts reacting to the man in front of it.

Guy had pushed the bowman back towards the storehouse without him realising. When Hood's back foot hit the door Guy took his chance, lashing his boot off the bowman's chest.

Hood flew into the door knocking it wide open, crashing onto the weak floorboards below. The smell of fermented alcohol hit Guy in the face, even the slightest spark could set a place like this off, causing the fumes to react and explode. Hood had shuffled back, his hands reaching out into the darkness of the storehouse, searching for his blade.

Guy slashed his sword across Hood's leg as he tried to manoeuvre himself up, causing the bowman to fall back. Dim light from the window reflected off Hood's eyes. They were serious, deadly. "This ends it all, Hood," said Guy, looking down at the injured man.

"Well, let's hope we both find some peace now," replied the bowman, his words strained, his breath shuddering.

The words angered Guy. "You have no right to peace. Your soul will burn, just like all the others."

Before Hood could reply, Guy's sword was once more upon him, cutting the side of his torso, causing a gash that bled instantly.

Hood gripped onto his side as Guy backed away. The bowman was groaning with pain and his attempts at movement had ceased. Before Guy closed the door, he looked down at the bowman, his enemy, taking in the sight of him one last time. Guy pulled the metal mask from his face and threw it at Hood's feet, the item clattering from the boards.

The storehouse door was shut now and Guy walked beyond the fire where Hood's bow lay. He picked up the bow and found the arrow he had pulled from his chest. Guy pulled a strip of material from the tunic under his dark vest and wrapped it onto the tip of the arrow. He heard a noise from the storehouse, loud and sudden. The sound of barrels falling perhaps? Guy dismissed it and imagined Hood panicking, knocking things over in a doomed frenzy.

The burnt man lowered the wrapped arrow to the fire and watched the material light with ease. Guy notched the arrow to the bow and took aim at one of the small windows on the front of the storehouse. The arrow flew with grace and smashed through the thin pane of glass. Within mere seconds the building exploded, a huge fireball bursting through the roof. There was a second explosion, bigger than the first, which completely blew the sides of the building away. The fire burned brightly from the alcohol and splinters of wood were blasted past Guy's face.

His eyes narrowed at the brightness and he felt the warmth of the fire touch his skin. He felt something else at that moment, something inside was extinguished and replaced by peace. Was it peace? He was not sure. Whatever it was, it was not a familiar feeling.

Guy smiled and looked up at the sky, the glittering stars staring back at him. The action this time did not break his skin; instead it soothed his soul.

Epilogue

Hood stood at the top of the hill looking down at the small town, the sun glinting from his eyes. The last time he was here, he and his brothers were not entirely welcome and Hood himself was of different mind.

The bowman walked down the hill and the decline caused a dull ache to form in the old wound on his thigh. He thought back to the night he last saw the man who gave him that wound. The storehouse door had been shut and Hood knew what Guy had in mind. The bowman had shuffled backwards, attempting to make his way to the cellar door he'd seen earlier. He knew it was a long shot, for his pace was slow and his body would not move well. Then he heard his saving grace; the floorboards beneath him ached and groaned. Hood lifted his leg and threw it down hard. The wood below his body splintered and broke, allowing him to fall through to the deep, damp cellar below. The bones in his body had jarred as he hit the hard floor, but that was momentary. What followed was a huge explosion, cracking most of the floor above him wide open, covering him with old debris.

Hood had blacked out from the pain of his wounds and the sheer volume of noise. He woke, to his delight, to find that he was staring up through the floor at a dark sky with twinkling stars. The fire had died down and only smoke remained. That's the thing about fires fuelled by fumes and spirits, they start big and die fast. The cellar around him was hardly touched, for it was wet and only filled with the odd empty barrel or bottle.

He'd heard movement above him as his ears adjusted. His heart sank as thoughts of Guy entered his mind. Instead, a dog's face peered over the broken floorboards above him, it was the old man's dog Hood had sent away. Its eyes were large and its tongue hung from its mouth. The hound barked and padded its paws. Voices followed and he saw Eustace's face appear beside it.

"Monk!" said Hood, his voice small and croaky. "Get me the hell out of here."

Eustace smiled. "Good to see you well, bowman."

It'd taken weeks for Hood's wounds to heal and months before travel was possible. Over that time, they'd never heard from Guy of Gisborne, the man had faded away, his revenge seemingly satisfied. Athella had been found miles away from the burnt storehouse, her throat slit and her body bloated in a stream. Hood believed Guy to be responsible, Eustace pinned it down to bandits.

"Watch it, bowman," said an old man walking past Hood as he looked down at the settlement. "Don't be causing trouble here; Robin Hood will see to you if he smells a hint of it."

Hood smiled. "Is that so?"

"Aye, he took on the old Sheriff and burnt Guy of Gisborne just in that house over there," the old man said, pointing to the burnt ruins of a huge house at the east of the village. "Rumour is, he's still keeping peace in the city and in the forests. Lords keep to themselves these days because of him."

"I'll keep that in mind," said Hood, walking further down the hill. The bowman rubbed at his clean-shaven face and removed his hat, pulling back his dark hair as he looked up at the house before him.

His gaze was drawn to the top window and his heart dropped to his stomach. Standing there he saw a woman with hair red like fire and eyes of dazzling emerald. She lifted her hand and waved, sheer delight on her face.

"Marian," he whispered under his breath, as he rose his hand and gave a bewildered wave.

Made in the USA
Monee, IL
05 January 2026

41030014R00194